SLEIGHT *Mistake*

SCARLETT FINN

Copyright © 2016, 2021, 2023 Scarlett Finn
Published by Moriona Press 2016, 2021, 2023

All rights reserved.

The moral right of the author has been asserted.

First published in 2016

No part of this book may be reproduced in any form or by an electronic or mechanical means, including information storage and retrieval systems, without permission in writing from the publisher, except by a reviewer who may quote brief passages in a review. It may not be used to train AI software or for the creation of AI works.

All characters in this publication are fictitious and any resemblance to real persons, living or dead, is purely coincidental.

ISBN: 9781914517884

www.scarlettfinn.com

Also by Scarlett Finn

GO NOVELS
GO WITH IT
GO IT ALONE
GO ALL OUT
GO ALL IN
GO FULL CIRCLE

EXILE
HIDE & SEEK
KISS CHASE

WRECK & RUIN
RUIN ME
RUIN HIM

**THE BRANDED
SERIES**
BRANDED
SCARRED
MARKED

**FORBIDDEN
PREQUEL DUET**
ALL. ONLY.
ONLY YOURS

THE FORBIDDEN NOVELS
FORBIDDEN DESIRE
FORBIDDEN WANT
FORBIDDEN WISH
FORBIDDEN NEED
FORBIDDEN BOND

**BOMBSHELLS & BILLIONAIRES
(ROXIVERSE)**
NOTHING TO HIDE
NOTHING TO LOSE
NOTHING IN BETWEEN: ONE
NOTHING TO DECLARE
NOTHING TO US
NOTHING IN BETWEEN: TWO
NOTHING TO SAY
NOTHING TO GAIN
NOTHING IN BETWEEN: THREE
NOTHING TO YOU
NOTHING TO THIS PREQUEL: ONE WILD NIGHT
NOTHING TO THIS
NOTHING IN BETWEEN: FOUR
NOTHING TO DO
NOTHING TO NO ONE
NOTHING TO FEAR
NOTHING TO DENY
NOTHING TO BEAT
NOTHING TO THE WEDDING
NOTHING TO TELL
NOTHING TO IT
NOTHING TO SEE
NOTHING TO WIN
NOTHING TO OFFER
NOTHING TO PROVE

**LOVE AGAINST THE ODDS
STANDALONE COLLECTION**
SWEET SEAS
HEIR'S AFFAIR
RESCUED
MAESTRO'S MUSE
GETTING TRICKY
THIRTEEN
REMEMBER WHEN...
RELUCTANT SUSPICION
XY FACTOR

KINDRED SERIES
RAVEN
SWALLOW
CUCKOO
SWIFT
FALCON
FINCH

MISTAKE DUET
MISTAKE ME NOT
SLEIGHT MISTAKE

LOST & FOUND
LOST
FOUND

**THE EXPLICIT
SERIES**
EXPLICIT INSTRUCTION
EXPLICIT DETAIL
EXPLICIT MEMORY

TO DIE FOR...
TO DIE FOR TRUTH
TO DIE FOR HONOR
TO DIE FOR VIRTUE
TO DIE FOR DUTY
TO DIE FOR LOVE

**RISQUÉ & HARROW
INTERTWINED**
TAKE A RISK
FIGHTING FATE
RISK IT ALL
FIGHTING BACK
GAME OF RISK

ONE

Lacie

"IT COULDN'T HAVE been that bad," Lacie Hart said to her best friend.

"You've met my mother, have you ever known her to be speechless?"

"It might have something to do with Bump," Lacie said, eyeing Sorcha's belly over the square aluminum table between them. "You're six and a half months pregnant and you're only just now telling your parents about the baby. Of course they're surprised."

"We had to wait for Bruce to… you know."

Bruce Booth was Sorcha Reynold's baby daddy. Their relationship had ended three months before Sorcha discovered she was pregnant. When she did, Sorcha sent Lacie on a mission to seek out Bruce, who had gone missing. Sending her to another of her exes, Sorcha had assured her that Seth Sheppard, PI, would help Lacie track Bruce down. Having never met Shep herself, Lacie had mistaken Ryder Stone—her now boyfriend—for Shep when she discovered him snooping in Shep's office.

The journey Lacie went on with Ryder did end with them finding Bruce, although they found him engaged in crime with Ryder's best friend Jamie Wallace who then kidnapped Lacie in a vain attempt to keep his secret safe. It didn't work. Ryder found Lacie, although by then, Bruce Booth was believed to be dead and Jamie Wallace was arrested. It was only later when one of Jamie's men, Eric, turned on him that they found out Bruce wasn't deceased at all.

"The bruises have healed and the statements are in," Lacie said to reassure her friend. "Wallace's bail was refused. It's all a waiting game now."

The pair sat in this unassuming coffeeshop enjoying one of their frequent girlie lunches. Lacie had never been sure what was "girlie" about them, other than the gender of those present, but that was what Sorcha dubbed them. The sun was pouring through the huge windows at the front of the café, which was situated on a busy street in the center of town. Sorcha still enjoyed being a girl about town. She hadn't quite come to grips with how motherhood might change her lifestyle.

Lacie had no children and no experience with them, but even she knew that long, relaxed lunches would be a thing of the past as soon as Bump made an appearance.

"How are things going at SW?" Sorcha asked, finishing her food, and wiping her hands on a napkin. "Are you going to finish that sandwich?"

Lacie switched plates with Sorcha in answer to the question. "The sale's done. Two weeks left until the exchange."

SW was also known as StoneWall, the company Ryder had run with Jamie Wallace for years before the whole debacle.

"How's Ryder doing with moving on?" Sorcha tucked into the remnants of Lacie's lunch.

"He spends most nights at my new apartment," Lacie said.

"I wonder why," Sorcha said, her playful eyes glowed and her sleek smile giggled.

Lacie averted her attention from her friend's suggestive expression. "The SW boys are taking the hiatus as extended vacation time, though none of them are venturing out of the city."

"You're still coming to the party at my parents' house tonight, though, aren't you?"

"Yes, don't panic. I said I would, didn't I?"

"Bruce says he's got a family thing. Some baby daddy he is," Sorcha said, gobbling down the food. "He's not coming."

"I knew that," Lacie said, rubbing the corner of her paper napkin between her thumb and forefinger. "That's why I'm your date tonight."

"It will be the first time I've seen my parents since I told them about the baby. They didn't seem very impressed with Bruce."

"You haven't sounded impressed with him yourself recently."

"It's difficult, he's…"

"He's what?" Lacie asked.

Their friendship had endured every negative experience they'd encountered and now that the friends were paired off, this should be a time for happiness. But from their conversations, she didn't get the impression that Sorcha was enamored with the man she was supposed to be spending the rest of her life with.

"I just don't know…" Sorcha exhaled. "He says he's always busy. I can't get him to engage. He's just… no fun."

"It's grown up, though," Lacie said. "That's what you told me when you demanded that he buy you that diamond."

"Which he bought with his parents' money, you should add"—Sorcha licked her fingertip to smudge up the crumbs from her plate into her mouth—"his accounts are still frozen. He has no money; he's just freeloading now and I don't think that even bothers him."

"You dumped Shep. You chose Bruce."

Sorcha had been decisive with the men in her life once it became clear that Bruce was alive. Being associated with the Reynolds family gave Bruce some credibility, but he still hadn't found himself a job.

"Shep was a loser," Sorcha said, wiping her hands again. "He was as annoying as hell… he wasn't a forever guy. But he was a lot of fun."

"You can't compare Bruce to Shep," Lacie said as Sorcha drank from her water glass. "You wanted different things from them."

"I know, but… do you remember what I said I would want from a partner?"

"Fidelity," Lacie said, sipping her water while watching a group of women enter the coffeeshop and take up position at three broad tables in the corner.

"He hasn't asked me to move in with him."

"You're lucky," Lacie said, switching focus back to her friend. "Ryder blew a gasket when I told him I was renting my place. He still smarts about it."

"That's because he loves you," Sorcha said, finishing Lacie's sandwich. "You're still not eating right."

Trying not to roll her eyes, she made herself smile because Sorcha meant well and didn't know about how Ryder always hounded her about taking care of herself. "Ryder's got you covered on that too."

"Do you ever worry about Ryder's fidelity?"

Lacie laughed, almost spitting out the water she'd just tipped into her mouth. "Sorry," she said, wiping her chin with her napkin.

"You're laughing," Sorcha huffed. "You think the question is hilarious." Sorcha dumped her napkin on the table and her petulant lower lip made an appearance. "You have to help me."

"Help you what?"

"Bruce keeps disappearing," Sorcha said. "Sometimes he calls, and sometimes he doesn't. Sometimes I see him every day, then sometimes he's nowhere."

"What are you thinking?" Lacie asked, but worried that she already knew the answer. "Do you think he's getting himself in deep water again?"

"No," Sorcha said. "None of that was his fault. He'll never get mixed up in crime again. Jamie Wallace certainly scared him straight."

"So what?"

"You need to go to Shep."

Lacie's wandering attention snapped back around to Sorcha. "You're kidding. Please, tell me you're kidding. We've been here before."

Sorcha held her palms open at head height and framed her expression of joy. "Yeah and look how well that turned out for you after…" her hands and her glee fell. "You know, other than the kidnapping thing."

"What do you want me to say to Shep? If you need information, Ryder will get—"

"As long as you two are seeing each other, Ryder will be socializing with Bruce, and they've met. Bruce will notice Ryder watching him."

Lacie had followed through on Sorcha's request for her to seek out Shep before. Back then, it sort of made sense as Shep was the only PI either of them had personal contact with. But since Sorcha had dumped

Shep to go back to Bruce, Lacie had noticed how mopey her friend was and she'd feared that Shep was the reason, now it seemed she might have been right.

"Ryder knows how to be covert. He presently has a team sitting around on their asses. They could help. But what do you want Bruce watched for?"

"He disappears," Sorcha said, rubbing her fingertip back and forth on an inch of the table surface.

"And you want fidelity." Lacie exhaled and leaned in. "You think he's cheating on you?"

"I don't know," Sorcha said and Lacie hated to see her friend look so defeated. "I'd like to know."

Lacie had to make sure that Sorcha knew she was playing with fire that could burn her if things didn't turn out the way she wanted them to. "Are you sure you want Shep involved? He wasn't happy when you broke up with him… again."

"That's why Shep can't know I'm involved," Sorcha said and the way her eyes grew more alert and her tone lowered told Lacie that Sorcha had thought this through… maybe a little too much.

"So why would I—?"

"You're a concerned friend," Sorcha said with a shrug and open expression like she was showing Lacie how to react if asked the question.

"My boyfriend is better at this than—"

"Bruce knows Ryder, and Ryder's got enough on his plate with the sale of the SW premises, and getting a new business started while trying to find somewhere else to live. Oh, and he has a girlfriend who demands his body at every opportunity."

Lacie couldn't hide the width of her smile behind her glass. "He provides plenty of opportunity. I have to do my part."

"Look at you all happy and smiley," Sorcha beamed. "If I wasn't so insanely jealous, I'd be over the moon for you."

"You have the diamond and a child on the way. Your future is set. This is a time for you to be happy."

Sorcha's happiness was important to Lacie. They'd been friends since college and been through a lot. Sorcha's respectable family and Catholic upbringing made her believe that marrying the father of her child was her only option. They hadn't been back together for more than a few weeks and the relationship had lost its sheen already… if it had ever had any. If Sorcha wasn't enamored with Bruce now, Lacie couldn't imagine her friend walking down the aisle carrying that kind of unhappiness.

"Bruce and I haven't had the time to… figure things out."

"Like how you feel about each other?" Lacie asked, considering this the most important question facing the couple at this time. "Ryder and I only had days together before I was abducted, but it was him I thought about constantly."

Losing some of her glum, Sorcha peered at her friend with curiosity. "How did you know that Ryder still cared? He could have hooked up with dozens of women while you were locked up."

"Wallace told me that you and he—"

"After that I mean," Sorcha said, glazing over the lies Jamie Wallace had fed to Lacie during her captivity. "After all the drama was done and when you two decided to make a go of it."

"I never asked him."

"You just…" Sorcha didn't finish. She turned her attention to her water glass before she spoke again. "Either you're super secure, or super naive."

Lacie smiled. "Could be either, I suppose."

"So you'll find out?" Sorcha asked, some of her sapped color had returned now that she had been fed.

"If Ryder had sex while I was chained up?" Lacie asked, being deliberately obtuse.

"No," Sorcha said, rolling her eyes. "Go to Shep, hire him to find out if Bruce is screwing around on me."

"Have you asked Bruce?" Lacie asked.

"I can't do that," Sorcha said as if this was the craziest suggestion in the world. "If he's messing around, he won't be honest, and then he'll be super careful. I have to know."

"I can ask Ryder—"

"Please," Sorcha said, launching her hand over the table. "We trust Shep, and Bruce doesn't know him. Please."

Lacie took a long breath. "Fine, I'll go and see Shep, but he's not going to be happy."

"Thank you," Sorcha sighed. "And you can't tell Ryder."

"What? Why not?" Lacie asked, snatching her hand back.

"He'll think I'm a nut," Sorcha said with a dismissive wave. "Men never understand these things. Plus, he and Bruce will socialize for as long as you and Ryder are seeing each other."

"You've said that twice now. Why do you say it like that?"

"I don't see a diamond on your hand."

Lacie looked at her hand but thought better of telling Sorcha the story of conversations she and Ryder had on that subject.

"Men understand that women have their secrets, especially between girlfriends," Sorcha said. "You will do this for me, won't you?"

The main door opened and the man that swaggered in stopped every woman mid-chew. Whatever their previous task, it was abandoned when their drooling attention became more enthralled with his every stride. Sorcha was the exception; she was busy eyeing the muffins at the counter.

Lacie admired the man too. Enraptured by those long, strong legs in his faded jeans and the crisp white tee shirt that strained across his broad chest and shoulders, she smiled at the sight of his biceps testing the stitching. Ryder was ripped to perfection and she knew that from up close, personal experience.

He'd said he needed to cut his hair, but Lacie liked it wild. She also liked his stubble-roughened chin that made him look so dangerous, especially with those new reflective aviators hiding his eyes.

When one corner of his mouth tilted up, she knew exactly what was on his mind.

"Baby," Ryder said to her when he stopped beside their table.

Sorcha was talking again, but Lacie couldn't tear her eyes from Ryder's still-shrouded ones. She didn't need to see his eyes to feel them trail down over her body. He undressed her slowly, exposing her in his mind for his mental visual consumption. It sent a shiver through her body, snapping her nipples to attention and moistening her core in preparation for his welcome intrusion.

"Uh, hello!" Sorcha shrieked. "I'm sitting here, and you're in a public place, stop with the foreplay."

Lacie blushed and dropped her eyes.

"Hey, Sorcha," Ryder said.

Removing his sunglasses, he hooked them into the neck of his tee shirt. It didn't matter that Lacie hadn't looked at him again. He scooped her up and sat on her seat, moving her to his lap in the process as though she was his napkin.

"We're having lunch," Sorcha said.

"You've been in here nearly two hours," Ryder said. "You spent most of that on the coffee course while you decided what to order."

Lacie looped her arms around his neck and rubbed her nose on the stubble on his cheek. The hiss from the women around them was audible, but it didn't put Lacie off. His hand slid from the small of her back all the way around her body to her abdomen. He didn't have to switch his focus to her, the reaction in his jeans against her thigh almost made her squeal. Her body pressed closer, her peaked nipples crushing themselves into his chest.

"Are you stalking us?" Sorcha asked.

"Don't have to," Ryder said. "My girl and me got the comms down."

"I didn't know you were joining us," Sorcha prickled.

Though she could tell by Sorcha's tone that her friend was unhappy, Lacie couldn't stop herself from rasping her teeth against Ryder's jaw. His smile spread, and when he glanced down at her, she pulled herself closer, still conveying without words exactly what was on her mind.

"Remind me to sneak out on you more often," he said, bumping her nose with his.

They'd had dinner in front of a movie last night and gone to bed early. Since her return from Wallace's lair, she'd had several issues at night. Nightmares and restlessness, as well as an increase in her sleep talking.

Last night after a bout of lovemaking, she'd settled to sleep in Ryder's arms. When she'd awoken in the dark, he was gone. But he was here now, sliding that hand on her lap up her skirt.

"You ate?" Ryder asked her with a squeeze.

"I ate," Sorcha said. "Can we help you with something?"

"Actually, I have to go," Lacie said, lifting Ryder's hand to read his watch.

"You do?" Sorcha asked. "You better not be running off to get laid."

"We've been here for two hours, Sorch," Lacie said. "I'll be over at eight."

"Make it seven and come to my place."

"Will you give me a ride?" Lacie asked Ryder.

"I'll leave you the truck before and drive you home after," Ryder said. "We're working security at the party."

"What?" Sorcha screeched.

"We've done Reynolds' events for years," Ryder said. "They haven't been impressed with the other contractors they've used while SW's been on hiatus. Your father called me this morning. I didn't want him to beg, and he was offering big bucks—five times what we usually charge."

"You're extorting my father?" Sorcha asked.

"I'm not taking the money," Ryder said. "I told the story to demonstrate his desperation."

"Sounds like my dad," Sorcha said, tidying up her place setting. "Always wanting the best of the best."

With an amused smile, Ryder waited a beat. "Why Sorcha, are you paying me a compliment?"

Sorcha didn't look too sure about that. Her friend and her boyfriend clashed, but their conflict was suppressed for her benefit and Lacie was grateful for that. Though it did lead to frequent displays of passive aggression.

"Why are you smiling?" Sorcha asked Lacie. "How are you going to get to my house now?"

"I'll drive us," Lacie said.

"In that monster of a truck?" Sorcha stuttered.

"I've got other vehicles," Ryder said. "You're welcome to any of them. Lace has full security access."

"Really?" Sorcha glowed and her eyes began to dance. "You've got a Spyder convertible."

"Yeah, it was a gift from a client," Ryder said.

"No," Lacie said, digging her nails into Ryder's neck.

"Dusty has a thing for the truck," Ryder explained.

"You know how I feel about loyalty. We've made some memories in that truck," Lacie murmured, flicking his earlobe with her tongue.

"We have," he said.

After he squeezed her thigh, his fingers extended, tracing his knuckle over her panties—the man was a covert pro.

"Stop making gooey eyes," Sorcha tsked.

"You're engaged," Ryder said. "Gooey eyes come with the territory, don't they?"

Lacie raced in before her hormonal friend either cried or stabbed someone, though she was sure Ryder could deflect her if it came to it.

"I should get going," Lacie said.

"You'll do that thing?" Sorcha pleaded when Lacie bent to pick her bag from the floor, squeezing Ryder's hand between her thighs.

"I said—"

"Today," Sorcha said.

Lacie looked at Ryder's watch again. "I'll try, but it's already after three, and—"

"Please," Sorcha said, placing a hand on her swollen abdomen.

"Okay," Lacie said. Sorcha beamed. "Do you need us to drop you somewhere?"

"No. I've got a nail appointment next door in ten minutes."

Lacie nodded, locking her fingers between Ryder's while they stood together. "I'll see you—"

"I do need a chocolate muffin," Sorcha said.

Ryder sighed but he released Lacie's hand and went to the counter to purchase the muffin without further complaint.

"Shep might say no," Lacie said, keeping her eyes on Ryder to ensure he didn't come back while they were talking. "You broke his heart the first time you dumped him."

"I did not! Hearts were nothing to do with it. That was only sex. We both knew that."

"Maybe. But we all went through a lot together, and you dumped him again—"

"We thought Bruce was dead," Sorcha said, but lowered her chin when Ryder approached.

Ever vigilant, Lacie knew that Ryder spotted the abrupt end to their words, but he didn't mention it. Both of them said goodbye to Sorcha, though Sorcha was more interested in beseeching Lacie with her desperate, innocent glances.

She would do Sorcha's bidding, because she always did. Lacie didn't mind dealing with Sorcha's messes because it allowed her a distraction from any mess in her own life. At the moment, she had it sort of together, but Jamie Wallace had taught her how quickly things could change.

She and Ryder left the coffeeshop, and he led her to the truck which was further down the block. After helping her into the cab, he rounded the truck to enter on his own side. But he didn't start the engine to get them moving. He leaned over to kiss her thoroughly and got his hand up her skirt again.

"People can see through these windows you know," Lacie said when he pushed her skirt all the way up and shoved his arm behind her hips, forcing her to the front edge of the seat.

"I thought we could make a memory."

"On a public street?" she asked, leaning in to kiss him again. His finger slid under the cotton of her panties and it was inside her before she could breathe out.

"Ryd," she gasped, grabbing at his shoulders for stability.

Slowly he slid his finger out only to join it with a second digit. "Mm," he hummed.

Resting his head on her shoulder, he buried his mouth on her neck and sucked as his fingers increased pace.

"What… are you… oh God, Ryder…"

Lacie grabbed for the door, and her other hand landed on his thigh, grasping for some kind of anchor. When he sucked her neck, she recognized that the sting would leave his mark on her. His fingers almost left her completely but his thumb grazed her clit.

"Do you like that?" he murmured against her.

"Uh, uh… I…" Her heart wanted out of her chest, so she tried to measure her panting, to slow it and breathe through the pleasure. But Ryder's digits delved back into her and his thumb curled around her nub, squeezing her hard.

"Talk to me, baby," he said, lowering his head further.

But she'd lost all perception of the situation, his teeth grabbed her nipple through her blouse and she shouted his name, then whispered it on an exhale. The fireworks in her gut bubbled to her aching breasts. The permanent clench of her inner muscles locked his fingers in place, but that didn't prevent his thumb from massaging her off the cliff again.

"Yes, baby," he whispered. "Good, more?"

Her eyes remained closed. Breathing became harder, and clenching again, she pulsed around the fingers he used to torment her with. Pushing them deeper, he curled around to push the cushion of her G-spot, while spiking her clit.

"Baby?"

Wriggling further down in her seat, Lacie rode his hand, rocking her hips against his digits. "You like that," he exhaled.

Dragging his teeth on her shoulder, Ryder made her blouse flutter down her arm. Her fingers twisted into his hair to direct his mouth upward as hers descended. Leading the kiss with her tongue, Ryder gratefully received her initiation, accepting her battling intrusion with his own.

He slipped a digit into her again. Her arousal forced her to push back, while rubbing herself on the pleasurable pressure he offered. "Good," he said on her mouth. He nipped her lip, then pushed her head aside to suck her earlobe.

Sliding her hand up his thigh, Lacie pressed her palm to his solid length, and at the discovery of his equivalent arousal, her moisture seeped over his digits. Ryder hummed against her again and took her hand from his lap. She tried to resist, but he held her hand away from his groin by pressing her hand over her own knee.

Just as she was sure he'd brought her to the brink again, his fingers slid out, causing her to yelp. Blinking stars from her eyes, Lacie looked at the stores and the greenery of the plaza where a smattering of people went about their business.

The truck started up, and Ryder pulled into the flow of traffic. Shaking off the mist, he carried on like nothing had happened.

"What was that for?" she said, when she was ready to attempt speech.

"What?" he asked.

"That."

His lips curled at one corner, and he rested his hand on her still-exposed thigh. "I love you."

"Ryder," she sighed with a smile. Taking his hand in both of hers, she lifted it to her mouth and covered his knuckles with kisses. "I love you too."

"You like orgasms," he said. "And I wasn't around to serve any up this morning."

"Our bed feels odd without you in it," she said, receiving a smile. Kissing his hand again, she laid it on her thigh and covered it with her own hand while the other reached to his tee shirt and snaggled his sunglasses. "What time do you have to be at work?"

"The boys are over there just now," Ryder said. "I'll join them in an hour."

"Really?" she asked. "You have a free hour?"

"You're not interested in how I knew you were still at lunch or why I crashed it? We haven't talked all day."

"Is everything okay?" she asked.

"Yeah."

"If there was anything wrong you would've told me as soon as we were alone."

"Yeah."

"So I knew there was nothing wrong. And I was happy to see you. I like it when you surprise me. I have nothing to hide, Ryder. You're not going to catch me in the act of anything untoward."

He laughed and squeezed her leg. "Not when I'm the one acting with you. If you want to have a tempestuous affair, you just let me know."

"What did we just do?" she asked when he pulled up outside her new place.

Ryder jumped out and came around to lift her out of the truck before he answered her. "What we're about to do again."

Locking the truck, he took her up the building stairs to unlock the communal door with his own key.

"You know I have a date tonight," Lacie said, struggling to keep up as he increased his speed on the stairs.

"Yeah, I met her at lunch, she's cute. The kid yours?"

She came up short at his back when he halted to unlock the front door. Once it was open, he swept her feet from under her to take her inside, past the door to her workroom and up the stairs to the loft with the mezzanine bed.

When he came down on top of her on the bed, she rubbed her hands from his chest to his shoulders. "Are you getting this out of the way so that you don't have to come home with me later?" she asked, running her hands into his hair.

"I'm coming to bed with you tonight too."

"I'll probably crash at the Reynolds' tonight with Sorcha," Lacie said, kissing him and reaching for the hem of his tee shirt.

He frowned. "Why?"

"It's what I usually do after a couple of glasses of wine. I don't like to drink and drive."

"Mm," he grinned. "You're going to be lubed without a ride home? I have to stay sober."

"So I get sex now and later?"

"Anytime I get the chance, you get it."

"I love you, Ryd," she said. "Promise me that you'll never let me screw this up."

"What?" he asked, brushing her hair from her face. "What would make you say something like that?"

"Just… if I do anything wrong, or… insensitive, give me a chance to fix it."

"Baby, I'll fix it for you, guaranteed."

Speech was forgotten when their mouths merged in prelude to what their bodies were about to mount. No matter how many times they were intimate, it got better every time.

TWO

Lacie

LACIE WOULD HAVE happily spent the rest of the day in bed with Ryder. But he had to work. If she had kicked up enough of a fuss, Ryder would have stayed in bed to pleasure her, but they had to move past their infatuation with each other and find a way to settle into normality. Though having such a man so thoroughly devoted to her was humbling.

Part of the ethos of the SW men had been Semper Fidelis, just as they had been reared by the military to follow. Jamie Wallace had been Ryder's business partner. More than that Jamie Wallace was Ryder's best friend. At least that was what all of them had believed.

What none of them could have known was the resentment building inside the sociopath that was Jamie Wallace. Where Ryder thought they were part of the same team, Jamie saw Ryder's success as highlighting his contrasting pathetic failure.

That resentment had increased throughout the years from when Jamie Wallace and Ryder Stone went to school together, through their time in the military together and beyond. After they departed the forces, Ryder started StoneWall, a security and investigation company. Ryder put Jamie's name over the door with his own even though Jamie contributed nothing, being all but penniless. Ryder believed that was what best friends did for each other, they were a team who supported each other.

Wallace coasted along in the easy life at Ryder's side for years before he began to dabble in illegal activities, which it turned out were his true calling.

Lacie hadn't known any of this, or any of the men, until Sorcha got pregnant by Bruce and she was sent to Sorcha's ex-beau, Shep. At that time, Lacie had hired Ryder who was in Shep's office doing a bit of snooping for a case. Lacie had thought he was Shep and Ryder hadn't corrected her. So their original adventure had gotten underway. It was an adventure that saw Lacie in captivity for almost six weeks until Ryder tracked her down.

The memories of that first experience with Ryder and what brought her here originally, played through Lacie's memory. Walking down the street toward the Sheppard Investigations storefront, she thought about all they had been through, about what Wallace had put them through.

Booth had been a reluctant member of Wallace's criminal gang. During the investigation into Bruce's location, Shep and Sorcha had restarted their affair. Except when Bruce was found alive, Sorcha dumped Shep again to do the right thing and be with the father of her baby.

Lacie had started her association with Ryder in this office and here she was again, under Sorcha's direction as she had been before. She pushed through the door into the small outer office with its plastic chairs and industrial grade carpet. A tall blonde with mousy features and a short red skirt stood at the side of the assistant's desk. The woman snapped the clasp of her purse shut and tucked it under her arm as she turned to face Lacie.

"We're closed," the blonde said.

"Office hours on the door say you're open until five."

The three and the zero that used to follow the five had long since been scraped off the door glass. The glue outline could still be deciphered by an attentive observer.

Though she didn't know the exact time, she figured that they had to be closing in on around five p.m. Ryder had left her place later than he had intended, meaning she herself had been late getting out the door.

"We're closing early."

The door behind the blonde opened and Lacie leaned to the side to see past the receptionist.

"Well, well, well, Lacie Hart," Shep said, falling sideways to prop his shoulder on the doorframe. "Didn't expect to have you on my doorstep, Little Lady."

"Hi, Shep."

Shep was just as Lacie remembered him from his first impression, tall, pale, and somehow lackluster without Sorcha. When he and Sorcha were together, Shep had a healthy complexion and carried himself with pride. But from his aura now he wasn't exactly over being dumped by Sorcha… again.

"Heather, this is Lacie," Shep said.

"Hi," the blonde said.

"Hello," Lacie said. "Shep, can I talk to you?"

Part of being a good PI was having a curious nature, she knew that from what Ryder had told her. He'd also told her that Shep wasn't exactly in that category; not because of his skillset, but because he was lazy. Except Lacie knew that went out the window when a certain woman was involved, Sorcha. And where there was Lacie…

Shep stepped back and gestured into his office. So Lacie skirted the receptionist and her desk to enter the office.

He closed the door and passed Lacie to sit at the desk angled in the corner in front of the closet. With the piles of papers, and a layer of dust on everything, the room was just as she remembered. This was the room she'd met Ryder in.

"What's up?" Shep asked. "Trouble in paradise?"

"Excuse me?" she asked, crossing to perch in the guest chair at the desk.

"There are only two possible reasons you could have for coming here. Either you think your boyfriend is messing around on you and you're here to ask me to catch him in the act…"

"You think you could tail Ryder without him noticing?"

"If it's not door A, then it's door B." Shep's eyes traveled south to her chest.

It was a good thing Lacie had known that Shep was crude and opportunistic when she walked in here or she might have been affronted by his leering. As it was, she smiled at his typical form.

"Who am I lashing out at by sleeping with you?" she asked. "Sorcha or Ryder?"

"I'd go with the boyfriend. I've told you before, Little Lady, I've got a feeling that facing the wrath of your boyfriend would be worth it. I know what you and the bitch are like, you'd never screw around on each other."

"So she's the bitch now?" Lacie asked, folding her hands over her purse in her lap.

"Tramp doesn't know what she wants."

The pair had a history of conflict. They had never been nice to each other; insults were a part of their foreplay.

But when Lacie had been kidnapped by Wallace's gang to prevent her from spilling the beans about his criminal activities, Ryder had gone into self-destruct. Her best friend, Sorcha, had turned to Shep, and he'd been there for her, he'd been a rock… then presumed dead Booth was revealed to be alive and Sorcha left Shep in the dirt.

The anger in Shep's expression now told Lacie that this wasn't the usual teasing, and it made her reluctant to speak up. This couple fed off each other's madness.

"How have you been doing?" Lacie asked him. "I haven't seen you for a month."

Knowing Sorcha almost as well as she did, Shep cut through the BS and said it plain. "She sent you, didn't she?"

"Yes."

"What is it she wants?" Shep asked. "She sure as shit didn't send you over here to ask how I was doing."

Lacie hesitated, momentarily considering backing out. "Why did you never tell Sorcha how you feel about her?"

"She didn't send you over for that either."

"Shep, you have to tell her."

"If you were matchmaking, you'd have led by bringing up Sorch. Either you tried it with her and she told you where to get off or you're winging it now because you don't want to tell me the real reason that you're here."

It appeared Ryder didn't give Shep enough credit. He was actually quite good at the detecting business. "Booth might be cheating," Lacie said.

Slowly Shep's posture changed, he became taller, yet more rigid. "You came here to tell me that my ex-girlfriend's new boyfriend is cheating on her?"

"I don't know if he is cheating, but he's not around, and Sorcha thinks—"

"She did send you!" Shep declared, swinging back in his chair, and running his fingers through his hair. "If this was your position, Stone would never let you near the competition."

Lacie couldn't argue that point because it was true. As uncomfortable as Lacie had been about coming here on Sorcha's behalf, this was what should've happened the first time she came here. If she had come here and met Shep instead of Ryder, then she'd have had this conversation with Shep months ago.

Shep wasn't the type to admit hurt feelings and Lacie didn't like to be the one doing the hurting. But after a momentary falter, he drew in a breath.

"I'll find out," Shep said.

"You will?" She hadn't expected him to be so compliant. Lacie considered whether or not she had misread the relationship because Shep didn't seem hurt. He was determined. That attitude didn't exactly marry with what she knew of Shep's practice.

"Yeah," he said. "I know enough about the guy and his background. I'll figure it out."

Curling her fingers around the edge of his desk, Lacie slid to the front of her seat. "Either you don't care about Sorcha as much as I thought… or you care more."

"Does it matter?" Shep asked. "She going to leave the guy?"

"Maybe if you told her how you felt and the both of you stopped playing these games."

"What games?" he asked, doodling on a nearby notepad. "We screwed around, we were both single, now it's done."

"Okay," Lacie said, not believing his glib attitude for a minute. "You know how to get in touch with me."

"Stone staying with you?"

"Don't you have my cellphone number?"

"Yeah, but I want to know if I'm likely to come across him," he said, glancing up from his handiwork.

"You and Ryder have more respect for each other than you let on," Lacie said, knowing their dislike for each other was more of a front than a reality. "You came through for him, for us. You worked together to find me, to set me free."

"I thought he was insane."

Shep didn't take gratitude or compliments well. She suspected that he cultivated his façade of being idle and apathetic to conceal his true insecurities. Insecurities which had no doubt taken a beating since his last experience with Sorcha.

"Ryder wouldn't have been there if it wasn't for you," Lacie said because it was important to her to show him that there were those who appreciated him.

"He's an arrogant ass," Shep said, tossing his pen aside.

"So why help him save me? If it wasn't him you were looking out for, it was Sorch. You didn't know me at all, so your motivation had nothing to do with me."

Shep pushed away from the desk to get to his feet. "I've got shit to do."

Lacie recognized the brush off, so she stood too. It wasn't really her place to push him into confessing his emotions. "Call me if you find anything."

"Don't phone the tramp or Stone. I hear you… don't worry, I'm not in any hurry to talk to them."

"Thank you, Shep, really."

Lifting her hand toward him, Shep shook it. But his smirk told her that the gesture was as pathetic to him as it was to her. "Come back tomorrow at noon."

Saying no more, Lacie left the office. The receptionist was no longer out front, which made Lacie wonder if Shep was sleeping with her. Usually Shep hooked up with the young, busty assistant he hired. But Heather wasn't busty, or as young as Shep would normally have chosen. Heather had left without him, indicating she was either in a sulk about something or she and Shep had no physical relationship.

Lacie didn't have the time to examine his motives. Luckily, Gabe had picked Ryder up from her place so she had the truck. Lacie departed Sheppard Investigations and picked up her speed to get back to where she had parked the vehicle. She still had to get ready for the Reynolds party tonight and time was running short.

THREE

Lacie

GETTING TO SORCHA'S early was always advantageous. Lacie loved how carefully her friend put on her makeup and did her hair with practiced and minute actions, all while her mouth moved at a hundred miles an hour. They'd been going through the same routine since college. Lacie took half the time to prepare for social occasions as Sorcha did, but Sorch always looked twice as good, even while pregnant.

Being raised in high society, Sorcha was every inch the refined lady that her parents had groomed her to be... at least she was until Shep was around.

When Lacie had arrived at Sorcha's apartment all she had been asked was if she had been to see Shep. In contradiction to what Lacie had expected, her affirmative answer didn't prompt any more questions. Instead, Sorcha wanted to run through some society gossip that apparently Lacie needed to know before they got to the party.

Often Lacie didn't know the people that Sorcha spoke about, but she let her friend tell the stories anyway. Having problems with her partner in addition to the usual pregnancy woes, Sorcha was having a tough time. Listening to her gossip like she had in the old days was comforting for both of them.

Much as Sorcha had griped about the truck, she spread out in the front while Lacie drove and Lacie was sure that her friend appreciated the space. When Lacie stopped the truck outside the grand Reynolds home, the valet appeared perplexed by this vulgar vehicle. But Lacie couldn't blame him for his surprise. Few people would expect two chic and accessorized women to jump out of a vehicle that the grounds staff would look more at home in.

Sorcha's father, Lawrence Reynolds, was loyal in who he hired and when the valet recognized Sorcha from previous functions, the youngster leaped to attention. The truck grumbled away leaving Lacie and Sorcha to traverse the stairs. Lacie tucked the valet ticket into her clutch and Sorcha sighed.

"I hate these shoes," Sorcha said, fixing the strap on her shoe before starting up the stairs to the Reynolds mansion. Set on twenty acres, it comprised of two and a half floors and contained twelve bedrooms.

"The place looks great," Lacie said about the twinkling lights flanking the stairs.

When they walked through the door Sorcha gave the attendant their invitation. One of Ryder's men, Ty, stood in the background wearing a black shirt and slacks with a wire in his ear. Lacie knew he was there in case of trouble and he had his company face on—ever observant, looking mean and serious. When his eyes stopped on her, he lifted his wrist to his mouth and Lacie knew her arrival had been announced to their security network.

The ballroom looked as magnificent as it always did. The string quartet played in the corner at the moment but the Reynolds always had an array of music throughout their famous evenings. All society's darlings were in attendance, corporate CEO's rubbed shoulders with celebrities in this immense, glittering, gilded hall. Designer clothes and sparkling jewels surrounded flutes of champagne being distributed by the white-jacketed waiters.

Sorcha snagged two glasses and Lacie must have looked judgmental when Sorcha sipped because she then tsked. "It's one glass of champagne," Sorcha said, rolling her eyes when Lacie took the flute away from her. "Do you know there's evidence now that alcohol in moderation during pregnancy can be good for the mother and child? It's a stress thing."

"They can prove anything if research is biased toward a desire for a specific outcome," Lacie said, doubting the merits of Sorcha's argument.

Completely ignoring what Lacie had said, Sorcha moved onto a different topic. "How did things go with Shep?" Sorcha asked, linking their arms, and smiling at those they passed on their circuit.

Those who noticed Sorcha were surprised by the bump under Sorcha's empire line dress, but Sorcha didn't flinch in the face of their stares.

"Just as I expected it would," Lacie said. Sorcha hadn't asked about the meeting with Shep earlier because she didn't want to appear too eager. Lacie now understood her friend's ploy. "He was surprised to see me, but he was nice to me. My appearance intrigued him. It didn't take him long to figure out why I was there. I really can't believe you'd want me to draw him into this. The man was nuts about you; it wasn't just a fling for him."

"Shep's not a forever guy," Sorcha said while surveying the room.

"You keep saying that, but I'm not so sure," Lacie said.

They paused beside a marble pillar on the periphery of the room. "Who was at the front desk?" Sorcha asked.

"Sorry?"

"Did he have some itty-bitty, big-busted teenager—"

"Her name's Heather," Lacie said. "And she's at least twenty-five."

"Oh, that makes a huge difference. Is she pretty?" Sorcha kept on scanning the room and Lacie knew that the lack of eye contact meant Sorcha was dealing with a little green-eyed monster of her own.

"Are you okay?" Lacie asked, wishing her friend would just face the truth of her feelings.

"Will he take the case?" Sorcha asked, obviously unwilling to address the truth of her motivation for this interrogation.

"Yes, I'm going to see him tomorrow."

"Good."

"Sorchie!"

The shrill call of Sorcha's younger sister made Lacie take another gulp of alcohol. Sorcha's eyes rolled as she turned and plastered on a wide grin. "Sweetie," Sorcha said and the pair air kissed before they took each other's hands.

"Isn't this party a dream?" Sadie exclaimed.

It was no surprise to Lacie that Sadie ignored her. For some reason, the woman had never been interested in making friends with her. Although from everything Lacie had observed of her through the years, she thought her flaky and frivolous. Sorcha claimed it was because Sadie was a through-and-through snob. But Sorcha could have claimed that title for herself many times and she still managed to lower herself enough to be friendly with those who didn't have her economic security.

"Everybody is asking about the baby," Sadie said with a little shake of her head as she trailed her eyes down to Sorcha's swollen abdomen.

Her smile never faltered, which suggested Sadie believed herself to be doing her sister a favor by pointing out her obviously pregnant belly.

"Great," Sorcha said, trying to take a glass of champagne from Lacie, but she held it back.

"And everyone wants to know where Bruce is… where is Bruce?" Sadie asked with a practiced pout. The woman was good at what she did, Lacie had to give her that.

"Oh, he was busy tonight," Sorcha said. "He's saving himself for the engagement party."

The sisters laughed a joyful titter that made Lacie have to conceal her own. They were so funny. Neither of them was the best of friends, yet, when they were together, they maintained the façade of sisterly devotion. It was quite a feat that they managed to be so snide while wearing such expressions of civility.

"Well, now that I have the goss, I better get back to the party…" Sadie said, twisting away. "It's funny being the center of so much male attention. I guess now they know your social life is over, they're interested in the newer, younger model. Ciao!"

Sadie flounced off back to the party and Sorcha again tried to take the champagne. Lacie moved away to put it on a nearby tray and then came back to her friend.

"She only does it to frustrate you," Lacie said. "Loosen up and see your future as the host of new experiences it's going to be."

"You're not helping," Sorcha grumbled but perked up to spread her joyful expression again, indicating that someone else was about to join them.

Turning to see what had caught Sorcha's attention, Lacie saw the tall, tanned Elijah Graden approach with his shorter, paler brother, Evan. The Gradens' had been in the mining industry for five generations and were the epitome of good breeding.

"I see we've missed our chance," Elijah said to Sorcha when the men reached them. "Where's the lucky fellow?"

"Working tonight," Sorcha beamed.

"I didn't get an invitation to the wedding," Elijah said.

Sorcha held up the diamond on her ring finger. "Engagement party is next weekend."

"Ah, cart and then the horse," Elijah said, shifting his gaze to Lacie. "Miss Hart, I'd appreciate a chance to talk to you in private for a minute. Sorcha, my brother will keep you entertained, if you don't mind excusing us?"

"Yes," Evan Graden said and offered Sorcha his arm. "Would you escort me around the dance floor?"

Never passing up a chance of attention, Sorcha departed with the younger Graden, leaving Lacie alone with Elijah.

"I've been trying to contact you for months," Elijah said, sidling in close to her.

"I know, I received your messages," Lacie said. "I'm sorry, things went off the rails for a while."

"I read about it in the newspaper," he said with endearing concern. "You should have called me."

"There was nothing you could've done."

"I don't like to think of you going through that alone. What did Matt say?"

Matt Rhys was her ex-boyfriend, a man who hadn't treated her well and that she was glad to be rid of. "I haven't spoken to Matt," she said. "You know that because you'll have spoken to him yourself."

"Under duress," Elijah said. "I told you he was a fool when you went out with him."

Lacie had met Matt at one of the Reynolds other parties and their relationship had started with Sorcha's blessing. "I told you then that you were biased," Lacie said, smiling at Elijah. "I stand by that."

"Have you thought about my offer?" Elijah asked.

"I've been fielding a few commission possibilities. I'm not committing to anything right now."

"I'm not talking about commissioning you. You know what I'm talking about. I meant what I said. I meant every word I said that night."

The night he was referring to was another Reynolds event that had taken place months ago, before Ryder, before her captivity, in a time that felt like another life to her now.

"And I thought it was the Scotch talking," she said, seeking out the still absent Sorcha. Except Elijah's finger curled around her jaw to bring her attention back to him.

"We have to talk about it, Lace."

"We don't, Lija. We really don't." Raising her chin, she backed away from his touch.

"You have to let me advise you," Elijah said. "We spoke about a business plan. We were working together—"

"I know and I appreciate what you were trying to do. But you had ulterior motives. I might be socially inept but I can't believe you would genuinely be that interested in my professional profile."

"Believe it or not I am. You're a good person, Lacie, and you're sincere but you're vulnerable. You are terrible at PR and have zero business acumen. If you trust me, I can help you."

"I'm not interested in money or fame."

"No, but you do have to be protected from exploitation. Your public profile was already rising, but since your abduction… People want you, Lace, you need a decent lawyer, and a manager, a—"

"Elijah, I appreciate this, but we're at a party. It's not like I have a pad and pen at hand to take down the particulars of your ace team."

He took the champagne from her and discarded it on a table. Taking her hand, he led her to the door which led to the family's wing.

"Where are we going?" she asked when Elijah closed the heavy door behind them.

"To find a pad and pen, you hate these crowded parties anyway."

Agreeing with his observation, Lacie let herself be led down the Saxon blue hall carpet of this wide corridor.

"I'm sorry but there's no access to this part of the house."

Elijah stopped. Lacie came up short and peeped around him to see the wall that was Will in their path. She hadn't known anyone else was there when Elijah blocked her view. Now she wished that she'd stayed ignorant behind him because Will was another of Ryder's men.

"I'm a family friend," Elijah said. "You have no security concerns here."

Will's stern expression didn't falter but his eyes did travel south to fixate on their joined hands. "Due respect, sir," Will said. "Your word is nothing to me."

"That didn't sound very respectful," Elijah said. "But I understand if I was a security concern, I wouldn't announce it." Elijah must have noticed Will's consistent focus on her. "She's no security concern either. Where do you think she'd fit a weapon in that dress?"

The attempt at a joke only made the situation worse for him, not that Elijah knew it. The satin gold dress she wore hung on inch long straps over each shoulder and skimmed to mid-thigh. It wasn't skin-tight but it molded to her slight figure.

"We're looking for paper," Lacie said.

"You don't have to explain anything to him," Elijah said, glancing around at her.

"It's a courtesy," Lacie said. "We're not running amok around a house that he's protecting."

"Not this weekend at least," Elijah teased, then turned back to Will. "May we pass now?"

"You're not on the list," Will said. Lacie didn't miss that Will didn't include her in that statement.

"Let's go back to the party," she said.

"No," Elijah said and she knew this was alpha-male combatting alpha-male. "We're at liberty to—"

"No, you're not," Will said.

"I'd like to speak to your superior," Elijah said in the tone she guessed he'd use with the board of his company.

Horror at his request made her eyes flare and her heart speed up. Jumping in, she wanted to dispel that request as quickly as she could. "No," she said to Will. "No, we absolutely do not want to speak to your superior."

"We do," Elijah insisted.

There was a whisper of a smile on Will's face when he lifted his wrist to his mouth and backed away a couple of steps to talk to the team.

"I'm going back to the party. Sorcha will be missing me," Lacie said, dropping Elijah's hand to try to retreat, but Elijah got hold of her again before she could get two feet.

"Sorcha will be fine," Elijah said. "She'll enjoy the attention."

An unseen door opened further down the corridor behind Will. A moment later, Ryder appeared and strode toward them, stopping a few feet behind Will, who didn't flinch. The blank look on Ryder's face adjusted to something much harder when he saw her, Elijah, and her hand that Elijah held.

"Problems?" Ryder asked on a growl she knew was never good.

"No problem," Will said. "He requested my superior."

Ryder scrutinized the scene. "Come here," he murmured, focusing his concentration on her hand in Elijah's. Lacie wasn't going to argue. She went past Elijah, but he didn't release her. That he held on and hindered Lacie's progress intensified Ryder's focus, which pounced up to Elijah's face. "It's okay."

Ryder's words were aimed at her but his menace toward Elijah heightened.

"We're going to the office at the end of the corridor," Elijah said.

"No, you're not," Ryder said.

"This is ridiculous," Elijah said.

"Let go of the lady," Ryder said, shoulder to shoulder with Will.

"This isn't about the lady," Elijah said. "This is about your man and autocracy gone haywire."

"Would you please all stop looking at each other as though this is going to turn into a bar room brawl?" Lacie asked, amazed at how quickly the mood of a situation could change.

"Lace, we've put this off long enough already," Elijah said.

"It'll keep," she said, trying again to free her hand.

"These men are not in charge of—"

"Tonight they are," Lacie said.

"We've spent dozens of hours in rooms in this building. We've spent months—"

"Please," she whispered.

Elijah wasn't happy, but he sighed and shrugged. "The lady has served you well tonight, gentlemen," Elijah said. "Now it's just drinking and dancing."

He tried to maneuver her around, but her gaze found Ryder's and she couldn't move. "You go on, Elijah," she said.

"No, I must escort—"

"No, you must not," Will said, moving in.

"Are you threatening me?" Elijah asked. "How dare you—"

"I know these guys," Lacie said. "I'll be safe. Would you just go, Lija, please?"

Again unhappy, Elijah frowned at the men. "I'll go and check on Sorcha."

After more glaring exchanges between the men, Elijah relented and let her go before he went back down the corridor and out of the door they'd entered by. When she turned back to security, Will was doing a disappearing act of his own.

FOUR

Lacie

ONCE WILL HAD retreated through the door Ryder had entered by, Lacie folded her arms and frowned at Ryder.

"What was that?" Lacie asked.

"You tell me, who's the suit?" Ryder demanded, adopting a wider stance.

He was angry with her?

Lacie scoffed. "Why are you pissed? You and your staff—"

"My staff?" he snapped, crowding in close.

She didn't shrink because of his proximity. She kept her eyes trained to his, ready to argue if that's what he was spoiling for. "You and Will both knew we were no threat of any kind. So why get in the way?"

"I've watched you be kidnapped by one mad man; I'm not going to watch it again!"

"If I'd been in danger, I would've told Will."

"Have you got your panic button?" Ryder asked, checking his watch with his eyes and his ear.

"Yes," she said, picking up the clutch she had looped onto her wrist and waving it in the air. "It's in here."

"Funny, because my watch hasn't vibrated," he said, holding it up for her to see.

The panic button he'd given her weeks ago linked to his watch and computer. It had built-in GPS tracking. If she pushed the button, he got alerts and his software could track her.

"I wasn't in danger," she said, losing her patience.

"So you wanted to be alone with him?"

The argument veered in a new direction that renewed her frown. "What do you think was going on?" she asked. "You and I had sex this afternoon, Ryd. Do you think I was suddenly horny again and just grabbed the closest man I could find?"

"I don't know, "Lija" certainly seemed at ease with his hands on you."

"I don't believe this," she said. Holding her hands up in the air, Lacie turned around. "I'm walking away before you accuse me of anything else."

Being that it was her intention to head for the exit, Ryder seized her waist and wrangled her to the wall where he pinned her with his body. He was no longer tense and frowning. In fact as he brought himself close to her, he kept a hand on her waist to keep her near him.

"I'm sorry," he said, insinuating his lips against hers, but she tipped her head away.

"You're pissed off, ruled by your caveman brain," she said. Being with an alpha male who was best friends with a bunch of other alpha males meant Ryder wasn't always the best at being rational when it came to his primitive urges.

"Baby," he muttered, sending shudders down to her bones. "I'm sorry. Don't punish me."

"You're working," she said, keeping her mouth down and her attention away so he couldn't kiss her.

"I'm due a break," he said with his lips against her temple.

Making eye contact, she sought a straight answer. "Do you think I'm sleeping around?"

"I don't," he said. "But I don't want any man putting his hands on my girl."

"He's a businessman," she said, exasperated by Ryder's continued dislike of Elijah. "He was talking about setting me up with a lawyer."

"He wants you."

"No, he doesn't."

"You're vulnerable," Ryder said, stating his position with an equally serious expression. "It's my responsibility to look out for you. Reading people is part of my job and believe me, that guy wanted you. I'm trying to look after you, Dusty."

"It turns you on to look after me, doesn't it?" she asked, finding her smile.

"That and the dress," he mumbled and she tried to dampen her amusement.

Not quite ready to forgive his behavior, Lacie made sure he knew he was still in the doghouse. "I hope you enjoy seeing it hanging in my wardrobe the next time I invite you over."

"Mm," he hummed, crouching to take his mouth to her shoulder. "My girl's not happy with me."

"Don't," she said, pushing her shoulder into his to try to move him away. "I've had to cover your earlier exploits with make-up." She thought she was beyond the age for hickeys, though she hadn't had many in her youth. But Ryder liked to mark her body, maybe because the reminder of their connection turned both of them on.

"Mine?"

"You don't trust me," she said. That was the truth of her sulk. Ryder had seen Elijah with her and had been jealous, but he should know that he had nothing to be jealous of. "I love you so much and you don't trust me to—"

"I do," Ryder said. "Look at me, Dusty. Come on, baby, you know I—"

"I don't," she said, finding his eyes. "I've spent hours with your men, late at night, most of them have seen me almost naked in your bed. They've seen us… together. I thought we were secure. I thought we knew—"

"Baby," he murmured, cutting her words off.

"Don't think that you can "baby" me and that will make things easier," she said. "I have been with insecure men in the past and it never works out. I spend all my time trying to make them feel better even when the relationship isn't giving me what I need."

His brows came down, erasing his contrition. "Are you saying I'm not giving you what you need? That our relationship—"

"Of course not," she said, moving into his arms and softening herself a little. "I love you and our relationship. You give me the confidence to be bolder than I ever have been and that's why I can be honest with you about this."

"Okay," he said, running his hands up and down her back. "Then be honest with me."

"I like it when you're possessive. I like it when you talk about forever like it's a foregone conclusion that we'll always be together."

"It is," he said.

He still hadn't relaxed his frown, but her smile loosened, so she reached up to graze his cheek with her thumb. "That being said, I don't want you starting a fight with every man who dares to come near me. You don't like it when Sorcha takes up more of my time than she should, but you never confront her about it in an aggressive way like you did with Elijah just now."

"Let me be honest with you," he said, letting his arms settle around her. "It's not unusual for me to get a call at a party like this, when a guest thinks he's entitled to more freedom than he is. And it's not a power trip, by the way. Keeping everyone in one place keeps them safe. If we let guests wander to every corner of the house then we couldn't possibly be expected to keep them all safe. If we let people wander all over then while we're trying to keep lots of little groups safe, we're spread thin. That means the bulk of the group—who stayed where they were supposed to—is more at risk."

That made sense and she hadn't thought about it that way. These men were trying to do a job that they should be respected for because if it came to it, it was their job to step in front of the bullet.

"I understand," she said.

"It can be frustrating when a guest patronizes us and believes he can overrule us because he's worth more money than we are."

"Elijah—"

"When I came through that door, into this corridor, and I saw that it was you with this guy… I had no idea if I had been called because there was a situation in progress. If we're face to face with a threat, we have codes we can use, but that's not always an easy thing to do when the threat can hear you and is listening for signs he's been detected."

"You thought I was in danger?"

"I thought there was a possibility of it. When we face dangerous scenarios, we have to get amped, we survive on the adrenaline. That's what causes us to fight instead of fly."

"Okay, but surely when you came over and there was no trouble, you should've known I was okay."

"I don't know anything," he said. "Making assumptions gets people dead. You might think that I acted inappropriately, but I could've put my hands on the guy and forced him to do what I said. We try to be as respectful as we can be. But if I have to throw someone out then Lawrence Reynolds is not going to argue with me. He never has, we have a history. I've worked closely with him before. I spent a few weeks protecting Sadie a couple of years ago against a stalker we eventually brought down. Lawrence trusts me and has respect for what we do."

"I have a respect for you too," she said. "That doesn't mean you can accuse me of screwing around when you eliminate the possibility of physical threats."

"Okay," he smiled. "Understood. Can I say I'm sorry now?"

Still holding her smile at bay, she rolled her eyes like she was considering his request, but eventually relented. As soon as she nodded, he pulled her close and ducked to merge their mouths.

What she'd said about him being at work was true, but she was happy to help him pass the minutes of his break. Sliding her along the wall, he backed them into a recessed doorway and ran his hands down her arms to her hips where he began to gather her skirt.

Breaking their kiss, she grinned and tried to push down his wrists. "We're not getting busy in my best friend's parents' house. What if someone saw?"

"Best part about this job," he said, kissing her smile. "Security is the first to be told of any incidents."

"That's just what I need," she said, lifting her arms to drape them over his shoulders. "The guys getting another good laugh at my expense."

He wasn't as worried if his next act was anything to go by. He kept lifting her skirt, and when he reached flesh, he spread his hands on her hips and toyed with the elastic of her panties, teasing the possibility of what could happen next.

Their relationship was still new and had been founded in an intensity that hadn't yet waned. Learning each other and exploring their still fierce physical attraction was strengthening their bond. He made her more confident, giving her the chance to explore a new boldness in her nature, which hadn't existed before she'd met Ryder Stone.

A door opened in the corridor and she tensed, fearful that they'd be discovered. Her panic made Ryder turn to conceal her in the nook at his back while he peered out into the hallway to see where the sound had come from.

"Hey, Boss," Rocco chortled. "On a lap of—oh, you got company?"

"What?" the second voice was angry in its exclamation, whereas Rocco had been surprised.

The men must've noticed someone was behind Ryder's back, but they hadn't identified her. "Got a problem?" Ryder demanded.

"Might, yeah," the angry second voice was Gabe.

The man who'd taken on the role of her protector since she'd been the catalyst to renewed trust between Ryder and his men after the Wallace betrayal.

"Yeah?" Ryder asked.

"Yeah, I got a problem," Gabe said. "Have you forgotten about Lace? What are you going to say—"

She poked her head around Ryder's arm and managed a smile at the guys. Rocco grinned, as he was quick to do anyway, and Gabe took time to reorient himself out of his snit.

"I didn't know we got paid to fool around," Rocco snickered. "I've seen a few debutants in there I might like to sample on my break."

Gabe managed a smile once he'd absorbed the details. Lacie didn't know why but Gabe liked seeing her and Ryder together and happy.

"I should get back to Sorcha," Lacie said.

"We're having a goodbye party for SW next week, are you coming?" Gabe asked.

"Sorcha's engagement party is next Friday."

"We'll do it on Saturday, just for you," Rocco said.

"I'll bring Sorch," Lacie said. "Have a good night, guys."

Slinking out of their den, Lacie intended to go back to the party, but Ryder caught her hand and stalled her. Pressing a finger to his lips, she didn't let him speak because their make-out session had provided all the explanations they needed. When she lowered her finger, Ryder took her hand to his mouth and kissed the back of it.

It might seem odd that so much of their communication was unspoken, but her blush must have provided a translation for outsiders because Rocco snickered again. Ryder glared at his colleague, giving Lacie the chance to slip away.

Steeling herself before she re-entered the bustling ballroom with its classical music and refined socialites. Lacie took a breath then opened the door to join the party again. Sorcha was upon her just as Lacie selected a glass of champagne from a passing tray.

"What happened?" Sorcha whispered. "I heard you and Elijah snuck off together."

"I'd rather not talk about it," Lacie said, downing half the glass.

"I saw him thirty seconds ago over there at the buffet. He didn't look like a man who just got laid."

"If it's that obvious try not to catch a glimpse at Ryder."

Sorcha sucked in a gasp and crowded her. "You didn't! In my parents' house? I thought you were meant to be the sensible one."

"We didn't," Lacie said. "But we might have if we weren't interrupted. Ryder brings out the wild in me I guess."

"How does he do that?" Sorcha asked. "I could use a bit of that influence with Bruce."

Lacie thought about it because she had never been bold when it came to sex. Even just making out with Ryder in a corridor, a door away from a crowded party, was something she would never have considered before him. Not a single atom in her body had resisted his kiss or even wanted to. If he had tried to take things up a level, she might just have let him.

"Trust," Lacie said, which was odd in light of what they had argued about before their kiss and grope session.

Ryder's problem wasn't believing she would cheat on him. Ryder's problem was the guilt he still carried about her abduction. He saw others, especially outsiders, as threats who could hurt her and he never wanted her to be hurt again. "Ryder would never compromise my honor or disrespect me and knowing that relaxes me into being a bit more daring."

"I'd settle for a little spontaneity," Sorcha sighed. "You're having all the fun these days.

"I know you're fed up," Lacie said. Sorcha swiped a flute of champagne from a waiter, but Lacie stole it from her before she could drink. "It will get better."

"When?" Sorcha demanded. "I can't drink. I can't flirt. Any guy who smiles my way runs a mile when he sees the bump. No one wants to dance with me, and I'm stag so I can't even fawn over the guy whose fault this is."

"You mean have him fawn over you?"

"Is that too much to ask?" Sorcha asked. "I'm carrying his baby, and half the time he doesn't even show up!"

"Sorch—"

"I can count on one hand the number of times he's stayed over at mine in the last month. Three times we've had sex, Lace. Since we found out he was alive, that's it, three times!"

"Three," Lacie said.

She and Ryder had sex before sharing dinner last night and had made love before falling asleep too. In the truck, after lunch, Ryder had delivered her another orgasm, and they'd enjoyed some afternoon delight. Lacie had never had sex so frequently in her life, not that she was complaining. She swallowed more champagne then put the glasses on a side table half finished.

"Do you want to go up to your room?" Lacie asked. Sorcha still had a bedroom here at her parents' house, which the women used sometimes to get ready in or crash in after festivities were over. "We could go to the AV room and watch videos."

"There's a party on," Sorcha said. "We're not supposed to wander around the house."

Lacie had experience with that. "It's okay. I've seen the security—we can take them." Sorcha didn't react to Lacie's joke.

"I used to rule these things you know," Sorcha said, with slumped shoulders, she frowned into her hunch. "I was the belle of the ball. Every guy wanted to dance with me and the women wanted to talk to me. I was the center of the party, everyone wanted to be with me."

"Your life is going to be different now that you're engaged and going to be a mother. That doesn't mean it's going to be bad."

"It's easy to say that when you're on the outside looking in. My life is over, completely. I'm going to be one of those sad, pathetic women with no personality or interests of my own. I'll be stuck in a loveless marriage, burying myself in a bottle, surviving on a dozen Xanax a day."

"It's not going to be like that," Lacie said. Sorcha ripped her hand away when Lacie tried to take it.

"Easy for you to say!" Sorcha snapped. "If you were knocked up right now, you'd be singing a different tune! I didn't want this baby, or a husband, and now I'll be lumbered with both!"

Speechless, Lacie absorbed the vision of her wide-eyed friend who was breathing so hard that her chest heaved with every labored inhale. "You have to embrace the—"

"You're with a guy who adores you, and serves up sex at breakfast, lunch, and dinner! He told us already that he didn't take this gig for the money! He took it because he can't bear to be apart from you!"

Sorcha had been with men who were obsessed with her and when she was in those relationships, she complained of being suffocated, so her venom right now didn't make sense to Lacie.

"Sorch, I—"

"Forget it, Lacie, go be with your adorer. You hate these things anyway."

Sorcha was angry but Lacie couldn't fathom why. Knowing how Sorcha could be when she got herself in a mood, Lacie knew that trying to talk to her friend now would accomplish nothing. People didn't shy from reminding her that she disliked these kinds of social occasions and they were right. And since she had come here for the friend who didn't want her now, it was time to leave.

Lacie wouldn't risk driving with even a sip of alcohol in her system, so she scanned the room for a man in black. Toby was closest and as luck would have it, he was darting into the outer foyer. Crossing the room to follow Toby's path, Lacie found Toby and Ty alone in the space now that all the guests had arrived.

"Can one of you lend me twenty dollars?" Lacie asked. Both men reached for their rear pockets but carried on whispering to each other. "What's going on?" Lacie asked.

"Nothing," Ty said, doing a double take when he noticed the dress. His frown cleared to a grin. "Wow, Boss got a treat tonight. Has he seen the dress?"

"And what's under it," Toby muttered, earning him a swat with her clutch.

Ty was the flirt of the group and Toby had a terrible poker face, which was why he was mostly found at home hiding behind a computer screen.

They both held two tens toward her, so she took one from each of them. "Did you lose a bet or something?" Ty asked.

"Tell Ryder I'm going home."

"Wait, wait," Toby said, closing rank with Ty to block her exit. "Take the truck."

She fished the valet ticket from her bag and handed it to Toby. "Give this to Ryder. I've had a drink. He can bring the truck home when you guys are done."

"We'll take you home," Ty said, lifting his wrist toward his mouth.

Lacie caught his arm before it reached his lips and lowered it for him. "I can get myself home," she said. "You all have a job to do, and your numbers are already down." No one ever mentioned Wallace around her but she could do the math. Jamie Wallace was in jail and he'd taken another of the SW men, Eric, with him. So they were two men short of what they were used to working with.

"Boss won't like you going home alone," Ty said. "We'll be skinned if he hears we let you out that front door by yourself."

Opening her clutch, she appeased them by fishing out her house keys. Holding them up, Lacie showed that her panic button was attached to the key chain. "I have my panic button. If bad things happen, I'll push it."

"And we'll be far away from the danger and won't be able to help you," Toby said.

"I do walk down the street alone," Lacie said. "Tell him I've gone but if he chases me down, I'll know who to blame, and your boss won't get laid for a month."

As serious as she played it, she was just teasing about holding them accountable and punishing Ryder. But these men were here to do a job and she didn't want Ryder rushing after her.

It was nice to have someone care about your wellbeing, but they both had lives and work, which meant they couldn't be together twenty-four hours a day, seven days a week. Ryder couldn't do anything for her at home now anyway, she wanted to have a long soak in the tub before Ryder finished with his duties and came over to pamper her.

He could still go back to SW as he did still own the building, but after slipping out of her bed last night and rushing their encounters today, she knew he would come over to her apartment. Tonight would be about kissing and caressing. He'd spoil her with hours of devoted foreplay designed to torment her and prove that adoration Sorcha alluded to.

Lacie did have a lot to be proud of, and happy with in her life. Sorcha was scared and confused. Lacie would take the hits if Sorcha needed to vent. There had never been a more important time to be a good friend to Sorcha and Lacie would step up to the plate.

FIVE

THE PHONE HAD been ringing when she got into her apartment and she spent the better part of an hour telling Ryder that she was fine and that he could come over when he was finished working. He had.

Lacie had her bath and went to bed, just like she'd planned. She awoke in her favorite way, with Ryder's head between her thighs. The pampering lasted hours. They made love until neither could anymore and fell asleep wrapped in each other.

Her sleep was disturbed by nightmares, which often woke her. No matter how she tossed and turned during the night, she always woke up in Ryder's arms. It was a wonder that he got any sleep at all through her fitful escapades.

After fooling around in the morning, he left her to get more sleep while he made breakfast. Lacie didn't get much shuteye because she was preoccupied by her argument with Sorcha. Checking her phone for messages from Sorcha left her disappointed. It was clear that Sorcha wasn't ready to make-up just yet.

"You look worried."

Startled by his voice, Lacie looked up from her phone to see Ryder at the top of the stairs with a breakfast-laden tray.

"You didn't have to do that," she said, pushing herself up into a seated position. "I could've come down to the kitchen."

"I was a jerk last night," he said, presenting her the tray and straightening the pillow behind her back while she steadied the food. "I'm groveling."

Examining the warm pancakes, the hot coffee, and the single rose in a narrow vase, she almost didn't want to disturb the beautiful sight.

"We had a lot of sex last night," she said. "I didn't think I'd have to engrave my forgiveness into stone."

"You and Sorcha had a falling out?"

"How did you know that?" she asked, picking at a blueberry on the edge of the pancake plate.

Ryder launched his length onto the bed beside her. "You're easy to read," he said, sitting up to take his coffee from her tray. "What did you argue about?"

"We didn't argue," she said, disappointed that she wasn't in the mood to enjoy Ryder's efforts from the kitchen.

"What was it about?" he asked, blowing steam from the top of his cup.

"Men," she said, wrinkling her nose as she tried to think of how she could be more specific without betraying Sorcha's confidence. "Sort of."

After taking a mouthful of coffee, he put his cup back on the tray. "What did we do wrong?" he asked, cutting her pancake with the side of her fork.

"I don't understand it," Lacie said then he fed her the pancake.

"Understand what?"

"I understand that she's scared because everything in her life is changing… but she's so angry."

He speared another blueberry and put it to her lips. "So it wasn't an argument as much as a one-sided tirade."

Lacie breathed in the berry and popped it between her molars before she swallowed it. "She's scared."

"She takes advantage of you," Ryder said, watching the breakfast tray as he cut a few pieces of pancake into bite sized chunks.

Lacie wasn't sure what she wanted Ryder to say. She knew that he and Sorcha weren't close, so she felt the need to defend her friend. "Her life is upside down."

"She made the choices."

"She's pregnant."

"Women all over the planet are too," Ryder said, showing no sympathy for the turmoil in Sorcha's life.

Hoping further explanation would prompt some empathy, Lacie edged into the truth. "Bruce isn't helping her."

"She chose to marry the guy," he said, forking more pancake into her mouth. She chewed and swallowed then opened for more. "What's wrong with him now?"

"He doesn't love her. They spend no time together and they've had sex three times this month. I can't imagine how… you look after me all the time."

"I like looking after you."

"I know. But imagine if I was pregnant with your child." His grin flashed up. Her hand came up in a halt gesture as her eyes landed on his to convey her sincerity. "I'm not propositioning you. Don't get ideas."

His grin didn't fade. He actually came closer. "So you're pregnant with my kid, what else am I imagining?"

Trying to explain Sorcha's distress, she summarized her situation in terms she hoped he'd understand. "Imagine you're ignoring me and we never spend time together. We never make love."

"Not possible," Ryder said, shaking his head. "We all knew Booth was an idiot before this. Why is Sorcha surprised?"

He didn't seem any more understanding in the situation, he just sipped from his coffee cup. "It's not the fairy tale I suppose," Lacie said. "She's scared."

"That's not your fault," he said, putting his cup back down.

"I know that," she exhaled and fixated on the tray again to admit her own guilt. "But I'm so happy with you, and we're not in the position Sorcha and Bruce are."

"We're together by choice."

This time when he offered a fork full of pancakes she didn't open. Ryder took this as a sign to discard the fork and put the tray on the floor out of the way. When that was done, he gathered her into his arms and laid them down.

"I can't imagine marrying a man who didn't love me," Lacie said, appreciating the warmth of his embrace.

"Because you never will. We're already crazy in love, now all I have to do is get you down the aisle."

"Not this again," she said, sorry that she had managed to give him the perfect segue. "We're not talking about us."

Turning his mouth down against her, he mumbled into her hair and she heard the enjoyment in his voice. "I'm still on the "pregnant with my child" bit."

Moving on from a conversation she didn't want to have. Lacie took her thoughts to the future to see if she could envision a happy future for her best friend. "I can't imagine Sorcha with a baby, maybe it will change her. She'll step up when it's time… won't she?"

That was apparently a question Ryder didn't want to answer because he body swerved it entirely and changed the subject. "What do you want to do today?"

Happy not to push him when he didn't push her, she went with this new conversation tangent. "I have work to do, and a meeting before lunch. Darwin wants to meet tonight."

"You told me."

"Dinner at eight he said," she said.

"I'll be there. I thought we could do something together today."

"You have a debrief to do." Nudging him with her head to prompt him into action had no effect, he stayed put. "And you still need somewhere to live. Shouldn't those things take priority?"

"Nothing wrong with this place," he said, snaking a hand around to grasp her breast.

"You can't live here," she said, turning her head up, but she didn't have the scope to see his face.

"I stay here all the time," he said, fondling the flesh under his palm.

Determined to make her point and not be distracted by sex, she stayed on point. "Staying here and living here are two different things."

His hand stopped playing, but it stayed curled around her. "You have a problem with us living together?"

"No," she said, trying to wriggle out of his embrace.

"Where do you think you're going?" he asked, pulling her back to roll her body under his. "What are you not saying to me? Speak that mind of yours I love."

"I laughed in Sorcha's face at lunch yesterday."

His expression turned curious. "That's not like you."

Trying not to look him in the eye, she lowered her chin. "I couldn't help it, she… she asked if I ever worried about you—"

"And that made you laugh?"

Drawing her eyes upward, she stared truth into his wondrous gaze. "Cheating on me, she asked if I worried about you being unfaithful."

"And you laughed in her face?" Lacie nodded. "I love you."

His lips were headed for hers but she spoke to forestall him. "But last night… I was heartbroken when you accused me of messing around with Elijah."

"I trust you," he asserted, determined not to break eye contact. "Last night wasn't about you, it was about him. I only want to look after you."

Lacie wasn't sure she was buying that. "You were ready to murder Elijah. I saw it in the way you looked at him."

"While you were doing that, I was looking at him looking at you."

"Can you read minds?"

"I didn't have to," Ryder said, some of his ease morphed into that disgust of last night. "The guy was all over you. He wouldn't let you go."

"Are we going to argue like this?" she asked, the breakfast might have been forgotten but she still lay naked in their mussed sheets on her back under her hulk of a man.

"I don't want to argue at all," he said, smoothing her hair and softening again.

"We argue," she said, though it was a rare occurrence and she wondered if they were still blinded by the haze of new love and sexual attraction.

"Not about this," he said. "I love you. I trust you—"

"How can I be sure when—"

"I was ready to walk away from everything, my work, my men… you were the one. I trusted you and you, you trusted them. You're my world, Lace, and I'll never do anything to endanger you. I'll look out for you because you are my number one priority. I won't apologize for that."

He really did adore her and she couldn't doubt that. Taking a breath, she opened her hands on his sides. "I don't want you to apologize," she said. "I want you to know beyond a shadow of a doubt that I love you, and I have no interest, or inclination toward any other man. I want you."

"Then we agree," he said and returned his grin. "I do believe it. I just want to look after you, it's my priority."

This time she let him kiss her, and his hand found its way under the cover to fondle her bare breast.

"No funny ideas," she said, twisting her head away from their kiss. "I have a meeting."

"What kind of meeting?" he asked, rolling off her to let her depart the bed. Except she didn't. She had a meeting, but it wasn't as imminent as she had led him to believe.

"I'm not allowed to tell you," she said. Reaching for the snap on his jeans, she unfastened them and squeezed her hand around his immediate reaction to her intrusion.

Locking his fingers behind his head, Ryder stretched out to allow her perusal. "Who says?"

"My best friend," she said, pulling his tee shirt up from his abs. "Your body is amazing."

Commando, she got a good view.

"Thanks, what is your best friend keeping from me?"

Leaning in, she dipped her tongue into his belly button. "You're asking me to betray my friend's confidence."

"Yeah," he said, casting his eyes down to hers.

"If I'd betray hers, how do you know I won't betray yours?"

Leaning in again, she kissed the tip of his penis then sucked the head between her lips. He inhaled through his gritted teeth.

"You're killing me, Lace," he said and her smile curled around his member told him that she knew it. "You would never betray me, baby. Our bond is real. It's deep. Sorcha's confidence probably doesn't work both ways."

"I love you," she said, drawing her tongue down the underside of him to his base.

"What kind of meeting?" he asked, snatching her up and pinning her down.

"I was enjoying that," she grinned. "Best start to the day I could ever have."

"What kind of meeting?" he said, parting her legs with his.

"With Shep," she said, arching upward but he pulled back, teasing her as she had done to him moments ago. "You can't tell…"

Pushing his pelvis down to hers, his thickness pushed against her center and her moan was automatic. "Doing what with Shep?"

"She thinks…" Lacie said, trying to wriggle down but Ryder kept her pinned. "Bruce is cheating."

Satisfied that he had his answer, he freed her only to pull back and slam into her. Grabbing his hair in her fists, Lacie forced their mouths to unite while their bodies moved together. Her life had never been better than this and she could only hope she would have this forever.

SIX

Lacie

SHE HAD BEEN so tempted to stay in bed with Ryder, but life kept them busy. Knowing they would come together at the end of every day warmed her from the inside out. So with a languorous kiss in the front seat of the truck she and Ryder said goodbye and parted.

For the second time in as many days, Lacie entered Sheppard Investigations for her noon meeting. Heather wasn't at her desk and Lacie knew about Shep's loose work ethic and how he liked to wander off to the pool hall in the middle of the day.

Hoping that he hadn't forgotten about their appointment, Lacie went straight for the office. Figuring that they'd all been through enough with each other to negate the need for niceties, Lacie didn't knock and instead burst through the door then came up short.

Heather was in the office with Shep, in his lap, with her arms around his neck, and their mouths joined. Or Lacie assumed from the swollen lips and shallow breaths that's what she had walked in on because right now they were fixated on her.

Frozen in the moment, Lacie fumbled for words. "We had an appointment."

"Noon already," Shep said, giving Heather a shove to put her on her feet. Heather paused for half a beat then scurried across the room wearing a frisky grin and exited behind Lacie.

"Have you had an assistant that you haven't had sex with?"

"If you think what you saw was sex then Stone's been doing you wrong… My door is always open if you need a better demonstration." Shep ran his hands down his shirt then pulled himself into the desk.

Lacie closed the space between her and the desk to take a seat. "What did you find?"

"I've been on it less than twenty-four hours."

Already discouraged by his lack of professionalism, Lacie would not cut him any slack. "You told me to come today. Why would you have done that if—"

"I've been poking around… There was a big party at the Reynolds' last night. He wasn't there."

"I know," Lacie said. "I was at the party with Sorch. Where was he?"

"I didn't find him… I've pulled his credit report, family documents, employment history, though he doesn't seem to be working anywhere right now."

Losing some of her patience, she sighed. "I asked you to get information, not recount things Sorcha will have told me. Bruce has been going through his physiotherapy. Rehabilitating after what he went through. There hasn't been time for him to find work."

Sorcha wouldn't appreciate Lacie disparaging her fiancé, even if Sorcha wanted to disparage him herself. So in the face of other parties, Lacie would defend

Bruce… though she herself was running out of excuses as to why he was still sitting on his ass feeling sorry for himself.

"You want me to feel sorry for him?" Shep asked, displaying a lack of empathy similar to Ryder's.

"No," Lacie said. "I'm offering an explanation."

"Good, because he's the fucker that got himself, and all the rest of us, involved."

"Just what exactly did you go through?"

"You're snippy this morning. You and Stone fighting about something?"

"Not everything is your business," Lacie said, though she knew her attitude wasn't Shep's fault.

Being there, talking about Bruce, it was a reminder of what she'd seen, what she had experienced, and that changed her whole mood. Lacie had watched Wallace taunt Bruce. She'd watched the men beat him until she was sure he was dead. She couldn't make excuses for how Bruce treated Sorcha, but it was easy to forget he'd gone through a traumatizing experience of his own.

"I'll go by Booth's place this afternoon," Shep said, spreading his hands on the papers that were covering his desk. "Try to find out where he is."

"Then?" she asked, wanting to be sure Shep had an actual plan and wasn't just blowing smoke.

"Then I find out what he's been up to."

"I appreciate this," she said. Shep could've told her to go to hell, he probably should have. But when you cared about someone the way he cared about Sorcha even negative contact was better than no contact.

Lacie guessed they were at the end of their meeting, but Shep picked up a pen and ran it through his fingers a couple of times and she paused, expecting him to say something else. "Why did the tramp send you here?"

"What?" Lacie asked.

"Stone could've done this for you."

"I know. Sorcha didn't think it was right that Ryder be asked to… if we're all going to be socializing."

"Right," Shep said, pressing the pen into the tabletop. "But it's fine to yank my chain?"

"Ryder knows. He knows I've spoken to you, and what we spoke about. If you need help—"

"I don't need help," he sneered. "You're Sorcha's big protector. She can't do anything wrong in your eyes, can she?"

Now she had to switch on her defense of Sorcha button for the second time today. "She's going through a lot at the moment."

"When is she not?" he muttered. "The woman's a drama queen."

"Never stopped you from taking her to bed."

"She's hot," Shep shrugged then peered closer. "You don't think it's weird that she sent you to me?"

"No odder than you agreeing to take the case," Lacie said. "I know Sorcha feels for you, just like I know you feel for her. But she believes she's doing the right thing by securing a relationship with her child's father."

"Doesn't seem too secure to me if he's screwing around."

"If you don't want to do this, say it and I'll figure something else out."

"She'd like that, wouldn't she?" he said, returning to his sneer. "You trot back and tell her I refused the case, what's she going to take from that?"

"Maybe the truth?" Lacie said, losing another thread of her sanity.

The relationship between Sorcha and Shep had been hailed as "superficial" sex without the strings. But every time Lacie experienced either of them with, or talking about, the other, the same thing happened, tensions ran high and they got snarky.

"I'll take the case," he declared. "Your money is as good as anybody else's."

"Thank you," Lacie said.

An awkward moment passed between them. The silence vibrated with the truths that weren't being faced.

"Stone was okay with you using the competition?"

"This isn't about Ryder, and this isn't about me. But he knows I'm here, though Sorcha told me not to tell him," Lacie admitted and acknowledging the betrayal made her cheeks burn.

"You're taking a risk telling me that," he muttered, reaching for his pen which he took to his mouth.

"No, I'm not," she said. "I want you to know that Ryder is at your disposal. If you need resources or help—"

"I'll call you when I have something," Shep said, not interested in reading into, or rather acknowledging, Lacie's point. "Later in the week."

Shep and Sorcha needed their heads knocked together. Lacie knew that they cared for each other. They probably knew it themselves too. But Sorcha believed that being with her baby's father was the right thing to do. Her family thought it was the right thing too.

To Lacie's knowledge none of them knew Shep, but he wouldn't be the kind of man the Reynolds would expect their eldest daughter to marry. Shep wasn't the marrying kind. Imagining him with the house, the car, and the kids was tough for Lacie. She had to trust that Sorcha was doing the right thing, and as long as Sorcha believed it, Lacie would support her.

SEVEN

Lacie

BY FRIDAY, LACIE hadn't heard from Shep. She would have expected to hear something but knew better than to harass him. Sorcha had other things on her mind this week and hadn't followed up. A couple of times Lacie had thought it was in Sorcha's mind to ask about Shep because there had been a few unfinished sentences. But Sorcha always changed the subject and avoided talking about Seth Sheppard.

"I'm ready to go home," Ryder said as he closed the truck door behind her.

Lacie linked her fingers between his to lead them toward the hotel where the Reynolds-Booth engagement party was being held. "We just got here," Lacie said. "Besides we booked a room to spend the night. I'm looking forward to living in luxury for a night."

"We reserved the room because Sorcha insisted we join her and her parents for breakfast tomorrow."

"And when you griped about that the first time, I promised you'd get laid as a reward for your compliance, didn't I?"

He leaned in close to speak. "I got laid before we left the house."

She didn't need the reminder of why they were late. "You won't need to be again then, will you?"

Picking up the pace, they got to the sidewalk. "I didn't say that," he said. "My point is I'd have gotten laid whether we were at home or in this hotel."

"Really?" Lacie asked, hurrying along the street. "You might find it difficult to get laid at home now that I'm here."

"Which is the only reason I'm here right now," he said. "Sorcha drives me nuts at the best of times and Bruce is an idiot."

Ryder opened the sleek glass door of the hotel and guided her in with a hand at the small of her back. "We don't have to stay at the party late," Lacie said over her shoulder. "As soon as we're done with the glad-handing and have ensured Sorcha has got a bunch of great presents. Then we can say goodnight and head for the bed that we have in the building."

The lobby was large and shiny, everything was polished to within an inch of its life. Ryder went toward the check-in desk and Lacie admired the proud easel providing direction to the Booth engagement event. The large black canvas was conspicuous but the golden lettering shone like everything else here.

A group of sleek socialites moved in the direction of the indicated function room. They were glittering and beautiful, demure in their conversation. They smiled as if this was the most thrilling event they'd been to all year, when Lacie knew most of them were only here for the gossip. Turning up pregnant and unmarried was scandal gold in the circles Sorcha grew up in. That may have been the reason why Sorcha had distanced herself from her family in recent years, favoring instead "the real world" as Sorcha called it.

Ryder handed over a spare car key to the bellhop so he could retrieve their luggage. He then came to her side with the intention of going straight to the event. Ryder took her hand and began to move in the direction of the hall but Lacie stayed put.

"Are you okay?" he asked, coming back to her.

The sudden reality of going into a room of strangers made her temperature drop. If these people loved scandal, her kidnapping was going to be a hot topic of the night too. "Can we go upstairs first, please?"

"Sure." Switching trajectory to the elevator, Ryder took her inside and selected their floor before gathering her into his arms. "Talk to me," he mumbled into her hair.

"I don't know," she said, her voice quivering. "I just—"

"Your anxiety is normal. I've told you that. If you're not up for it—"

"I could never let Sorcha down," Lacie said, closing her eyes and trying her best to shirk this madness that had overcome her.

"She wouldn't offer you the same courtesy."

"That's not fair…" Lacie found some of her buoyancy when defending her friend. "Sorcha's unhappy with me already. I don't need to make the situation any worse."

"Why is she unhappy?"

That was a question that Lacie didn't want to answer, so she changed the subject. "How would you feel about going away? Just us."

"I love it. Let's go now," he said. Either he was easily distracted or he really did want to jet off and leave their responsibilities behind without any notice.

"I meant later in the year," she said. "We could plan it all out and give ourselves something to look forward to."

"We could get married," he said. "We could look forward to that."

"Sorcha would never forgive me for getting married before her."

The elevator doors opened. Lacie moved to exit but Ryder caught her arm and bounced her form back to his. "Is that why you keep saying no to me?"

"You haven't asked me, not properly."

His frustrated confusion melted to a satisfied curiosity. "Is that right?"

Lacie wasn't sure that she liked his sly tone. "Why are you looking at me like that?"

"No reason," he said, sliding his fingers between hers and taking her out of the elevator to a wide hall. The thick carpet and fresh cut flowers were lush but the clue came with the single door to the left, and the grand double doors in front of them.

"Ryder," she said with a tone of warning. Sliding the key into the lock on one of the double doors, it beeped, giving him leave to open both doors and urge her inside.

"It's a treat," he said.

The space in front of her was vast. Glass doors led to a wide balcony and the view beyond was spectacular. The furniture was leather and oak. Her heels sank into the carpet pile making her wobble on her feet.

"I can't believe you…"

"Penthouse," he said, passing her to take the champagne from the ice bucket on the central foyer table. Beyond, the room opened out to a lush living space.

"You booked the penthouse?" she said. Kicking off her shoes, she crossed to him to take the filled flute he offered her. "Sorcha will kill us."

"I reserved it on the proviso that if the engaged couple requested it, they could have it. They didn't want it."

"Sorcha will kill Bruce if she ever finds that out."

"A toast," he said. "To the most beautiful woman in the world. May she continue to take pity on me and allow me to be the man in her life."

Their glasses connected with a satisfying ting. "We shouldn't stay up here long," Lacie said, taking a drink and acknowledging that her heart rate was beginning to return to normal.

"Why is Sorcha mad at you?" he asked.

Exhaling, she should have known better than to assume he'd forget something or let a difficult subject drop. "Because I told her that I told you about Shep," Lacie said.

"Ah."

"I didn't tell her what I walked in on Shep doing in his chair with his assistant."

"You think he set it up like that?" Ryder asked. "So that you would see him with Heather?"

"I don't know," she said and shrugged. "You know him better than I do. He's fooled around with most of his assistants, so I suppose it wouldn't be unusual for him to be intimate with them in the office."

"He's also conniving. If you're right about his feelings for Sorcha, then he no doubt wanted you to pass on details of the encounter in hope of provoking a reaction in Sorcha."

"It's all so complicated," she said, appreciating the alcohol in her hand.

"It's pretty simple, but if neither of them will get their heads out of their asses…"

Lacie admired the engraving on the ice-bucket and the sweet scent in the room. "Sorcha has more important things to worry about than Shep," Lacie said.

"Are you sorry you told her the truth?" he asked.

"I wasn't going to lie to her. After telling Shep he could use your resources, well, it seemed like the truth might come out," Lacie said. "I figured it was better to tell her up front."

"It was," he said. Taking her hand, he led her to the couch and seated her at an angle so that he could sit behind her and massage her shoulders.

His fingers kneaded the knots and her tension began to recede. "But she's not happy with me. I can understand why."

"You didn't do anything wrong," he said. "You trust me and we're honest with each other. Sorcha should be happy that you found yourself a secure relationship."

"She's embarrassed," Lacie said. "She made a song and dance about confidentiality between girlfriends, but I think the truth is, she's embarrassed. We haven't talked much about what happened at her parents' party last week. She says her hormones make her erratic, which I guess is true."

"Doesn't explain why she was like this before the pregnancy," he mumbled.

Letting one of her hands rise to still his, she peeked over her shoulder at him. "She's terrified about becoming a parent. She thought Bruce was a better bet, that he would be there for her and have the means to support her, and now she fears he's cheating. Sorcha could find herself alone if Shep comes up with evidence to support Bruce's cheating."

"And if he does, are you sure that Sorcha will leave him?"

She wasn't. Sorcha might be too afraid to embark on this journey by herself and she had been raised to believe that appearances were important. Not marrying the father of her child would send Sorcha into uncharted territory. As bold as her friend could be, Lacie wasn't sure that Sorcha coveted the role of pioneer.

"We should go down the stairs," Lacie said, patting his hand. "I feel better."

"Are you sure?"

"Yeah," she said.

Rising from the couch, she used her link with his hand to bring him to his feet too. With another gulp of her champagne, she put the glass aside.

"If you start to feel anxious or you need some time out from the party…"

"I'll be fine," she said. Smiling, she took his glass away from him and they headed out for a return trip downstairs.

By the time they walked into the party, they were almost an hour late. After being delayed at home and then their trip upstairs, time had mounted. Sorcha would have been expecting them at the commencement of the party, and Lacie could only hope that Sorch had been too busy basking in the adoration of the guests to notice their tardiness.

"We don't have to do this," Ryder said, as they followed the sign indicating the engagement party location.

"Sorcha's going to kill me," Lacie muttered, looking around for the familiar face of her friend.

"I care about you, not her," Ryder said. "If you're uncomfortable—"

"Why would I be uncomfortable?" Lacie asked, turning to walk beside him so that she could look into his eyes. "You're here. You're not going to leave me to the hounds if there are any, are you?"

"No—"

"My boyfriend's a bodyguard," Lacie said, squeezing his hand with both of hers. "Sorcha got it right. How many ways do you know how to kill a person?"

"One's enough," Ryder said. "But I believe in variety."

Lacie leaned in close. "I know. I share a bed with you."

Ryder dipped near her when she stopped outside the open function room doors. But Sorcha's sudden arrival stopped him before they could seal their kiss.

"Lacie! Where have you been?" Sorcha exclaimed and rushed up beside them to grab Lacie's arm.

"Sorry we're late," Lacie said, but Sorcha wasn't listening.

"It's a nightmare in here. Bruce is too busy drinking with his cousins to notice everyone staring at my stomach."

Sorcha wore a sand-colored dress that draped beautifully but she was very pregnant and there was no way to disguise that now.

"You get over there and tell him to get with it," Sorcha commanded Ryder. "Lace, you're with me."

Sorcha began to walk with Lacie in her clutches but Ryder didn't let go so Lacie rebounded against him.

"Not tonight, Sorch," Ryder said.

"Uh, it's my party," Sorcha said.

"Cry if you want to," Ryder said, not swayed by Sorcha's declaration. "But I'm not leaving Lacie tonight. You get two for the price of one right here."

"Who's going to tell Bruce to forget about his stupid cousins?" she asked, at a loss as to what to do if Ryder wouldn't step in.

"Bruce and I don't exactly know—"

Lacie cut Ryder off. "I can talk to him if—"

"You're not going near him," Ryder said and his ease became anger.

"Which reminds me," Sorcha said, coming nearer and decreasing her volume. "Ixnay on the… you know."

"No one knows about what happened?" Lacie said, finding it difficult to believe no one knew about Bruce's involvement with Jamie Wallace and her kidnap.

"Except they do," Ryder said, cutting through the bullshit. "They know what happened to Lacie. They must know about Bruce's involvement as well."

"Well… yeah…" Sorcha said. "But we're not talking about it."

"It's fine," Lacie said. Their group of three began to move into the sparkling room filled with champagne, and finely dressed society, which were all encompassed in the melody of the string band.

Sorcha snagged a glass of champagne and downed half of it. "I thought this was supposed to be fun," Sorcha grumbled when they stopped just inside the door. "Bruce just ignores me. This isn't how I expected…" She trailed off and gulped more champagne.

"I wish you wouldn't do that," Lacie said, scowling at the champagne in Sorcha's hand. "You know how I—"

"Ryder Stone."

The booming voice drew their attention away from Sorcha's drinking. Tellingly, Sorcha shoved the flute into Lacie's hand. The man approaching was Lawrence Reynolds himself, not a man known for being easily impressed or won round. At his side was his smaller, but by no means meek, wife, Amelia Reynolds, Sorcha's mother.

"Lawrence," Ryder said, accepting the hand Lawrence held out. The men shook hands like old friends—like close, trusted compadres.

"I didn't know you'd been invited to this thing. It's good to see a friend." Lawrence Reynolds didn't need to vocalize his boredom. This was a man who pandered to his girls, or at least enabled his wife to.

"I'm plus one tonight," Ryder said, lifting his hand joined to Lacie's, while Lacie put Sorcha's flute aside.

"So I see," Lawrence said, smiling at the couple. "Lacie, this is a surprise. Stone's a vast improvement on anything we've seen you with before, though I have to say we rarely see you with anyone."

"And you won't," Ryder said. "No one but me." Ryder kissed the back of Lacie's hand.

"Is that so," Lawrence said, nodding in approval. "You've been tight lipped about this, both of you. How did it...? Oh, your disappearance, were you—"

"She's here where she belongs," Ryder said.

"Shame for you, Sorcha," Lawrence said. "You've missed a great one here. It's a shame you didn't find this one first."

"Before our Sorcha found Bruce, or before Lacie got to our Ryder?" Amelia Reynolds said.

Lacie saw the way Amelia Reynolds smiled at Ryder. The woman hadn't lost that sparkling flirtation of her youth but Amelia kept her hand in the crook of Lawrence's arm proving that she adored her husband. Sorcha on the other hand was positively fuming, though she kept her plastic smile in place.

"I love my girl, Lawrence," Ryder said. "She turned my head. I knew it in that first minute."

"You're a serious man," Lawrence said. "I know what happens when you've made up your mind." Lawrence turned his attention to Lacie. "It's about time for you, girlie, you're a good girl. You're a lucky man, Ryder." The men shook hands again.

"I know it."

"Shame you don't have your friend's taste," Lawrence said to Sorcha.

"Lawrence," Amelia chastised with a smile. "Our daughter's taste is…" No one knew quite how to finish that thought.

"Where is Booth?" Lawrence asked and they all looked around to no avail.

"Daddy, he's hosting. This is our party," Sorcha said, starting a trend that would no doubt continue through her marriage of making excuses for her groom.

"Stone, come and sit at our table," Lawrence said, slapping a hand to his shoulder. "There are some people I want to introduce you to. And I want to talk shop with you for a while."

"Not tonight, Lawrence, like I said I'm plus one."

"It's okay," Sorcha said, grabbing Lacie. "We'll do a few laps together."

"I'm Lacie's date," Ryder said.

"I can go with Sorcha," Lacie said, but Ryder didn't release her hand. "I'll stay in your eye line."

"Wow, how insecure are you, Ryder?" Sorcha asked, not disguising her snort of disapproval.

Before Lacie looked to the floor, she saw that each face around them was flabbergasted by Sorcha's words.

"He's looking out for me," Lacie said, revealing more of herself than she ordinarily would in such a large group. "I was uncomfortable tonight. I have some trouble with strangers."

"Sit with us," Lawrence said. "No one will approach you at our table."

"Uh, who's going to work the party with me?" Sorcha demanded.

"Find Booth," Ryder said, noticing that Lawrence was muttering to himself as he glared around the room, presumably trying to find Bruce.

"He's busy," Sorcha said.

"Hello all, you guys keeping the party all to yourselves?" Sadie approached from the side to invade their group. Sidling up close to Ryder, she widened her smile.

"There, take your sister," Lawrence said to Sorcha and held his arm out for Lacie who linked her hand into his elbow while keeping the other hand in Ryder's.

Sorcha wanted to argue and Sadie wanted to say something to their father's command. But Lacie didn't leave the protection between these men. She'd save Sorcha in a while, once she had her bearings.

EIGHT

Lacie

OF ALL THE Reynolds' parties Lacie had been to, this engagement party was the best by far, with the last one coming a close second. The fact that Ryder was at her side for the duration wasn't lost on her. Just having him around made a host of activities more fun.

Ryder and Lawrence spent most of the night in conversation but Ryder's hand remained on her thigh throughout their discussions.

"How you doing?" Ryder asked, turning his lips down to her temple. "Do you need anything?"

"You," she said.

The corner of his mouth slid upward. "Right here?"

"I meant in life," she said, nudging him. "Everything you're doing, that's what I need."

"Lawrence wants an invite to our party."

"What party?" she asked.

"Our engagement," Ryder said.

"StoneWall's party is tomorrow night," she said, reminding him of the event. "Invite him to that."

"That's not a classy event like this," Ryder said, scanning the door. "It will be one step above a frat party."

Taking her attention away from the partygoers around her, she did a little teasing of her own. "Thanks for the warning," Lacie said. "I wasn't warned about the mandatory alcohol poisoning and group sex."

His hand found its way under the hem of her dress. "Get as drunk as you like," Ryder said, leaning in closer. "Sex is required but the group part is plain absurd. Do I seem like the sharing type?"

He kissed her but she deliberately tipped her chin down to keep it chaste. "A party like this isn't us," Lacie said, looking out into the room.

"No?"

She observed the faces and the glamour surrounding them. The details of the environment emphasized the highly convoluted situation.

"You have to get the business up and running again before we can think about having any kind of party for ourselves," she said, not ready to start planning their own engagement party.

"We exchange on Tuesday," Ryder said. "We'll never have to see that place again."

"What happens next?" she asked. "Have you decided?"

"I have," he said and she stopped moving to blink up at him.

She hadn't expected him to respond in the affirmative. He hadn't hinted to her about any plans he'd made or places he'd scoped out.

"You have?"

"Yes," he said, keeping his head up, though his smug smile teased her.

Squeezing his thigh, she was too intrigued to play with him. "Tell me."

"I'm going to let you see the place when it's finished," he said, pulling her closer and kissing her head. "I want it to be a surprise."

"I'm not sure I like surprises," she said, accepting that he was keeping her in the dark about this development.

He did seem pleased with himself, so she took it on faith that he was doing something positive.

"You'll like this one," he said.

Ryder was confident. When it came to business, and to her, he knew what he was doing. Being involved in the process would put pressure on her and ultimately, this was his place of business, so it was right that he made all the decisions about it. That didn't mean she wouldn't be eagle-eyed in her search for clues as to what he was setting up.

NINE

Lacie

THE KNOCK ON her apartment door had speared Lacie with hope. When she opened it to reveal Sorcha, Lacie was frustrated with her foolish hope that Ryder would have dropped by. He wouldn't drop by unannounced, not when he delighted in teasing her about what he was doing at his new place of business. It had been a week since the engagement party where he'd revealed the existence of this secret plan. Despite her attempts to wheedle more information out of him, she was no further forward in deciphering what he was up to. Ryder knew how to be covert.

Seeing Sorcha happy boosted Lacie's mood. Bruce had been more attentive and Sorcha had spent the morning with her future mother-in-law buying clothes for the baby. While showing off her wares, Sorcha beamed, and Lacie dared to hope that they'd been wrong about Bruce's infidelity.

Ryder had been manic, so busy in fact that Lacie had spent the majority of the week alone, which reminded her of how empty her life was without him. He could be overprotective sometimes, but he was a bodyguard who had seen the worst of life and he wanted to shield her from those things. Lacie should have been more grateful for the man who adored her and could think of nothing worse than losing her again. She felt like she hadn't truly appreciated him, not until he was too busy to spoil her with his attention.

Her days had been filled with work and her muse had always been with her through every peak and valley in her life. In spite of all those hours alone with her clay, Lacie was still preoccupied by Ryder, where he was and what he was doing.

Usually when she was worried or distracted, a few hours with her clay would make the world right again. Ryder had become her grounding point and as much as she missed him, she was also excited by what he had in store. It was important to her that he had focus and this new venture, she hoped, would be it.

The two women had been seated in Lacie's apartment for a little more than an hour. Sorcha had been talking for a while, but Lacie had no idea what her friend was saying. When her eye caught the clock on the windowsill, she tensed and straightened her posture.

"I should get going," Lacie said, cutting Sorcha off mid-sentence.

"You have that thing with Monty today," Sorcha said, taking another cookie from the plate Lacie had brought from the kitchen for her on her arrival. "For the exhibit. Are you excited?"

"I should be," Lacie said, mustering a pathetic smile.

Sorcha admired her cookie as she chewed a chunk then swallowed it. "Are you doing that piece for Darwin? He's been very understanding about the delays and everything."

"He met Ryder," Lacie said.

It turned out he could be quite a useful weapon in her arsenal.

"Ryder scared him?" Sorcha asked, brushing crumbs from her thigh.

Ryder was more of a diplomat than Sorcha might give him credit for. During their dinner with Darwin, Ryder had been attentive and managed to win Darwin's favor despite the businessman appearing perturbed when they sat down together.

"Ryder didn't scare him, but… Darwin is happy being patient," Lacie said, focusing on the cookie plate. "I'm not really in the mood to work on commissions."

"You agreed to do the exhibition with Monty."

"He's a friend and he hasn't put any pressure on me," Lacie said. The agreement had been made weeks ago and the date had seemed so far away, Lacie had been sure she would be back in top form. But work still took a lot out of her and she knew she wasn't yet back at her best. "He's marketing it as a career re-launch. Since the abduction there has been more interest in my work. Monty's been handling the press interest. He's been great."

"He runs a small, private gallery," Sorcha said. "You're a star. He gains notoriety with you."

"He's been good to me," Lacie said, not happy with the implication that Monty's motives had been anything other than noble.

"I know," Sorcha said, swaying toward Lacie to snag her hand on her knee. "I love him, you know I do."

"Jimmy too," Lacie said, never forgetting the hard work Jimmy had put in over the last couple of months for her.

Jimmy was Monty's young assistant at the gallery. He'd been obsessed with Lacie for years, but it was harmless infatuation that usually manifested in the youngster losing the ability to form complete sentences whenever she was around. His admiration never failed to humble Lacie.

"Yes, of course. Jimmy is a misguided sweetheart," Sorcha said.

"I have to get going," Lacie said.

If they got onto a new topic of conversation then she would be delayed and she didn't want to be late. Monty might believe something had happened to her and she didn't want to cause anyone to worry.

Sorcha gathered up the baby clothing, and Lacie helped her pack it up. They folded each item back in its crisp paper and boxed it or bagged it where necessary. The baby was due in eight weeks. A new human would be in the world, and Sorcha would be responsible for that new life. Seeing Sorcha engaged with that reality filled Lacie with hope, but she couldn't join in the joy.

The cookies and cups were cleaned up in the kitchen, then both women donned their outdoor gear. They were approaching the door when there was another knock.

"Doesn't Ryder have a key?" Sorcha asked, stopping just a few feet from the door.

"Yes," Lacie said. While she wasn't expecting anyone, Lacie didn't hold out hope that Ryder was on the other side of that door because she hadn't seen much of him during daylight this week. Passing Sorcha, she opened the door to find that she was right. "Shep?"

"I've been trying to get in touch with you," he said, making no move to come inside. If he was frustrated by coming here, then his annoyance only grew when Sorcha moved into view behind her.

"What are you doing here?" Sorcha demanded of him, rounding Lacie and straightening her back so as to better present her chest.

"Me and the Little Lady are having sex. What's it to you?" he sniped.

Lacie opened her mouth and lifted a finger to refute his claim, but Sorcha spoke before she could.

Sorcha scoffed and moved toward him. "Lacie is a sane, rational human being. She's way too smart to get mixed up with the likes of you."

"What does that make you?" Shep asked Sorcha, his brow furrowed, but his mouth stayed relaxed.

The baby bump was the only thing between the pair now. "Charitable," Sorcha snarked.

Now it was his turn to scoff. "You don't make a guy work for it if you're handing out charity."

"You didn't work for it!"

Nodding, he agreed. "True, you do hand it out pretty easy." Shep glanced down at the bump.

"Don't look at my child that way!" Sorcha exclaimed and wrapped her arms around her stomach.

"You're seeing things," Shep said, drawing his eyes back to Sorcha's face. "It's all in your head. Doesn't pregnancy mess with your mind or something?"

"Yeah, I'm the crazy one," Sorcha said, dismissing him with the tilt of her chin.

Crossing Lacie's threshold, Shep forced Sorcha to take a step back. "I think you might just be, sugar-hips. You've been ga-ga in love with Booth for the last couple of days. I don't know anyone in their right mind who would be attracted to that loser."

Sorcha's jaw swung loose as she made an affronted squeal. "You were spying on me?"

"Ordered to," Shep said, glancing at Lacie before he narrowed his eyes on Sorcha. "You want to pay me to watch that kinda shit, it's going to cost you more."

Sorcha's frown joined the revulsion in her words. "You're disgusting!" Sorcha declared.

"Guys!" Lacie shouted. If she didn't take control of this now then it was likely the pair would mount each other there in her living room with her present. "Keep arguing if you want but you can't do it here. I have a meeting to get to."

"Pick up your damned phone once in a while, Lacie," Shep snapped. He fixed on Sorcha for a score of seconds and although he wanted to convey anger, it was obvious that his expression was a mask for a true hurt. His feelings went unspoken though because he turned on his heels and marched off.

"Yuck, I can't believe I let him near me," Sorcha said, moving outside for Lacie to lock up.

Lacie saw through her friend's indignation but chose not to needle her about it. In her own time, Sorcha would come around to the truth. The possibility existed that Sorcha already knew it, but Bruce was from a good family and was the father of her child. Sorcha believed she had made her bed.

If Shep had been working on the case over the last few days, he'd have seen Sorcha and Bruce playing at being a happy family. Lacie couldn't blame him for being irked. A part of him had to suspect this was all just one big joke meant to exacerbate his unhappiness.

Witnessing Sorcha and Bruce's happiness would be tough on Shep, but in a perverse way, Lacie was encouraged. Shep couldn't have found evidence of cheating or he would have delighted in presenting both women with it.

Sorcha skulked down to the car and gave Lacie a ride to the gallery for her meeting with Monty. Few words were exchanged during the journey which told Lacie Sorcha wasn't half as detached from Shep as she'd want the world to believe.

TEN

Lacie

"YOU'RE NOT YOURSELF," Monty said.

Their meeting had gone well. The idea was to talk about plans for the exhibition. They'd covered the basics but Lacie's heart wasn't in it, which apparently Monty had noticed. They sat together in his office, drinking tea, and usually they'd be chatty, but shooting the breeze was beyond her ability this day.

"I'm sorry," Lacie said, trying to shake herself into the moment.

Monty was an astute man who had all the time in the world for people. "You have to talk to Ryder."

She shook her head and sipped her tea before replacing the cup in its saucer. "No, he has enough on his plate," she said. "He's setting up a new business and… I'm just tired."

"Do you want to talk more about your exhibition? I can't tell you how grateful I am that you chose us to stage your re-launch." His joy perked her up some.

"You're one of my closest friends, Monty," she said, proud that she had put the grin on Monty's face. "I trust you. You've always been there for me."

Monty had a large office with a bistro table set in the bay window just for this type of occasion.

"The tickets sold out within the hour."

Lacie lifted her teacup to her lips. "Tickets," she said.

"For launch night," Monty said. "Everyone is waiting with bated breath. We've added another week but we're still selling tickets for the viewing engagements."

"That's good," Lacie said, turning the cup on its saucer. Tea in the States didn't taste the same as it did at home, even when it was made to her specification. To be honest, she had never noticed or minded the difference, until today. Maybe it was her separation from Ryder that was making her crave the comfort of her mother's brew or maybe it was the idea of people buying tickets to gawk at her and her work.

"There's been a lot of interest in you as well as your work," Monty said. His tone was meant to encourage, but the edge to it told her he knew it was unlikely to improve her ease.

"Yes—what?" Lacie asked, realizing that she'd only been half listening.

"We've had calls here and people showing up looking for information. Elijah Graden has also called repeatedly requesting contact. I wasn't concerned when I thought Ryder was at your side. But since your disappearance you've garnered a lot of interest and I'd worry that it's not all positive or at least sane. What works in your favor is that you've recently moved to a new apartment. I presume that's made you harder to track down."

"I've had calls," she said. "A couple of hang ups and some heavy breathers."

His grin was long gone. Monty was a great comfort in many situations and knew when to be serious. His advice was sage and almost always right. "The fact that you're telling me that in context of this conversation means they are not particularly pleasant," he said.

Monty was worried about her and about those who might want to gain her favor or at least attract her attention. Ryder's fears were not just his, all her friends were worried about her and it was possible that they had a point. Sometimes less than savory characters fixated on those who had been traumatized or those who had the limelight.

"It's nothing sinister," Lacie said, hoping to reassure him. "It's just tiresome. The media asked for interviews, as you know, we refused all requests. People want to offer support or to ask what happened. It can be overwhelming… the interest has died down and I had hoped it was over. I suppose this exhibition is drawing more interest than I thought it would. I've had the odd fan letter in my time but nothing on this scale… It's unsettling that so many people know who I am."

Monty leaned across the small circular table and elbows on the table weren't normally his thing so Lacie knew what he was about to say was serious. "I don't begin to pretend to know what you went through out there," Monty soothed. "I don't pretend to know the ins and outs of your relationship with Ryder either. But the man knows what he's doing, and he loves you, not even you can deny that."

"I never would. He's been so busy this week that I haven't wanted to… do you think I should talk to him about it?"

Monty shuffled to the front of his seat to get closer. "I think that it won't work out in your favor if you hide things from him."

"I'm not unsafe," she said, trying to show it wasn't fear as such that the interest caused. "I'm unsettled. There's a difference… Without Ryder around all day, I'm… I'm more aware of my vulnerabilities."

"I have a little surprise for you on that score and I hope it will cheer you up." Monty slid a business card across the table and let his smile turn sassy. "Their business is through referral only, mention my name."

Lacie frowned at her friend's smile then turned her attention to the black cardboard rectangle. The initials S.I.S. were embossed in a dark gray with a phone number she didn't recognize etched beneath.

"How could they—"

"Turn it over," Monty said.

On the other side was an address only a couple of streets over. "They're set up?"

Monty shrugged but his smile was knowing. "Getting there from what I understand. The office just opened for business yesterday. Ryder came by this morning and asked me to pass that on after our meeting. Why don't you go over and take a look for yourself?"

Lacie turned the card around to examine in more closely. "Why that…" Smiling, she traced her fingertips over the lettering.

"He's expecting you to go over there. I suppose this is the big reveal."

Monty drew her to her feet and gave her a hug, which gave Lacie the time to re-plan her afternoon. After that, saying goodbye was swift. When she was out on the street, she thought about going home to change her clothes. But the building address on the card was only a couple of blocks, so she decided to forego freshening up.

Maybe it had been her eagerness to see Ryder, or maybe it was her desire to see what he was cooking up, but whatever her reasoning, Lacie was determined in her gait when she set the new S.I.S. address in her sights.

ELEVEN

Lacie

S.I.S. WASN'T DISPLAYED on the building's list of premises. Either it just hadn't been added yet or Ryder liked it that way. The full address was on the back of the card, so Lacie got into the elevator, confident that she was in the right place.

The elevator pinged when it reached the penultimate floor. The doors whooshed open to reveal a slick lobby with a wide white reception desk where a woman sat behind a computer. Behind the receptionist was a white wall emblazoned with the S.I.S. initials in large black lettering. Gray light emanated from behind each letter making the sight professional but striking.

Flanking that screen were two glass walls, which were each garnished with a wide constant waterfall. These premises were modern, professional, and expensive. Ryder had put all of this together, in less than a week.

"Can I help you?" the little blonde behind the high reception desk asked. Though the woman wore a smile, Lacie read her feigned sincerity. This place was expensive, so was the clientele. Right now Lacie was not, which was probably why the receptionist had her nose turned up.

She tiptoed out of the elevator, keeping the strap of her purse in her hand. "Uh—"

"Do you have an appointment?" the blonde asked when Lacie didn't answer with enough speed.

"I'm looking for Ryder," Lacie said, with a tentative step toward the desk. "Ryder Stone."

The slope of the receptionist's brows became steep and her lip quivered. Lacie was just pleased the girl didn't laugh right in her face because it was obvious that her request had amused the youngster.

Her brows didn't come down but her smile became sympathetic though it was also undeniably smug. "Mr. Stone is busy, as I'm sure you can imagine. He owns the company. He runs the business," the receptionist said. "I can make you an appointment to meet with one of his associates if you give me the details of who referred you. As I'm sure you understand, we have to corroborate the referral personally before you can be allowed to meet with anyone."

"You check references?" Lacie asked, thinking of how she'd stumbled through the front door of SW— Ryder's previous company—that early morning months ago.

"Of course we check references," the receptionist said, offended by the suggestion they might not. "This is a very elite company. We offer an exclusive service. Can you tell me who referred you? And what the matter is in relation to?"

The blonde produced a form from a drawer in her desk and smoothed it onto the desk. Lacie tilted her head to get a better look at the document that appeared to be in triplicate.

"There are a lot of questions on that form," Lacie said, approaching the desk. "Toby already has me on file. He's got all my background information and a credit reference on me."

"If you're a returning customer then you'll be on the computer," the blonde said, moving to her mouse and keyboard. "Is there a reason you chose not to phone ahead for an appointment?"

Lacie hadn't considered the possibility that she might have to take a pop quiz before she was allowed in the door. "If you tell Ryder I'm here all this administrative stuff will be unnecessary."

"I can't really take your word for that, can I?" the blonde said with distinct condescension. She was so good at it that Lacie wondered if she practiced her contempt in front of a mirror. "People come in here every day requesting the CEO's attention. He would never get anything done if I granted every request for an audience with him."

Lacie hastened to cover her mouth, but she hadn't been quick enough. It was obvious that the blonde had registered her smile.

"CEO? There's no way Ryder told you to call him that."

"That's what he is, isn't it?" the blonde said, showing no shame for her statement despite Lacie's reaction.

"Is this your first day?" Lacie asked.

"My first week, why—"

"This place hasn't been here for more than a week," Lacie said. "The office only opened to the public yesterday, so you can't have had that many requests for Ryder's time."

"There are protocols to follow. They're there for a reason."

"Everyone's safety," Lacie said, nodding because she was all too aware of how strict the men's protocols could be—especially if Gabe was watching. "I know."

The receptionist put her pen and the form back in a drawer. "If you are not willing to follow procedure, I suggest you look elsewhere for your investigation and security needs."

"Like I'm allowed to use the competition," Lacie mumbled.

The blonde was steadfast and Lacie wasn't sure what to do. It hadn't occurred to her that she might not get over the threshold. She didn't particularly want to discuss her personal business with the blonde and she certainly didn't want to make an appointment.

But right then Lacie wasn't sure of Ryder's location. There would be more than one exit on a building this size so staking it out wasn't an option. Besides, she didn't want to be crazy stalking woman, especially when she might have a stalker on her tail too.

Making a scene or a threat was an option, the receptionist probably had a panic button built into her desk somewhere and if security came running then they would recognize her... unless Ryder had hired additional men, which was a distinct possibility.

Coming here with the aim of seeing Ryder, Lacie was eager to lay eyes on him. "Is he in the building?" Lacie asked. Opening her purse, she regretted not packing her cellphone. "Can you tell me that?"

"What?"

The receptionist sounded flummoxed, but Lacie kept searching her purse. "Is he in the building? At least tell me if he's doing something important."

"I can't possibly reveal—"

"Of course not... Can I sit over there?" she asked, pointing to the leather couch in the corner.

"Why would you—"

"I probably won't need it." Lacie retrieved her keys from her purse and did the thing she'd always vowed she would never need to—she pressed her panic button.

Nothing happened. Not that she expected it to, the thing was built to be discreet. Its purpose would be moot if it started blaring or flashing, thus letting the bad guys know she'd raised an alarm. That would take away the element of surprise, which could be crucial to a rescue mission.

The blonde was more confused than ever and looked ready to raise an alarm of her own. The possibility existed that Ryder had taken off his watch to work out or something. Before she could panic about that, he stepped into view from behind one of the waterfall walls.

Fixating on him, Lacie forgot about the receptionist who was no doubt confused by this turn of events. "Hi," she said, moistening her dry lips.

"That's supposed to be for emergencies," Ryder said, nodding at the button in her hand.

"For when I needed you," Lacie said, curling her lips into a smile. "That's what you said to me."

"You need me?"

"Every day," she said.

"Come here," he murmured.

He nodded once and stepped back. The blonde leaped from her desk. "She doesn't have an appointment, Mr. Stone."

"She doesn't need an appointment." Ryder watched Lacie's every move as she walked toward them and around the reception desk. "Ever." Lacie stopped in front of him and rolled her eyes upward to peek at him through her bangs. "Get back there," Ryder growled, not drawn in by her expression of innocence.

Slipping a hand to the small of her back, Ryder guided her around the partition bearing the S.I.S. logo.

The space was open. The center of the area had couches and a coffee station then a pool table beyond. All around the perimeter were glass walls with their blinds closed and solid doors in equal distance from each other. The furthest wall had only two doors but like the others the walls were glass but blind shielded.

Ryder took her to the remotest door and opened it then urged her inside. The walls of the corner office were floor to ceiling tempered glass and gave her a sense of vertigo.

"Wow," she whispered, rushing to the window trying to absorb the vastness of the city they were in.

When the door closed it shattered her abandon and she was reminded that he was there with her. She turned and drank him in, standing there just in front of the door they'd used to enter.

"You've had a busy week," she said.

"I wanted to get the place up and running," he said. "It's amazing how much time daylight abstinence frees up."

His smile grew and she laughed. It was comforting to know that she wasn't the only one who had missed their days together.

"I've missed you," she said.

"I've missed you too," he said. "I'm sorry it's been so crazy this week."

"I love you," she said. "I know that we can't be together every minute of the day and this… this is a step back toward normality and that's something we both need."

"We're almost there," he said, crossing the room to erase the distance between them. "I have to show you around and I have a surprise for you… I hope you like it."

She went into his arms and was encouraged by the ridge against her abdomen. Wriggling as close as she could muster, the rumble of his chest vibrated her cheek and without removing her body from his, Ryder's hand slid up her back and he took hold of the zipper of her strapless dress. The buzz of her zipper descending increased her heart rate. She knew what was coming next and her body thrummed in anticipation. When the zipper reached the bottom, she stepped away allowing the dress to pool around her feet leaving her in nothing but a pale thong.

Ryder growled again and reached for her, but she stopped his hand. "Being without you so much this week, it's put some things in perspective for me. We're a team, a unit. Now that you have the business on its feet, I want us to find a place where we can live together."

"You got it, baby," he said, stepping into her and stealing her mouth with his own.

There were things to say but none of it would be said until they expelled the need from their bodies. Desire devoured them, he stumbled forward, catching her weight with his strength. Then he had her up and lay her down again on the solid desk.

"I love you, Dusty," he said, breaking their kiss to stroke her hair from her face.

"Ready to break your daylight abstinence vow?"

"It was never a vow," he said. "Just a lack of opportunity… and now that I have that opportunity…"

His lips curled up and he pressed them to hers. This was what she had missed, and stealing these precious times together were more important now that there would be fewer of them. Lacie planned to remember every detail, so she'd never be without him again.

TWELVE

Lacie

AFTER THEIR DESIRE was sated, they were lying on the floor of his office together wrapped in each other and basking in the glow of the sun pouring into this professional space.

"Your body is amazing," he said, trailing his fingertips down her ribs to her waist then her hip, she curled when he caught her ticklish spot but that only brought her deeper into their spoon.

He had a deep rug laid out in the corner where the two glass walls met and there, they lay naked, spooning. Ryder kissed her shoulder and kept on going to her neck.

"You're not self-conscious that we're naked in front of the whole city?" she asked, struggling to take in the features of the city before them.

"You have nothing to be self-conscious about," Ryder mumbled against her. "But I'll protect your modesty." Ryder's hands moved around her and he covered her breasts with his palms.

She laughed again and his erection prodded her rear. "You're such a gentleman."

"I'll do my best by you."

"I know you will," Lacie said, rolling to her back.

"These windows are one-way," Ryder said. "They reflect light back from the outside. No one can see us. I thought you'd enjoy the view."

"The view," she said, admiring his chest letting her hands test the texture of his hair. "I like the view of you. I like being in your arms."

"Where you belong," he said, touching his lips to hers. "Now about that surprise, I hope it's a positive—"

Catching his arms, she didn't let him pull away. "Before we get to that there's something I should say."

"What's that, baby?"

"We're going to get married someday. We'll have the wedding. We'll buy a respectable family home, have a dozen kids, the responsible family car, the dog, the works. We'll have parent-teacher nights and anniversaries, and we'll go to bed arguing about whose turn it was to take the trash out. We'll have boys you'll teach how to pitch a baseball and girls you'll never let date."

"Sounds good to me."

Stroking his face, she wanted to make him understand. "My point is, my reluctance wasn't uncertainty. I'm still dealing with what happened and getting back to who I was. I want you to myself for a while. I want us to make memories of our own together. This time we have with each other is precious and it's what we'll have to look back on in years' time when we're up to our knees in dirty diapers, arguing about how we'll pay the gas bill. We should value this time we have together. I guess I've realized this week that… since I've had you, I've taken you for granted."

Exhaling, he pulled her close. "If you'd just said that to me…"

Explaining why she blanched when he brought up engagements or changed the subject when he talked about them co-habiting, liberated her from her anxieties. "I don't think I knew it myself until this week or put language to it at least," she said. "But we will both have to give each other time to work through our own issues. Your best friend did a horrible thing to you and you haven't processed that. We have to help each other through this and not ignore what happened thinking it will go away."

"I'll try," he said, kissing her. "Do you want to get an early dinner?"

Shirking the remnants of her profound revelations, she returned to her motivation for coming. "I actually had an excuse for coming here today."

He was stroking her body and admiring its reaction to his attention. "You don't need an excuse to see me."

"I know," she said.

"What was it?"

"It's business," Lacie said. "Can we get dressed?"

"We can talk shop naked," he said. "I'm a professional."

"You know about the exhibition at the gallery—"

"Stone!"

The shout came from outside the office. Ryder groaned and rolled to his back. "Give me one minute," Ryder said, kissing her forehead. Springing to his feet, he grabbed his jeans and hopped his way into them. Before he exited, he stopped at the door to look back at her naked form laid out on the rug. "Beautiful." He winked then slipped out of the office, closing the door at his back.

The sky was blue, only a whisper of a cloud drifted in it, and she could be happy living her life in this place forever. But her man wasn't here. While she hadn't picked out the identity of the shouter beyond the door, she'd missed the boys. Here they were in a new place and she hadn't congratulated them on what they'd achieved. Picking Ryder's shirt from the floor, she got to her feet and buttoned the shirt from the bottom up. She snagged her thong too and stepped into it while going for the door.

She expected one of the boys, maybe a few of them. When she opened the door and stepped out of Ryder's office they were there. All of the men that she knew as Ryder's colleagues… plus half a dozen others whom she didn't recognize, along with the blonde receptionist.

The men she didn't know checked her out, while the blonde visibly faltered at this out of place person who was partially dressed in their place of business. Lacie didn't have a chance to seek out Ryder because the men she did know were moving in.

"Hey," Rocco said, lifting her from her feet when he hugged her.

Many of them hugged her but it was Gabe who got to the heart of the matter.

"We haven't seen you at all this week. Are you okay?" Gabe asked, scowling at her like a concerned father. "Have you had any trouble?"

"I'm better now that we're all back together again," she said, accepting his hug.

"We've missed you," Ty said and Will chucked her chin. "Loving the threads. You should come downstairs like that."

Her smile spread when the men parted and she saw her topless Ryder in the center of the group of strange men who were all dressed in S.I.S. black gear.

"You've expanded," Lacie said, through her motionless smile.

"That's what happens when you walk into the room, baby," Ryder teased and the men began to jeer.

His stance was wide and his strong arms were folded over his broad chest. Those things screamed man-in-charge, who was all business. But those eyes ate her up, replaying every second of their shared time in his office.

"You're Ryder's girl?" one of the new men asked.

"This is Lacie Hart," Ryder declared to everyone. "My number two, and your boss one day if she offs me."

She drew in a breath, and their eyes locked. "The future Mrs. Stone," she said, flicking her brows up.

Any fear she had about losing herself in this man was nothing to the fear that she had of losing him. Saying the words, admitting the certainty of their future, as Ryder did, was freeing for her. The more she said these things aloud, the more she got used to the possibilities.

The corner of his mouth tipped up. "Future mother of my children."

"Did he finally put a ring on your finger? Are you guys for keeps now?" Toby asked.

"Always were," Gabe said. "I don't think they need a ring to indicate that."

Pinning Gabe in her sights, she stepped back to scrutinize him. "I'd have pegged you as the traditional type," she said to Gabe.

"Should I…?" Sonny stepped forward, always close but never touching her.

"Should you what?" Gabe asked him.

"Collect Lacie's things from her apartment?" Sonny said.

"We haven't gotten to that yet," Ryder said. "We have shop to talk too, I haven't forgotten."

"I just popped out to say hello," Lacie said. "I didn't realize we had company." She included all their usual boys in the statement. "Can we do dinner tonight?"

Lacie touched Gabe then Will while looking at all of them. "Sure, Lace," Ty said. "Who's paying?"

"Ryder," Lacie said.

"Then definitely," Ty said.

"I've got business with my girl," Ryder said. A couple of the new guys snickered. "Take another shot at the training drill."

A few paled though they all still scrutinized her bare legs. "Guess that's what you get for ogling the boss's girl," Will said. "We all learned that lesson quick smart too."

Ryder crossed to her and hooked his arm around her. "Lacie is this company's first priority. Her safety will always be number one. It is the primary objective above all else, understood?"

Every male in the room took notice of the deep sincerity and gravity of Ryder's words and each nodded. Lacie just wanted to blush and the blonde was dumbfounded, but no one said anything more. Ryder guided her back into his office and closed the door.

"Where were we?" Ryder asked.

"I should get home and change but—"

"I live upstairs," he said. "We've got the three upper levels of the building, the three highest. The first is the training level where there's boardrooms and facilities for the new guys you saw out there. This floor you've seen, it's office space for me and the guys you know. Upstairs is residential space. I've always liked to be close to our resources in case of emergency. But we can live wherever you want."

"Upstairs is fine," she said. "But we have—"

"I have a surprise for you upstairs," he said and began to guide her toward the exit again. "I hope that you—"

"I need security," she said.

Ryder snapped around to face her, his brows were drawn down in a snap of anger. "You're in danger? You let me make love to you, and introduce you to the guys without thinking to tell me that—"

"No. Nothing's happened," she said. "Monty told me that the exhibition will be busy and he said it might be an idea to—"

"We'll staff the event; you don't have to worry about that. S.I.S. will be there for anything and everything you need. I meant what I said out there about—"

"I know," she said, taking his hand. "You will come with me though, won't you? I hate it when it's busy and all the people, and—"

"I'll be there," Ryder said, stroking her cheek. "I'll always be at your side. I told you that I'd be supportive. I'll rig the operation myself but on game night I'll be right there holding your hand the whole way."

"I love you," she said.

Ryder kissed her. "That was your excuse for coming over here?"

"Show me upstairs," she said not ready to burst the bubble of happiness around them. This was what she'd missed all week, being with the man she loved. "Show me my surprise… and where we sleep."

"Do you want me to send Sonny—"

"Yes," she said.

He noted that she didn't hesitate. His surprise and pride shone from his face to hers. "I love you," she said. "I don't want to wait."

"You got it, Dusty."

"I'll need somewhere to work locally. The gallery isn't that far but—"

"I've got you covered," he said. "Come upstairs with me."

When she did, he didn't let her down. He never did. Ryder rushed them through the upper level to a set of spiral stairs off what she assumed was the master bedroom. He pulled her up the stairs without thought for her wish to see the rest of the place.

But it was worth it when they reached a hatch. Urging her ahead, Ryder hung back to let her enter the space first. Climbing up the stairs and through the hatch, Lacie arrived in a glass dome on the roof, which had a full three-hundred-and-sixty-degree view of the city.

"There's a button," Ryder said, sliding his hand around her waist while pressing his foot to a button on the floor. The windows shuttered to black out the view and light glowed up from the floor.

"This place is incredible, how did—"

"It's the reason I picked this space. The rest was whatever, but when I saw this room and—"

"It's perfect," Lacie said. He gathered her against him as she leaned into that strong body and admired the space around them, her new studio. "You make me happy, Ryder."

She turned in his arms and hooked her hand to the back of his neck. "And I'll keep trying to do that for as long as you let me," he said. "I want you to consider this place your home. This is where you belong."

"Is that an order?"

Blowing her hair from her forehead, he leaned forward to kiss her. "Yes, it's an order. You belong here at home with me."

Breaking the intensity of the moment, she maintained their intimacy. "I'm looking forward to dinner with the guys tonight," Lacie said. "How about we go away soon? Can you get away?"

"Where do you want to go?" he asked, running his hands up and down her back. "I'll take you anywhere in the world."

"How about our motel?" she asked, kissing his jaw.

One of his brows arched, her request hadn't impressed him. "You might want to think bigger. I just offered to take you anywhere in the world."

"You're my world," she said. "What's the point in spending big money when we won't see anything outside? The point is to get away from all interruptions and signal our fresh start."

"If it's our motel that you want, then it's our motel you'll get," he said and kissed her. "Consider it done."

THIRTEEN

Lacie

BOTH OF THEIR schedules had been crazy since their stolen days away almost two weeks ago. But battling through life was easier with the knowledge they'd always come together at night—and they did come together every night.

Sorcha was preoccupied with her own life and hadn't asked much about Ryder's new business. Since Lacie had moved into Ryder's residence, Sorcha had phoned every single night to talk about Bruce, or rather the lack of him.

Sorcha hadn't seen him in four days and out of sheer desperation she had begged Lacie to call Shep, which she had, but he hadn't been focused on the task. Since Sorcha and Bruce's loved up phase a couple of weeks ago, it seemed he'd been put off working the case. Though he did assure Lacie he would get back on it. During her phone conversations with Sorcha, Lacie had yet to work in the information that Shep was coming to her exhibition.

Somehow, Lacie had arrived at the gallery for opening night. With Monty working out the event details and Ryder protecting them, all Lacie had to worry about was the art and not falling on her face.

In a dark gray shirt with a black-tie Ryder looked good enough to eat, or at least he had before she'd left him at home. She hadn't seen him since they arrived at the back entrance of the gallery. Alone, Lacie paced in Monty's office while Monty and his cronies spoke in the outer office. They were over schedule. The doors were supposed to be open already. The masses would be impatient. But there was no sign of her escort, Ryder.

Sorcha was on her way but had never been on time to anything in her life. Her Aunt Elise had volunteered to come and offer moral support. But Lacie had insisted it wasn't necessary. She wouldn't have felt right about leaving her aunt alone at the function and Elise didn't have many friends who would enjoy this kind of night.

Still pacing in the office, Lacie distracted herself with thoughts of what needed to be done. When this exhibition was over, she'd have to decide about the commission Darwin wanted from her. Her mother wanted her to spend some time at home. Emails from her parents were becoming more frequent, but Lacie didn't want to leave the country again until Wallace's case had been heard and he was sentenced.

Through the glass doors of Monty's office, Lacie saw the door to the outer office open. Ryder came in with Gabe and Rocco at his back. They spoke to Monty while Jimmy came around them all to make for Monty's private office where she was ensconced.

"They've opened the doors," Jimmy said, hanging through the door. "Do you want to come through to the—"

"I have to speak to Ryder first," she said, rubbing her hands together then linking her fingers only to stretch them again to bounce her hands together.

Jimmy came in to wait with her. But as he came toward her, the men in the outer office walked in the opposite direction and departed. Jimmy glanced back in time to see the outer office door close behind those who had just abandoned her here.

"There will be time later," Jimmy stuttered, perhaps sensing her discomfort.

On a sigh, she took Jimmy's arm much to his astonishment. "Stick with me," she said, resolved to the fact that she had to make an appearance at her own show. "I don't like to be alone at these things."

Jimmy led her out and remained at her side while various people came over to congratulate her. Maybe forty minutes had passed when she saw Elijah enter the gallery. Their eyes met but Sorcha appeared in front of her, breaking the moment.

Having just arrived herself, Sorcha was still absorbing the buzz in the atmosphere. "This is nuts," Sorcha said, taking her hand. "Can we talk?"

Lacie tried to seek out Bruce who was supposed to attend with his fiancée, while Sorcha looked Jimmy up and down. "What about?" Lacie asked.

"Where's Ryder?" Sorcha asked, twisting this way and that, trying to locate him.

"Right here." They turned to see Ryder approach from behind. "Sorry for the delay. Everything's in order now."

"Was there a problem?" Lacie asked.

Ryder dipped down to kiss her cheek. "Nothing to worry about."

He slid his fingers between hers. Immediately, her chest relaxed, her lips curled upward and she rested her face on his upper arm.

"You're here," she whispered.

Jimmy was an eager escort, but there was no replacing a trained one who had a vested interest in her safety.

"Scram, kid," Ryder said to Jimmy.

Removing her face from his jacket, she chastised her lover for his abrupt attitude.

"Jimmy has been my escort," Lacie said to Ryder. "Leave him alone."

Ryder's dismissal was a tease. In a way, it was nice of him to poke at Jimmy. Acting possessive probably gave Jimmy the idea that he might actually be a threat. The kid loved to be part of the gang too, even if he was socially awkward like her.

"I can't blame him for being crazy in love with you. I know what that's like," Ryder said and lifted his fist toward Jimmy, who bumped it with his own despite his surprise. This had been a night of firsts for the intern.

"Uh, has everyone forgotten I'm here?" Sorcha asked.

Focus went back to Sorcha, who was still in front of Lacie.

"What's wrong?" Lacie asked, but they were interrupted again before Sorcha could answer.

"Lacie." Elijah joined the group and everyone paused for a few seconds. His focus was on her and he afforded no civility to those around her. "Can we talk?"

"Do you know everyone?" Lacie asked, hoping to draw attention to the people around her who he was ignoring. "You know Sorcha, of course. This is Jimmy, he works here at the gallery, and this is Ryder—"

"I know you."

"He and I live together," Lacie said, dropping the not-so-subtle hint about their association.

"You were at the Reynolds party," Elijah said, clarity seized his expression.

"That's right," Ryder said.

Neither man moved to shake hands, making the mood in their group grow rather frosty. "Is that where you met?" Elijah asked.

"No," Ryder said without blinking.

"Lacie!" Monty rushed up to join them. "This is quite a party! Could you come and meet someone?"

"Who?" Lacie asked.

"He's a donor, at least he will be. He said he'll write a huge cheque for the gallery, his only stipulation is to meet you first," Monty said and the curator carried his own ball of hype in his aura. Watching him being so enthusiastic was contagious and that usually encouraged people to spend more money.

Lacie wasn't very keen on leaving this group alone together, not with Ryder and Elijah ready to face off. But Monty had been a good friend and had put this evening together almost single-handedly, so she wasn't going to refuse such a simple request. "Okay," she said.

"Great!" Monty exclaimed. The man could be an eccentric at the best of times, but that was one of the things that she loved about him. His energy was electric making his enthusiasm contagious. He wasn't at all like the sedate academics Lacie had met at some other galleries.

Behind Monty, near the far wall, something caught her eye. "Gabe's gesturing at you," Lacie said to Ryder, then popped up to kiss his jaw at the same time she released his hand.

"Do you want me to come and find you when—"

"Yes," Lacie said to Ryder, though she was aware of all the eyes on them. "There's something I have to talk to you about."

"Sounds final," Elijah said with either hope or satisfaction in his voice.

Proving her loyalty and her commitment to her man, Lacie quelled the speculation. "Quite the opposite," Lacie said and made sure to brush her lips side to side across Ryder's stubble to highlight their intimacy. "Be quick."

Ryder skimmed a hand down her arm and watched every step she took with Monty toward his office. When they rounded the corner and left Ryder's sight, Monty looped an arm through hers.

"This night has been a big hit," Monty said, linking his hands in front of him, so she did the same, though their arms remained twined. "The exhibition is amazing. It's a big hit."

"I know," Lacie said.

"You don't sound very excited."

Being around so many people who all wanted to question and compliment her was exhausting. She appreciated that she was lucky to have status in her field. But returning to normality after her abduction was still a bit of a struggle.

"Honestly," Lacie said on a sigh. "I'd rather be home curled up in bed with Ryder."

Monty laughed and leaned in close. "Who wouldn't," Monty whispered and laughed again.

Welcoming his joke, she let exhaustion ebb in the development of her smile. "I don't do well in big groups," she explained. "It's been a long night."

"No big groups in here," Monty said, touching his door with a fingertip. "Our prospective donor wants to see you alone."

"Alone?"

"Take a deep breath and say thank you, then you can get back to being adored… with Ryder at your side."

Monty knocked once on his own office door then opened it to urge her inside. A small lamp on the assistant's desk lighted the room. This outer office was vacant, but the glass door through to Monty's office was open. The sound of metal on porcelain in that room drew her closer.

Monty's office was dark. His bay window, where the bistro table was located, was barely illuminated by the light from the courtyard beyond it. A shadow seated at the table finished stirring liquid in a teacup then put the teaspoon aside.

"Hello, Lacie," a deep voice said.

"Hello," she said, unwilling to move further into the room. The hairs on her arms and on the back of her neck stood up. It was possible that this guy was just as eccentric as Monty, hence the unusual setup. But being wary was part and parcel of what she'd been through. "Monty said you wanted to meet me."

"I've been a fan of your work for a long time. Will you sit with me?"

"I don't know if that's a good idea," she said, remaining near the door. "I'm expected back in the gallery." This guy had promised Monty a check, so Lacie couldn't exactly declare that he was creeping her out with his sinister antics.

The cup rose from its saucer, but he had seated himself in the angle of shadow caused by the window frame, so she couldn't pick out any details of his form or his apparel. "There's more money," he said, holding the cup near his mouth so it almost muffled his words. "Much more money… Monty would appreciate that."

Monty could use the money and he'd been so kind to her that she couldn't waste this chance. The guilt would make it impossible for her to look her good friend in the face again. Moving into the room, she told herself that she was just being paranoid and that she shouldn't let her history with Jamie Wallace affect professional encounters.

Stopping short of the table, she reminded herself of the room full of people not too far behind her. "You've given generously," she said. "Monty is a good man who works hard. He's been very kind to me."

He replaced the delicate cup in its seat. "I could give you more. Would you consider a permanent collection?"

"I don't understand what—"

"Your own gallery," he said and although his voice was confident, he kept it low. "A place to show your work together in one place."

This was supposed to be a casual meet and greet, not an opportunity for someone to hire her. "No," she said. "That's never been an ambition of mine."

"Why not? You're an artist. A permanent center could include an artist's residence," he said and his fingertips edged into the light slicing across the table. "Then all of your needs would be taken care of."

"Why would—"

"You wouldn't have to move home as frequently as you have been."

Her frown coincided with him rising from the bistro table. That was too intimate a detail for a stranger to know. "How did you know that—"

"I've been following your career very closely, very closely indeed," he said.

"Why?"

"I think that would be obvious," he said, moving closer but remaining in the shadow that dominated this space. "You're beautiful and you're talented."

"I'm involved," she said. "Engaged, off the market." She wasn't exactly engaged, but Ryder wouldn't mind her exaggerating for the sake of a creepy buyer.

"He doesn't understand you."

"You don't know him," she said and that was the final straw. No third party got to judge her relationship with Ryder. Deciding her paranoia was justified, Lacie began to inch away. "And you don't know me. I'm going back to the event."

"Wait," he said and lunged forward to snatch her wrist. "We have to talk. There's something you have to know."

"Let me go," she said. If he had been following her career then he had to know about her kidnap. She was going to chastise him for his lack of decency when something stung her wrist. Lacie tried to recoil but his grip increased and he yanked her closer.

"I know what you're afraid of," he whispered into her ear when the fog spilled into her mind and light burst behind her eyes highlighting the shape of a familiar form.

"Ryder," she murmured, then her body gave out.

FOURTEEN

Lacie

LACIE TOLD HER eyes to open but they didn't. Her mouth was as dry as cotton wool and moving her lips didn't help the ache that seemed to be squashing her skull. Processing a mental list of her faculties, she wiggled her toes and accounted for her extremities but something was missing though it lingered on the edge of her consciousness.

"Ryder," she croaked.

"He's here," Gabe said. "But he's being an ass."

Lacie recognized Sorcha's perfume and Gabe's voice, but her hand was conspicuously empty. Forcing her energy to her eyes, she prized them open to see that she was in a hospital room. Gabe and Rocco stood near the door. Monty stood with Sorcha in the corner and Ryder's silhouette filled the window. His back was to her, and from his posture, she didn't need to see his face to know how his expression was set.

"Were you going to tell me?" Ryder asked without turning around.

Monty inched forward, worrying the Kleenex he had wrapped around his fingers. "I thought he knew about…"

"Knew about what?" Sorcha asked, asserting herself in this space and coming straight to the end of the bed.

"Maybe we should give these guys the room," Gabe said, reaching for the door.

"Know what?" Sorcha asked without showing any intention of leaving. "I want to know."

Ryder turned and fixed immediately on Lacie. "Give us the room," he murmured.

No one objected aloud though Gabe and Rocco had to flank Sorcha to get her out with some gentle encouragement. Monty pulled the curtain partway around her bed to conceal her from the door, so she didn't see them leave but there was a finality to the sound of the door closing.

"What happened?" she asked, trying to sit up and failing.

"He knocked you out," Ryder said and she didn't like his discrete manner. "You hit the deck the second I walked through the door. He ran… I thought he'd killed you. So you tell me, what the hell happened?"

Closing her eyes again, she tried to recall the events that led her here. "He was talking to me then…"

She curled her fingers around the wrist her assailant had grabbed, which drew her attention to her IV.

"Were you going to tell me about the phone calls?" he asked.

Annoyed at herself for not being more forthcoming, she had played down concerns believing herself to be paranoid.

"There was nothing to tell," she said. "I told Monty that the attention had been unsettling. You knew

I felt that way after the kidnapping when we were getting calls and mail all the time."

"I thought that all stopped."

"I thought it had too," she said. "It was just a few phone calls… I really didn't think I was in danger."

"And you didn't think to discuss it with me?"

He might have reason to worry about her, but the likelihood of her repeating her previous experience was minute.

"Ryder, there was nothing to discuss. I was preoccupied with us. I did my best to ignore all of it."

"You ignored it?" he said, spitting out the words like an angry parent.

She wasn't going to let him take over, as he liked to do. But she wasn't going to lie to him either.

"Yes. The first day I came to you at S.I.S. I'd been with Monty, he said I should discuss it with you. We got distracted and then when I moved in, I didn't think there would be any further communications."

"But there were?"

"No, there's been nothing. The media has given up. I thought it was over."

"Over or not, you could have told me," he said, proving he wasn't yet ready to forgive her for the slight. "We sleep in the same bed every night. We talk to each other every day."

"I like it when we're happy. I've had obsessive fans before. How do you think I got to know Jimmy?"

"You think this guy is obsessed with you?"

"No," Lacie said. "I said that to demonstrate how I know the difference. People sending messages of goodwill and the media trying to get in on the gossip is a different thing to… being wary about my own personal safety."

"You're going to be wary now."

"There's nothing to worry about," Lacie said.

Placating him was as important to her as staying safe. Lacie didn't want to be apart from Ryder any more than he wanted to be apart from her. If anyone wanted to stay out of a lunatic's captivity, it was her. She'd been there once and that was enough for her. But Ryder would drive himself crazy worrying about her and she didn't need to live her life under watch every minute of the day.

Ryder took one step toward her. "We need to know who this guy was, and what he wanted."

His resentment gave way to his professional planning.

"I don't know what he wanted," she said. "He… he told me he'd been paying attention to my career…"

"What else did he say?" Ryder commanded.

"I don't know. I can't think."

Her mind was still fogged by whatever he'd drugged her with. When she tried to concentrate, she got dizzy. Bringing a hand to her head, she rubbed her forehead, but her headache grew to a pulse that made her ears ring.

"You better think," he said. "I need you, Dusty. I don't want to be blindsided. I trust you to tell me everything. Do you understand that? I trust you. Without you I have nothing. If I can't trust you to talk to me, I'll put a guy on you twenty-four seven. I swear to you I will. I love you. You are my responsibility. Your safety is important to me above everything else."

This was exactly what she didn't want. She would take his professional help of course. But there was a desperation in his voice that she knew came from the guilt that remained under his skin.

"I know you're angry with me," she said. "I didn't deliberately withhold or deny you anything. It wasn't my intention to—"

"I'm not angry at you, Dusty!"

Both of them registered his raised volume, which worked in contradiction of his words. He didn't stand down. His chest moved in time with shallow breaths, and his eyes burned with the fire she saw in him on only two occasions, in bed… and when he feared for her life.

"I love you," she said, raising her hand toward him. It took another five breaths before he came close enough to take her hand. Their linked hands hung in mid-air. He was still so far away that she had to lean to maintain the connection. "Why are you over there? You don't want to be near me?"

His expression loosened before his form did. "Don't talk crazy," he mumbled and brought her hand to his lips. Lowering to the side of the bed, he crouched and kissed her hand then rubbed his face across it. "I was so… seeing you fall like that… I've never been that afraid in my life."

He wasn't angry at her. Anger was just the easiest way to let out the maelstrom of panic and fear that he'd been languishing in since the museum.

"What happened with the exhibit?" she asked.

"Jimmy stayed to close up," Ryder said, still in his crouch, he spoiled her hand and arm with more kisses. "The ambulance was there in a minute."

She wouldn't be surprised if Ryder had one on standby for the event, or if he knew people who he could lean on for a favor in that moment of distress.

Raising himself, she met his lips and the potency of his kiss gave her strength. Bolstered by his presence and his attention, Lacie spread her hand on his body that was suspended over hers and curled her nails into him through his shirt.

"Oh good God!"

Ryder stopped kissing her to look up at the gang who were assembled at the end of her bed. Gabe was as stoic as ever, Sorcha appeared repulsed, Monty and Rocco were just amused.

"You're my hero, Boss," Rocco laughed.

"It's disgusting," Sorcha proclaimed, screwing up her face. "This is a hospital. You two are like animals. Can't you contain yourselves?"

"They don't have to," Rocco said and his easy grin relaxed the mood. "You got it made, Boss."

"Much fun as this is, are we going to talk about the issue?" Gabe asked, straight to business as was his way. "What do we have?"

"Do you have a record of any communications?" Rocco asked.

Everyone looked at Lacie who stretched her fingers on Ryder.

He straightened up at the side of her bed to switch himself into work mode. "No, I doubt there would be a record of any of the calls. I have a couple of letters that were written to me, but they're perfectly nice benign letters wishing me well. There was some correspondence from media outlets asking for interviews, but I trashed most of that when I moved. I didn't come across anything that looked in any way suspicious."

"Nothing from fans?" Rocco said.

Lacie shrugged. "The ones I still have are in the kitchen drawer. Look through them if you want. But I didn't see anything worrying in them, they were just normal supporters."

"Yet you kept them?" Gabe asked.

This was a subtle interrogation.

Happy to answer their questions, there was nothing for her to hide. "Only a few I wanted to respond to."

"Respond to?" Ryder asked, reaching down to link their fingers again.

She shrugged. "They were nice letters."

"We'll take a look at the letters," Gabe said. "What do you remember about the guy?"

"If I—" Lacie was cut off when Sorcha gasped and clutched her bump. "Sorch?"

"Just a twinge," Sorcha said, blowing out a breath. "Nothing to worry about. This little guy likes to dance around this time of night.

"Where's Bruce?" Monty asked. "Wasn't he supposed to be at the event with you tonight?"

No one answered. "Where is he?" Gabe asked. "We can get in touch—"

"I haven't seen him for a few days," Sorcha snapped and that point probably accounted for her foul mood tonight.

Her friend had wanted to talk to her in the gallery when Lacie had been whisked off by Monty to meet with the donor. She guessed that griping about Bruce was high on Sorcha's agenda.

Her memory of the night was blurred, but everything before her encounter with the maniac was clear as a bell. Something from the background of their phone call the previous night flared in her mind.

"But last night when I phoned…" Lacie trailed off. "Who was the guy?"

Sorcha didn't answer. She was suddenly transfixed by the plain hospital bed sheets.

Ryder found the answer for her. "Shep," he said, knowing how Shep and Sorcha were.

They delighted in insulting each other. But as soon as they were alone, somehow always ended up falling into bed together.

Lacie's jaw fell and she gasped in a breath. "You're sleeping with Shep again?"

"No wonder Shep didn't show at the exhibition tonight," Monty muttered. "If you two are sleeping together, you'd have screamed at each other most of the night and ruined the event. Argument is foreplay for you pair."

"I went over to his place a couple of nights ago," Sorcha said in explanation though she came across as quite defensive. "He's a friend. He was making me feel better that's all… It's no big deal."

Rocco widened his stance and folded his arms with glee all over his face. "This is entertainment," he said.

Although he should know better, Monty probed further. "I thought you were marrying Bruce," Monty said.

"Bruce is sleeping around," Sorcha bit back.

"And that makes it right?" Lacie asked, unable to hide her own judgment. Sorcha was her best friend and she loved her but getting involved with Shep when they already thought Bruce was cheating just caused more layers of drama. "Do you have proof of that yet?"

"Don't get high and mighty about this," Sorcha said, pointing at her. "You know how difficult it's been for me."

Unimpressed, Monty shook his head and took a step back. "Yeah, Lacie's stalker is nothing to complain about."

This revelation was more than she could handle. Her anxiety from earlier combined with the chemical cocktail she'd been assaulted with and the amalgamation took Lacie to the end of her rope. "Everyone should go," Lacie said, unable to look at any of them for fear she might break down.

"You're kicking us out?" Rocco said, losing his amusement.

Gabe stomped to the bed. "We need to know—"

"Please," Lacie said, unable to handle any more of the interrogation. "I'll answer your questions tomorrow. No one will hurt me in here."

"You've never kicked me out," Sorcha said, confident on the outside, but nervous on the inside as her folded arms attested to.

Standing in her corner as always, Ryder stepped in. "Everybody clear out," Ryder said, loosening his hand out of hers. "I'll be back in a minute."

"You can go home," Lacie said to him.

Ryder turned back to lean over her again. "You're definitely not kicking me out," he said, kissing the corner of her mouth and her smile twitched up. "See… everyone else out."

With wide arms, Ryder crowded everyone out despite their protests before he glanced back at her and closed the door leaving her peacefully alone. Settling back in the bed, she closed her eyes and counted her breaths. Rest would help her make sense of what had happened tonight, but she was struggling because it made no sense.

Nothing would be found in a couple of letters from people who said nice things and asked her for nothing in return. It hadn't been as though anyone had followed her around or stalked her. She had been living on the top floor of Ryder's complex and strangers didn't get in there.

Keeping her faith in Ryder would be easy, she just hoped he didn't drive himself crazy trying to get answers from a scenario that was senseless.

FIFTEEN

Ryder

IN THE RELATIVES' room opposite Lacie's private room, Ryder was talking with his men. Sorcha was fizzing mad. Monty was on the phone. Ryder kept his eyes on everyone.

Footsteps in the hallway between the rooms caught his ear, but he thought nothing of them until he saw Lacie's door open. Bounding toward the intrusion, Gabe and Rocco stayed on his heels to offer back up. What he didn't expect to see were two guards flanking her door.

"What the hell is going on?" Ryder demanded of the men dressed in black and standing at ease, but neither of them spoke.

Gabe and Rocco were at his shoulders. He could feel from their tension that they were as perturbed by this development as him.

"Are you sure you want to do this?" Gabe asked the two security agents before them.

"You're out numbered," Rocco said, offering his own intimidation.

The first stooge broke stance to smirk at them. "Not for long," he said and took his attention to the corridor to his left.

Ryder and his men followed his line of vision to see more security guys in the same garb coming down the hallway.

"Call in reinforcements," Ryder said to Gabe.

If a fight was what these guys wanted then a fight was what they would get. Ryder had to get to Lacie and after that, he'd figure out who set this up. Though he was already drawing up a short list and one name was prominent at the top: Elijah Graden.

SIXTEEN

Lacie

"WHAT'S GOING ON?" Lacie asked.

When fingers had brushed the apple of her cheek, she had known immediately that they didn't belong to Ryder. She'd heard the door and assumed Ryder was returning to her side, so she hadn't bothered to open her eyes and disturb the slumber that was tempting her. This man felt different, smelled different, was different.

"Everything's under control," Elijah purred from beside her.

"Elijah," she said, trying to sit up.

He clasped her shoulders and pressured her down to keep her on her back.

When she gave up her fight against his insistence, he began to stroke her hair. "I have everything under control. The chopper's on the way and we'll get you to a facility—"

"There's nothing wrong with me," Lacie said. Panic grew and merged with annoyance until she didn't know what to feel about this interference. "I'm not going to any facility."

His calm features became stern. "You're in danger, I heard about what happened at the gallery. I've got a full security detail—"

"You what?" Lacie asked.

Again, when she pressed her hands into the mattress to try to sit, he urged her back.

"I've got a team ready to watch you from—"

"I don't want that," she said, allowing her anger to supersede her worry. "Why would you—"

"You need to be looked after," he said, increasing his insistence. "This is a serious situation."

"Elijah, I don't need—"

"Of course you do," he said, not hearing a word she was saying. "I have the resources to look after you."

She couldn't believe that he was being so heavy handed and glib about her opinions.

"I have the resources to look after myself," she said, wondering how Ryder would react when he found out Elijah was trying to take over.

"You don't have to do that," Elijah said, and took his hands off her for the first time so he could look at his watch. "When the helicopter—"

Certain in her conviction, she took her chance to sit up. "I'm not getting into any helicopter. I want to go home."

Elijah glanced at the door in expectation of something while he righted his cuff over his watch.

Grabbing the IV in her hand, she eased out the needle and slipped out of the bed on the opposite side to where Elijah was positioned.

"What are you doing?" Elijah said when he noticed she'd gotten up. "Get into bed and you'll be transported—"

"You're being ridiculous." Happy he could no longer touch her, she was not encouraged by his belittling attitude. "What is any of this going to achieve? You don't need to be here. What are you—"

A shout from outside the room interrupted them. Scuffling followed and Lacie took two steps down the bed but Elijah mirrored her on the opposite side. Stuck on the side of the bed furthest from the door, she couldn't move. A draft of air reminded her of her apparel and made her clasp her gown closed at the back.

The door burst open and a pile of men fell into the room. She recognized three of them and didn't need to recognize the others to know what was going on. Elijah made for the door and hospital security appeared on the periphery with at least one actual cop behind with hospital staff.

"Stop it! Everybody stop!" Lacie shouted and the whole room froze in place. "Why has everyone gone crazy?"

The men who'd been fighting separated and everyone took a breath. The doorway cleared when a nurse and a porter appeared with a bed.

"Patient transport," the nurse said.

"No," Lacie said, waving one hand then quickly taking it to the back of her gown again. "It's not needed."

"Now, Lacie—" Elijah stopped when Ryder began to march toward him.

The only thing that stalled his journey was Lacie when she held up a halting hand.

"I don't need medical help," Lacie said to Elijah. "The transport is unnecessary."

Elijah still wasn't listening. "Let the professionals check—"

"They have," she said to Elijah, asserting her right to be heard. "Keeping me here over night was probably just a precaution. I was drugged not injured."

"Drugged by a mad man," Elijah said. "You're in danger. You need professional security."

Maintaining her position, she appreciated that Ryder didn't try to railroad her like Elijah did.

"I have professional security," she said to Elijah, opening a palm toward Ryder while the other hand kept hold of her gown. "I'm sleeping with professional security."

This didn't assuage Elijah who grew more insistent.

"You've known him for all of ten minutes," Elijah said. "You don't really trust—"

"I do," she said, stepping once before remembering her rear exposure. "And I'd come over there and be more vehement about it except I'm the only one in the room partially clothed."

Switching her focus to Ryder, his anger dissolved when their eyes met. Darting her eyes to one side in a hurried motion, Ryder snapped to attention.

"Would you get behind me, please," she hissed at him. "There are twenty people in this room. I'm feeling a little vulnerable."

Ryder did as he was told while Rocco and Gabe smiled.

Elijah wasn't giving up. "This is a serious situation."

Lacie returned to handling her unrelenting friend's objections. "The only person who takes this situation more seriously than I do is the man now standing behind me. I appreciate that you think you're helping, Elijah." Rocco and Gabe came closer and Ryder wrapped his arms around her shoulders. By keeping his body against her back, Ryder blocked any view of skin there might have been. "My family is protecting me," Lacie said. "Nothing will happen to me."

"I won't accept—"

"It's not your place," Rocco said.

He was the last of Ryder's men who would ever get riled and yet there was a tinge of anger in his tone.

Lacie put a soothing hand onto Rocco's arm then looked back to Elijah. "He's right," she said. "It's not your place… I'm sorry."

Elijah examined them all. "I'm reluctant to depart," Elijah said, failing to be deterred. "But I will do as you ask for now. I will contact you in the morning."

The testosterone in the room bubbled high, but everyone managed to stay quiet until the door closed behind Elijah and his men. Monty and Sorcha weren't present, so Lacie assumed they were in the waiting room. Lacie found herself alone with Ryder, Rocco, and Gabe.

"The guys are all on their way," Gabe said. "This place will be secure—"

"Get out," she said to Gabe then she looked at Rocco. "You too."

"You're kicking us out?" Rocco asked and she was encouraged to see his smile. "Again?"

"Scram," Ryder said and despite their hesitation his men complied, closing the door behind them.

Ryder released her shoulders to grab her hand. "You're bleeding," he barked.

Lacie tugged her hand free and walked away from him. Pulling the curtain around her bed, she left Ryder on the other side of it.

"What are you doing?" he asked and his anger had become pure concern.

"Getting changed," she said.

Her intention when pulling the curtain was to get dressed. Instead, she found herself sitting on the edge of the bed, tucking her hands over the edge of the mattress.

"I've seen you naked," he said in that infinitely understanding tone that told her he knew she was lying.

Lacie nodded to no one. Her eyes got wet and she knew if she opened her mouth that her pent-up emotion would escape.

"I know," she squeaked.

Five seconds passed, then the curtain began to slide back. When he came into view, she looked up and he had to notice the moisture gathering in her gaze.

"Hi," he murmured and stayed where he was, not pressuring her or rushing her.

Breathing in, she tried her best to explain the thoughts swirling inside her. "I came to live in a foreign country as a teenager," she said. "I've been mugged. I've been groped… I lived my life in captivity under threat of rape or murder, often starving or in pain. I've heard the man I love be threatened, seen him be imprisoned. My best friend has been in peril before my very eyes."

"Yes," he agreed with the slightest of nods.

Still lost, Lacie wasn't sure how to feel when the truth came to her. "I've been in life or death situations."

Ready to soothe her, he moved toward her. "I know, baby—"

Removing her hands from the mattress, she stalled him. "I love you; I tell you that every day."

His understanding hid behind an emerging frown. "I love you too," he said.

Aware of how her words could affect him, Lacie inhaled to give herself time to try to get it right.

"I didn't grasp how… we were apart. When the door opened, I thought it was you… but he touched my face and… It was terrifying," she murmured and touched her cheek where Elijah had. "When I realized another man's hands were…"

"Hey," he said, crossing to her, Ryder took both of her hands into one of his and used the other to stroke away Elijah's touch with his own. "I'm here. You don't have to be scared."

Tilting her head into his palm, Lacie caressed her cheek back and forth memorizing his texture. On closing her eyes, her tears skittered down. Wiping them away with the pad of one thumb, Ryder said nothing.

"Wallace kept us apart," she said, opening her eyes to seek his. "When we met, I knew our connection was there…"

"I know," Ryder said. "Being with you was electric from that first second."

"Being with you was liberating, I felt invincible. When we were torn apart, on that street…" For all the support he'd given her, she hadn't let herself be honest about how much turmoil her experiences had put her through and how grateful she was for this man. "You've been so patient with my nightmares, and insomnia—"

"It's my job. You're my responsibility." He didn't shy away; he kept his hands on her and didn't retreat. "I love you. I told you I want to help. I want to be there for you, for everything. You said I was easier to talk to than all the therapists. If you need—"

"You're missing the point," she said, shaking her head and covering his hand on her face. "My terror, it came from the obstacle between us. My night terrors, the darkness, it's not the isolation I fear or the threat of harm, it's you."

He didn't follow and she didn't blame him. "I scare you?"

"I…" Trying to make sense was difficult given her mental state. "I don't need to be with you every minute of the day, but I like knowing that you're out there… For me."

"What—"

"I wasn't scared until Elijah stood between us. I got out of bed and tried to get to you, but I couldn't get past him. He was an obstacle between us. His men wouldn't let you in… He wouldn't let me out. My throat closed. I couldn't get to you… just like on that street when I couldn't come to you… When they forced me to get into that car without you… I didn't know if I would ever see you again…" He hadn't said anything and she couldn't tell from his expression if he was following her train of thought or worried that she'd finally lost it. "You're quiet. Am I weirding you out?"

"No," he said, tucking her hair back behind her ear. "I don't ever want to be kept apart from you either. We belong to each other. No one gets in between us."

Pleased that he could decipher her, despite her confusion, she relaxed. "Take me home, Ryder, please. I want to sleep in your arms. I don't want people and hospitals and rules. I want you. Us touching all night with no interruptions or interference. All I need is you."

His lips curled upward. "You got it."

Ryder understood her and if there was real cause for concern about her physical wellbeing then Ryder would insist on her staying where there were doctors. Unlike Elijah, Ryder gave her respect and listened to her opinions. Being at home in their familiar bed would do far more to speed her recovery than being here in this sterile environment.

SEVENTEEN

Lacie

ON ENTERING THE kitchen, Lacie saw Ryder's men standing around, drinking coffee. They silenced when she came in and she took that to mean they were discussing something they considered might upset her.

"I woke up alone," Lacie said, expecting a response from Ryder.

Ty got there first. "Thought it was best I duck out before your old man caught me there," Ty said in his typically flirtatious way, then focused on Ryder. "Sorry, man."

Ryder wasn't in the mood to joke but he smiled along.

"Are you working?" Lacie asked them, expecting to be dismissed if they were.

"Getting everything in place for you," Will said.

Suspicious Will had taken his time in warming to her. Eventually, when he figured out she was sticking around, he grew to love her as much as the others did. He liked to needle her and she would needle right back, they had a sort of sibling-like relationship. Falling in love with Ryder had earned her five big brothers and Sonny's servitude.

"You're all here," Lacie said, moving toward Ryder. "I assume your conversation has been lively, it always is. The fact that none of you are continuing with it means you were talking about me."

Most of the men averted their attention, Will wasn't shy. "Your situation came up," Will said.

Satisfied that someone else had admitted the truth and she hadn't had a hissy fit, the others relaxed. "We have to keep you safe," Ty said.

"Which means finding the threat," Gabe said.

These men had been working together for so long that she wasn't surprised when they finished each other's sentences. "You have other cases," Lacie said because she didn't want them to feel obligated to prioritize her.

It seemed that she was too late to assert that fact. "Not anymore," Gabe said. "You get the elite team. The new starts can pick up the slack."

"You're going to take over my life, aren't you?" Lacie sagged against Ryder. His hand slid up her arm.

"There's a threat, someone wants to hurt you," Gabe said.

"We don't know that he wants to hurt me," Lacie said, using Ryder as her leaning post while she addressed the other men who were growing more serious. In a return to the conversation they had no doubt been having before she came in, they lost their ease.

"The guy wanted to get close to you," Will said, putting his coffee mug on the kitchen counter.

"He's got his eye on you," Ty said. "We were arguing the merits of how long he's been watching you."

"Does it stem from Wallace?" Rocco asked, Ryder's hand fell away from her arm. Lacie kept herself propped back against his chest but he'd been conspicuously quiet thus far.

Clearing her throat, she inspired herself to be as serious as these men were when they worked. "That was when the attention started. But that was when people outside the arts community heard about me, about what happened."

They had all been around when the media started calling and people tried to seek her out. They'd ridden the wave of that publicity together and had probably considered the matter closed, as she had.

"So you don't think last night is connected?" Gabe asked, returning to his interrogation tone.

"I don't know," Lacie said, feeling more like she needed to go to bed than she'd just left it. "The man last night didn't threaten me. This could all be a big palaver about nothing."

All of the men bristled. "You can't shrug this off, the guy made contact," Toby said.

"What did he say to you?" Gabe asked. "In person, in the museum last night."

"I don't even get a coffee?" Lacie asked. "You're straight into the interrogation?"

The phone on the kitchen table buzzed and began to skitter across the surface. Toby read the device screen, then looked past her to Ryder and her leaning post tensed further.

"What is it?" Lacie asked while the gang all exchanged a pissed look. Turning to look up at Ryder, Lacie expected an answer. "What?"

When she slid her hand up his neck, he brought his aggravated attention down to her. "Graden's been phoning your cell all morning," Ryder said.

"Ignore him," she said, rushing over to snatch her phone from the table. Once she had it, her intended destination was the sink to drown the device, but Ty stilled her progress. Grabbing her wrist, he took the phone away from her. "What?"

"He's eager," Gabe said.

Scanning them all, she observed a series of serious company faces ready to take on a fight. "You're kidding," she said. "You think Elijah could be behind this?"

"His phone calls are more persistent," Will said, stating fact.

Taking his turn, Toby highlighted another point. "Ryder says he's been pursuing you."

This was supposed to be her home, and these men were supposed to be her friends. Ryder wouldn't even look at her and the rest of them were looking at each other like there was some question they didn't want to ask, maybe because they were scared of how she'd respond.

Examining them all, she asked a question of her own. "Are you accusing me of something?"

"No," Ryder said in his authoritative tone. "Give us a minute, guys."

The men did as they were told, just like they always did, and they left her and Ryder alone. After a beat, he poured her a coffee then sat at the kitchen table.

"I didn't know we lived in an interrogation room," she said, annoyed that these men she trusted with her life might not trust her. "I don't like feeling unwelcome. I thought this was supposed to be our home. If you have something to—"

"Shh," he said. Stealing her hand, he pulled her into his lap. "We're pissed at Graden, no one's pissed at you. We're worried."

"None of them looked worried," she said, hooking her arms around his neck.

Lowering his mouth to kiss the mound of each of her breasts, Ryder exhaled as he rested his face in her cleavage. She stroked his hair and was unsure of the cause for this interlude, but it wasn't unwelcome.

Wriggling her rear over the growing lump in his jeans, she let him know that she was not only aware, but eager. "The boys are right outside the door," Ryder mumbled. His mouth was muffled, so she laughed at his moist breath seeping between her breasts, but that action made him groan. "Your laugh is…" He didn't finish his thought with words, he used actions instead. His hands crept under her skirt to curl around her ass, which was exposed by her thong.

Getting off his lap, Lacie didn't leave him with his disappointed expression for long. She re-adjusted, pulled up her skirt and straddled his lap. Unzipping his jeans, she reached inside to pull out his dick, then raised herself up. Meeting his eye, she sank down, spearing herself to his hilt. Her satisfied breath brought her head back.

Ryder's arms hooked under hers and around to her shoulders giving her a secure lever point to lean back. Squirming up and down on him, their union remained shrouded under her skirt.

"We should be talking," he grumbled and bowed forward to kiss her chest.

"Mm," she said, hooking her heels on the chair crossbar and pushing up then sinking down onto him again. "You once said you were my sex toy." She wrapped her arms around his neck and forced his face into her cleavage. "BOB doesn't talk."

"Bob?" he mumbled.

"Battery operated boyfriend," she said, lifting up and sinking down. "God, you feel so good inside me." She pumped up and down, Ryder kept kissing her breasts until she grabbed his hair and delved her tongue into his mouth. Rocking forward, she rubbed her clit between them and moaned out at the piercing pleasure that shot up inside her.

She froze when the kitchen door opened to reveal Gabe and Rocco. The men didn't get two steps into the room before they stopped, damming the others who traveled behind them. Rocco grinned, but Gabe made them back up, thus pushing everyone out and closing the door again.

"Oops," she said.

Luckily the door was at the far side of the room behind Ryder, meaning she was the only one to have seen the men, but Ryder's frown betrayed his knowledge. Of course he knew everything. Probably her cessation of motion alerted him. He was still sheathed inside her, but she'd been fixated over his shoulder. Still standing as proud as steel inside her intimate space, Ryder wasn't ruffled enough to stop. Lacie undulated her hips in a figure of eight and began to bounce that frown off his face.

"I'm removing their security clearance for up here," he said.

"Stop thinking about the boys," she whispered, brushing her thumbs over his lips. "You're in me, baby. You're fucking me."

Ryder stood up, forcing Lacie to grab for him to steady herself. Keeping an arm around her hips to keep them engaged, Ryder's chair clattered to the floor and he pinned her with his fierce glare.

"Not yet, but I will be," he growled.

Thrusting his other arm out, he cleared space on the table to shove her down onto it. Withdrawing, he slammed into her, and his arm around her body forced her to arch into his driving stabs. The ferocity of his propulsion brought her to climax after climax.

The men knew what they were up to, so they had the kitchen to themselves now and there was no point in hiding their passion. She whipped her top up over her head and he went immediately for her breasts. He sucked her nipple so hard that she squealed. His rough touch sent spikes through her until she yelled his name. Sitting up, the only way she could muffle herself was to close her mouth around his arm. The sensation of her teeth dragging on his flesh made him call out and shove into her again, holding until she'd milked him of every drop.

Both of them took a few panting breaths. She circled her arms all the way around him and rested her cheek on his torso.

"Baby," he murmured. Kissing the top of her head, he ran his hands into her hair, stroking it down her back. "I'm sorry."

"For what?" she asked, rubbing herself closer and kissing his tee shirt.

"I was rough."

"So?" she asked, leaning back on her hands while keeping her legs up over his hips. His sorrow faded a little when his attention was drawn to her bare breasts. "We just had sex half a minute ago." His penis grew upright between her thighs.

"You're so fucking hot," he said.

"I'm really not," she said, laughing. He hooked his elbows under her knees and drew a chair across from the side with his ankle to seat himself. "What are you—" When she tried to sit up, he pulled her legs higher, making her lie back on the table again. "Ryd!"

"I'm going to say sorry," he said. Snagging her panties, he pulled them down out of the way and dropped them to the floor. "I maybe should have done that already."

Running her hands over his, she soothed his worry. "You have nothing to be sorry about," she said. "We've been rough before."

"Not today," he said, hooking her legs over his shoulders and stroking his hands up her thighs. "Not after last night."

Managing to angle herself up, Lacie kept her weight on her hands to accommodate the awkward angle. "I love you," she said, testing the texture of his hair. "I trust you. I like it when you want me that much."

"I always want you that much."

Lacie wasn't ignorant to the feral force that compelled him to consume her. His intensity humbled her, but she didn't fear it. She enjoyed being such an integral part of it, of him. He'd chosen her as his mate and this was a guy who mated for life.

"Distract the guys for five minutes," she said, sliding her legs down his arms. "I'll get changed then we have to talk. I'm taking this seriously. I'll play nice."

Resigned to her sense of responsibility, he tried one more tease. "We could just stay home and have more sex," Ryder said.

"What will the guys do?" she murmured, bending to steal his mouth. "They've got nothing to do if the others are looking after the other cases."

"They can stand guard," Ryder smiled.

"I'm going to get changed."

Kissing him again, Lacie popped down off the table and grabbed her top from the floor. After she had it back in its rightful place, she slipped out of the kitchen with a huge smile on her face.

EIGHTEEN

Ryder

"YOU GUYS EVER think about knocking?" Ryder asked when he strolled through to the living room, which also served as an entrance foyer, where the guys were seated around in the various couches.

"You're a legend," Toby said. It was unlike their meeker member to say something so triumphant. Ryder could only assume that he and Lacie had made quite the impression.

"I agree with Toby," Ty said, nodding and pointing at his colleague. "You're a legend. You've been together a couple of months at least and you're still at it like rabbits."

Dropping down into an armchair, Ryder let his arms fall onto the wide arms of the red chair. "It's worse now," Ryder said, tipping his head onto the backrest. "I can't get enough of her. I want her more and more every day."

The elevator pinged and because everyone with clearance was present, the men fixated on the metal doors, waiting for them to open. When they did, Sorcha was revealed and she appeared to be more aggrieved than she had been last night.

Scurrying out of the elevator, she addressed everyone in the space. "What's going on? Did no one think to phone me?" Sorcha declared.

Always on the ball, Gabe straightened and slid forward in his seat. "How did you get in here?" Gabe asked.

"I watched Lacie put in the code last week," Sorcha said and the elevator doors closed at her back.

The men muttered and shook their heads. "Practicing your covert skills?" Rocco asked.

Ty didn't seem as pissed as the others, but he'd had very little interaction with Sorcha in the past. "You're hot," Ty said.

Rocco spoke again before Ty could slide into his practiced seduction. "She's pregnant, engaged, and having an affair. I think you need to take a number."

"I am not having an affair!" Sorcha exclaimed. "Where is Lacie? It's ridiculous that you would try to keep me locked out of here anyway. She's my best friend. There's nothing she wouldn't let me see."

"You weren't in the kitchen ten minutes ago," Rocco murmured.

"I have to speak to her," Sorcha asserted, ignoring Rocco. "It's extremely important."

It wasn't like the socialite to be flustered, but she was now and that intrigued Ryder into a frown.

"Has Graden been on your ass too?" Ty asked.

"Elijah's been in touch with me but this isn't about him," Sorcha said, righting her purse on her arm.

"So what's it about?" All of them turned to see Lacie loitering in the doorway. "What is it, Sorch?" she asked.

Rushing over to her, Sorcha flouted the men who had been questioning her. "We have to talk," Sorcha said, grabbing her wrist. "Let's go into the kitchen."

Lacie caught Sorcha's arm to adjust her trajectory with an obvious push toward the recreational space in the back of their home. "Let's go into the den. Ryder has to clear up in the kitchen."

Twisting to make eye contact with him, Lacie glared, and he huffed through his grin as though clearing up was an inconvenience. But he slapped his hands on the arms of his chair to push up to his feet. If Lacie wanted him to take care of the mess in the kitchen, then that's what he would do.

Sorcha and Lacie left the reception lounge. Only after they were gone did Rocco speak up. "Do you want us to listen in on the girls?" Rocco asked.

"No need," Ryder said, navigating around his men and the furniture.

"Slipping a bug in there will be no trouble," Gabe said. "Might be useful to know what—"

"Lacie will tell me," Ryder said, pausing by the entrance to the hallway to absorb his men's cascade of admiration.

"Are you sure?" Gabe asked.

"Yeah," Ryder said. "Damn sure."

Leaving to do as Lacie had asked him to, Ryder garnered pride in their relationship. Lacie meant the world to him and he had to trust her. Never again did he want her to question that trust. Communication was important, but he was positive that after last night, she was taking that fact much more seriously.

NINETEEN

Lacie

SETTLING HERSELF AND Sorcha on the doublewide slouch couch in the den. Lacie tried to erase her memories of lying on this couch with Ryder. It was almost as wide as a double bed and watching movies with Ryder here made her feel like a teenager with her first boyfriend, which had been a pleasure she was spared in her teens. Ryder was more than happy to fulfill every one of her lost experiences.

"What's wrong?" Lacie asked, focusing on her friend who was clearly in need.

Sorcha bounced to the edge of the couch and gathered Lacie's hands onto her lap, forcing Lacie to adopt an upright pose too.

"Elijah's been in touch with me," Sorcha said. "I told Ryder that this wasn't about Elijah because I know he's insecure."

"Ryder is not insecure and Elijah has been phoning here too, but I haven't answered any of his calls."

"You should hear him out," Sorcha said and her expression of concern was valued but not necessary.

Smiling, Lacie tried to reassure her. "I don't need to. We have things under control here."

"He's your friend," Sorcha said, releasing some of her grip on Lacie's hands. Her concern became annoyance and the groove between her brows deepened. "Just because you have a boyfriend now doesn't mean you should turn your back on your friends from before."

"I haven't," Lacie said. This wasn't going to be as easy as a few platitudes. She had some anger of her own that she would do her best to dampen for the sake of Sorcha's condition. "But last night he—"

"Because he cares about you," Sorcha said, leaping to Elijah's defense. "If Ryder can't accept—"

"This isn't about Ryder, it's about me," Lacie said, losing grip on the anger she'd tried to harness. "If you've come over here to lecture me about Elijah—"

"Matt wants to see you." Sorcha at least had the decency to appear contrite. She lowered her eyes and for a few stunned seconds, Lacie didn't know what to say.

Her first reaction to the utterance of her ex-boyfriend's name was to withdraw her hands from Sorcha's. "You spoke to Matt?" Lacie asked, feeling irrationally betrayed.

Sorcha stole her hands again. "He's been pestering Elijah, but Elijah's been standing in front of you. He's been trying to protect you."

Her old life, her very old life, included Matt and Elijah as key players. But after she and Matt stopped seeing each other, she had seen less and less of Elijah and others in their circle.

"He's not doing a great job of it if you're bringing it to me," Lacie said, she considered the new information. "Thanks for letting me know."

"That's it? You don't want to talk about it?" Sorcha asked, flummoxed and deflated that they weren't going to deconstruct every detail of what all this might mean.

Depressurizing her anger, she rubbed her hand on Sorcha's wrist. "There's no need," Lacie said. She would tell Ryder about Elijah and about Matt, and from there they would form a plan on how to move forward. "Have you heard from Bruce?"

When her body sagged, Lacie's interest was piqued. "I spent last night with Shep," Sorcha said with enough of a sigh to suggest she knew that she was acting inappropriately. That being said, if she really believed that, then she would not have spent the night with a man other than her fiancé.

"You have to tell your parents," Lacie said.

As though prodded in the spine, her posture righted. "That I had sex with a man who's not my fiancé? Why would I do that?"

It was becoming more obvious that not only did Sorcha and Shep care for each other, but that Bruce was not going to be the beacon of stability someone like Sorcha needed. "You have something with Shep," Lacie said. "Why are you afraid of that?"

"I'm not afraid," Sorcha said, but from the uppity shade in her manner, Lacie felt that she was being dismissed. "I'm marrying the father of my child."

"If you can find him," Lacie said.

Still the height of civility, Sorcha did spare her a brief glimpse of the stink eye. "Shep is going to find him."

If that wasn't preposterous, Lacie didn't know what was. "Your boyfriend is out to find your fiancé? Let me ask Ryder to—"

"Ryder is worried about you. There's a nut out there who wants to wear your skin as a cloak!"

Sorcha did have a flare for the dramatic. Lacie tilted her head to nod. "That's lovely. I'm not worried."

"Says the woman who was recently held in captivity for weeks," Sorcha said, returning to some of her concern. "And who still struggles to get through a night without flashbacks."

"Ryder won't let anything happen to me."

"You've said this to me before," Sorcha said. She lacked the faith that Lacie had. "Right before you were kidnapped."

"That's not going to happen again," Lacie said. "Ryder—"

"You're infuriating," Sorcha exclaimed and tossed Lacie's hands off her lap. "He's not a superhero. What's so great about him anyway?"

"He loves me," Lacie said. Ryder would focus on keeping her safe and wouldn't rest until whoever was responsible for the gallery incident was found and

"We know that. Every thing's just so easy for you, isn't it?"

"Easy?" Lacie asked. "You just said—"

"My life is a complete mess! What am I going to do, Lace? What do I do?"

Sorcha collapsed into her arms and began to sob. Lacie calmed her as best she could, whispering soothing words, and stroking her hair. Sorcha had always had a tendency toward tears and the pregnancy hormones hadn't helped.

Once the crying jag had dwindled, Lacie tried to offer a solution. "Do you want to stay here for a while and get away from things?"

"With you and lover boy? No thanks," Sorcha sniffed and stayed curled into Lacie.

At least if Sorcha was here, they could limit her exposure to Shep and Lacie meant that in the intimate way it sounded in her head. "Ryder won't mind," Lacie said. "Or if he does, I'll make sure he hides it."

Ryder wouldn't be wild about the idea, but he would put up with it. He always put up with Sorcha and her ways because he knew how important the friends were to each other.

"We should go away," Sorcha said, easing out of Lacie's arms.

"Away where?" Lacie asked, watching Sorcha open her purse to retrieve a Kleenex. "I don't think Ryder will like that idea with everything that's going on."

"Since when have you been ruled by a man? Getting away right now might be the best thing for you. The nut is here so you shouldn't be. We can keep the circle small and make sure no one but us knows where we are."

Torn, Lacie struggled to decide. "I'm not ruled by Ryder. It makes sense for me to stay here where I can be protected."

"We'll go and stay with my cousin Carlos," Sorcha said. With this new notion, Sorcha's mood was becoming much more buoyant. "He has security."

That was a no-go idea, though it was probably the best suggestion of where they could go to be safe. "You're pregnant, you can't fly."

"We'll take a train down to Florida. Mason will take us sailing," Sorcha said referring to another of her cousins.

"You on a boat when you've got about six weeks left of your pregnancy?"

Searching for other ideas, Sorcha didn't take long to come up with a new suggestion. "You want to be safe," Sorcha said. "It's that or we go up to the cabin in New England, we could get an airlift from there if necessary."

"The cabin," Lacie said. "You're talking about Elijah's cabin?"

Tutting, Sorcha flopped and shrugged. "Accepting a favor from a friend doesn't mean anything other than he's a friend. I don't have to tell him you're going to be with me… Come on, we could both do with getting away from things for a week or two. Once this kid is out, we'll never have the chance to get away."

That was a very good point. Sorcha deserved some rest and relaxation. After the baby was born, Lacie would have a competitor for Sorcha's attention, though she didn't mind when her opponent would be so cute. "I'm not sure—"

"Please, please, please," Sorcha begged, bouncing in her seat, taking Lacie's hands to bounce them with her. "We'll be in the middle of nowhere, there won't be any trouble."

Lacie drew in a breath and knew she was going to fold. "Let me talk to Ryder."

"Yeah!" Sorcha screeched and pulled her into a hug before she leaped up off the couch. "I'm going home to pack. We'll leave this afternoon."

Sorcha didn't give Lacie a chance to say anything else. She just ran out of the room and presumably out of the building. Lacie wasn't keen on this idea but Sorcha was her best friend and life wouldn't be the same after the baby was born. She just had to convince Ryder.

TWENTY

Lacie

"JUST US, no men," Sorcha hissed. "Who do you see crawling all over the property?"

Persuading Ryder that this trip was a good idea took some time. Lacie told him about Matt getting in touch with Sorcha and that Elijah wanted to help—which had been a tough sell. In the end the only way he would agree was if he could bring them here to check the place out for himself. So he and his men traveled up with the women and were putting security locks on the windows and a proximity alarm on the main road in, which was the only one wide enough for a vehicle.

They'd been in the cabin for an hour. While the men worked, both women unpacked their clothes and while Lacie felt quite at ease, Sorcha was restless. "They're nearly finished," Lacie said, sitting beside her friend in the large living room that the front door opened onto. "They just want a lay of the land."

"I thought Ryder was going to have a heart attack when he saw how close the trees were to the house,"

Sorcha hissed and lifted her legs onto the low table that stood between them and the view onto the front porch.

The house was beautiful though modest, especially for someone of Elijah's means. The wraparound porch was her favorite feature of the house. With the bedrooms upstairs and the kitchen dining area behind the living room, that was the sum total of what the house had to offer.

Lacie had to admit that Sorcha had relaxed just by being here although she was griping, probably because it was one of her favorite pastimes. As picturesque as the house was in its situation, it didn't have the same calming effect on Lacie.

Ryder came down the stairs, which were behind the couch, flanked by Rocco and Gabe. Toby kneeled on the floor beside the front window to close the plastic box that had contained his gadgets. As though they had some sort of psychic link, Ty and Will were moving toward the truck outside and Sonny came through from the kitchen.

"We're moving out," Ryder said when he reached the bottom of the stairs.

"Thank God," Sorcha grunted and didn't get up when Lacie moved over to open the front door.

All of the men kissed Lacie on their way out except Sonny who offered an awkward smile before he shuffled off. Sorcha wasn't budging from her spot on the couch, so she lifted her hand in a feeble farewell. Ryder was the last man to meet Lacie on the threshold and instead of requesting a kiss, she took his hand and led him onto the porch.

The men were heading across the front yard, such as it was, and gave Ryder and Lacie their privacy to say goodbye.

Drawing him over to the railing at the edge of the porch, Lacie exhaled and went into his arms. "You're tense," Ryder said, brushing her hair over her shoulder to her back.

"You're leaving," she murmured into him although that wasn't the sole cause for her negative mood.

"That's making you tense?" he asked, suggesting he knew there was more to her melancholy.

Taking her body away from his, she exhaled and prepared to tell the truth. "Honestly?" she asked, looking left and right, despite being under an awning she was very aware of the men in the truck.

"Tell me."

"It smells like"—unease tickled at the back of her neck, making her shiver—"where they took me that first night. The sounds, the moisture in the air, it's…" Distracted by the scene, she phased out and when he touched her hand, she gasped and stumbled back. Shaking her head, she reoriented herself and tried to smile while taking his hand, but Ryder wasn't going to be fooled.

Opening his fingers, he caught hers and that anchor point meant so much to her. "If you want me to stay…"

"I'll be fine," she said. "I'm overreacting."

"Your feelings are healthy," Ryder said. "If you feel unsafe—"

"I'm being ridiculous," Lacie said. "It's just the heebie-jeebies. I'll be fine. Maybe it's the prospect of sleeping alone, I haven't done that in a while."

She refused to let Wallace and what he did to her ruin her life. Ryder was right, her unease was normal, it was a healthy reaction to her trauma. But she wouldn't sit around in a cage for the rest of her life because she was stronger than that. Despite the difficulty, she had endured, their relationship had endured, and her faith in that gave her power to face her fears."

Ryder slid forward to bring their bodies into contact. "There's an inn a couple of dozen miles south. The guys and I are going to stay there for the night… maybe two. I can be here in half an hour… twenty minutes if you're naked." His tease made her laugh and that was exactly what she needed to chase her butterflies away.

"And here I thought you might introduce me to phone sex," she said, raising herself high onto her toes.

That idea made his brow rise in time with the corner of his mouth. "Dirty talk really works for you, doesn't it, baby?"

A flicker in her throat prickled down through her ribs making every millimeter of her skin become hypersensitive. Diverting her eyes didn't put him off, and he skimmed his hands up her arms to cup her face and bring their eyes back together. The intensity that bled from his gaze only made her body ache in hope.

"How do you do that?" she whispered. Completely enamored and ready to do whatever it took to get her man naked. "I'm ready to bend over and pull up my skirt."

"I can work under the skirt," he said and with another half-smile, he made her shiver again. It was the way he looked at her, with that all-consuming devotion and dedication, that seduced her.

Planting her hands on his torso, she slid them around his ribs to nestle her body on his. "I love you, Stone."

"Love you too."

Kissing the top of her head was a distracting maneuver. At the same time, he bent his knees and let his hands creep under her skirt to squeeze her ass. Protecting her modesty, he moved their bodies so that his blocked the view of the couple from the truck full of his colleagues.

This was probably the point that he was supposed to walk away. But he didn't. "My butt is getting a draft," she smiled.

"Want me to heat you up?"

"You flirt," she said, but didn't take her arms away from around him.

His mouth moved in her hair. "I'm flirting with you because I want you thinking about me. I want to be on your mind."

"You're always on my mind," she said. "It's five days, we'll make it."

"I think we'll need time away together alone after this."

"A week in bed at least," she agreed and enjoyed how their breathing levelled out in this shared embrace. "I love you."

"You've said that already which means you're ready to say goodbye."

"Never ready and never goodbye," she said, tipping her head back. "Just behave yourself, will you? And be careful. I still have use for you."

"I'll be careful," Ryder said. "We're going to track this guy for you, Dusty."

"I know it."

In unison, they brought their lips together and while they sealed their goodbye kiss, Ryder's hand came around to the back of her head. Slanting her head, he deepened the kiss and the moment they shared became more profound than any of their previous sexual encounters.

Parting from her, the encounter was forced to end. "Love you, baby," he said and with a final brief kiss, he squeezed her hand then dropped it.

Running down the stairs, he headed for the truck, but glanced back to wink in sync with his emerging smile. In that split second, she read his mind and her cheeks flushed because the mental images he conveyed were carnal. Too soon, he was in the vehicle and driving away from her.

Still watching the truck, Lacie felt Sorcha approach at her side. "Are they finally gone? I thought they'd never leave," Sorcha grumbled. Lacie couldn't take her eyes from their rear lights, which eventually disappeared round a bend. "Are you crying?"

"No," Lacie said. Sorcha peered around to examine her face and touched her index finger onto Lacie's cheek to show her the moisture. Being emotional was usually Sorcha's bag, not hers, and she couldn't explain this engulfing reaction to watching Ryder and his men depart. "You're going to hate me for this"—Lacie spun around to take her friend's shoulders—"I'm going to get drunk."

TWENTY-ONE

Lacie

THE FIRST NIGHT was tough, but night two was worse. By night three, Lacie had given up even pretending to sleep. Spending time with Sorcha during the day was great. The woman carried a beauty spa with her, so they had plenty to do. They walked, they talked, and they pampered themselves. Lacie was enjoying doodling on her sketchpad, and barbequing for dinner, something she hadn't done for years.

Ryder phoned her five times a day, but she would talk to him more if she could. Fearing he was already worried enough for her, Lacie played down her anxieties and the trouble she had with being in this environment alone. Sorcha could sleep for twelve hours straight without any bother. Although she still claimed to be worried about the state of her life, it didn't appear to impact on her shuteye.

Lacie couldn't argue with Sorcha's assessment. The baby would arrive in little more than a month and Bruce hadn't been in touch at all, which was a testament to his ability to be supportive. Shep had been calling and he'd begged to visit. Sorcha refused him and as much as Lacie wanted to praise her friend's strength, she wondered if it was more do to with Sorcha's "No men" rule, rather than an aversion to spending time with Shep.

It was late, maybe about three a.m., and Lacie was headed downstairs to get a glass of water from the kitchen. The place was dark and eerie, that atmosphere was made all the worse by how out of the way they were because even the moonlight couldn't penetrate the tree canopy. Tiptoeing across the exposed wooden floor, she resolved to phone Ryder when she got back upstairs. Her restlessness was lonely.

Often times when they were together, she would wake up but wouldn't wake him. Just his physical presence was enough to soothe her. If he knew the depth of her struggle, he'd take the burden upon himself to fix her and Lacie was beginning to fear that that wasn't possible.

She sipped her water and turned to head back up to her bedroom when something snapped outside the back door. Her inner paranoia made her freeze on the spot, she didn't want to breathe. An owl called. Vegetation rustled. And the roof tiles rattled. It didn't matter that she knew the noises could be attributed to the wind, the sounds still set her on edge.

Convincing herself it was nothing was harder than it sounded. Drawing on the strength she got from Ryder and his confidence, she pushed through the fear and made herself go to the back door. Her ears were tuned to be acute and were aware of every whisper and creak as she tried to seek out any proof of danger. If she found it then she'd be calling Ryder and waking Sorcha.

Sorcha had lost the back door key yesterday during one of her treks in and out with their dinner and drinks, so the rear door wasn't locked. Lacie pushed the back door open a few inches and was met with a rush of cold night air. Because there was nothing visible that concerned her, she began to retreat. Something metallic rattled, so she paused, but couldn't pick out a source in the vicinity. A hand clasped around her face over her mouth and she was lifted from her feet, she didn't have time to breathe let alone scream. Before she could think to fight, something nipped her arm and within seconds, she was out cold.

TWENTY-TWO

Ryder

BEING AT WORK while Lacie was on vacation shouldn't bother him. It wasn't that she was relaxing that worried him, it was that she was so far away. Their separation did have one advantage. He was free and clear to devote all his time and resources to tracking down the threat.

"Two more this afternoon," Ryder said, placing his hands, shoulder width apart on the board room table of the S.I.S. space they'd turned into their incident room. "I want these guys off the list before the primary returns."

His men all looked at each other before they smirked at him.

"It's just us here," Rocco said, pointing at his cohorts who were all former SW employees. "You do know that we all know who you're talking about? You know, the woman you have a helluva lot of sex with… Do you call her the primary in bed?"

Typical of Rocco to get a laugh even in the midst of this serious setup. "Most of us have seen most of Lacie through your exploits with her," Will said, bobbing his brows at the others, and causing Ryder's scowl to form. "You're a lucky man."

"I think the point Rocco was trying to make is that attempting to keep distance from the client in this case is redundant," Gabe said, not as swayed by frivolity as their colleagues, which was one of the things Ryder appreciated about his man in charge.

"I know what his point was," Will said, resting his weight on his forearms on the table. "I'm just saying that I like the art she presents… and I don't mean her work."

The others laughed at Will's attempt to rile him. Ryder cracked half a smile because he knew this teasing was his men's way of lightening the load.

Bringing them back to task, he thrust his hands up off the table. "Let's do what we can to keep her around then, shall we?"

Though the men quieted, they didn't quite return to sober. "Yeah, you're sure easier to work with these days now she's around," Toby said.

Everyone was smiling in united agreement when the door burst open and Sonny flew in panting. "The bathroom's the next one along if you need to knock one off," Ty jeered.

"What's going on?" Gabe asked, sensing Sonny's conflict as Ryder did and it was enough to scare him.

"Something's happened to Lacie," Sonny said to the table then brought his focus to Ryder.

All of the nerves in Ryder's body clenched in a hissing fizzle. "What?" Ryder asked. "What happened?"

No one answered because his team was already up and heading for the door. This was unreal. He had lost her once and vowed to never do it again. Snatching his phone from the table, he began to dial her as he headed out and he just prayed she would pick up.

TWENTY-THREE

"WHAT HAPPENED?" Ryder asked as soon as he got out of the truck.

Gabe and Rocco piled out too, but all he cared about was getting to Lacie who was sitting on the porch wrapped in a blanket.

"I'm okay," Lacie said and moved to stand up, but she was unsteady on her feet and wobbled before she sat on the bench again.

Running up the stairs, he dropped onto the bench beside her and had no chance to check her out because she immediately snuggled against him. Holding her for a brief moment, he began to run his hands over her to check she was uninjured and was actually there.

"Tell me what happened?" he asked and bent over to hook her legs up over his thighs to pull her into his lap.

"I don't know," Lacie said and her weight sagged onto him, reassuring him that she was here and it was a reassurance that he needed.

"Oh, you're here!" Sorcha exclaimed as she came out of the cabin carrying a tray of tea. How she could be so calm in light of what had happened, he was flummoxed.

Gabe and Rocco were propped against the railing at the edge of the porch. "Good to see you healthy, Hart," Rocco said. "What do you remember?"

Lacie stayed in his lap but turned her face out of his chest to observe everyone. "I wish I could tell you it was something useful… it's not."

"Tell us anyway," Gabe said. "You never know what—"

"I couldn't sleep," Lacie said, stretching her arms, then pulling the blanket tighter around herself. "I came down to get a glass of water and… it was stupid… I'm really lucky that…"

"That what?" Ryder asked her, stroking his arms down her body and onto her legs.

She didn't respond to him and turned her focus to Sorcha. "I want to go home, Sorch. I'm really sorry to cut our trip short but—"

"Are you kidding?" Sorcha asked, putting the tray of teas onto the bench beside them. "If I could reach the steering wheel, I'd have taken you home myself. I'm so sorry that…"

"It's okay," Lacie said and when Sorcha began to tear up, Lacie sprang up and pulled Sorcha into her arms, wrapping both women in the blanket.

Bereft without her, Ryder saw Lacie waver on her feet, so he stood up behind her to steady her hips while the women hugged. They were occupied with each other, so Ryder switched into company mode and spoke to Gabe.

"I want you and the guys to do a full survey. Find out what happened, where the bastard got in and how he got out. If there's any evidence, I want it analyzed, understand?" Ryder said and Gabe spoke to Rocco who then pulled out his phone to take notes.

"What about Graden?" Gabe asked. "Should we ask permission?"

Glancing at the women, Sorcha was still crying, so Ryder didn't disturb them. "I don't give a fuck what Graden thinks. We're going to be in and out before he knows anything has happened, understand?"

The men nodded and retreated to the truck to coordinate the op with the other S.I.S. men who were setting up a base at the inn they'd stayed in previously. Sorcha had answered Lacie's cellphone earlier and given him pieces of the story. Later in the drive Lacie had called back to assure him that she was okay. But he was not going to let this go.

TWENTY-FOUR

Ryder

PACKING UP THE women took no time at all and Ryder was pleased that Lacie stuck close to him. Gabe was running the evidence gathering, but before he left, he gathered all the men together on the porch. Keeping an eye on Lacie through the living room window, he'd told his woman that he'd keep this meeting brief.

"How is Lacie doing?" Toby asked.

"Good," Ryder responded. "Okay… I don't know. I'll figure that out once I get her alone."

"What happened?" Will asked. "What does she remember?"

He'd spoken to her about the incident again up the stairs while she was packing and it was clear that her memory was vague.

"Whoever he was, he surprised her," Ryder said. "Drugged her with something I'd guess. She woke up on the kitchen floor hours later, which means whatever he hit her with was stronger than the last time."

"She doesn't want to go to the cops?" Will asked. "Or the hospital? They might be able to find something in her blood."

"She spoke to the cops this morning. Sorcha called them right after she called Sonny," Ryder said. "But she's adamant that she doesn't want to go to the hospital. Whatever he used the last time didn't show up in a tox screen. It's tough to know what to test for when we don't know what's there."

"We test for everything," Will said.

After being one of Lacie's biggest opponent's, Will had made quite a turn around. "I'll talk to her about it again," Ryder said. "Gabe will run things here while I take the women back to the inn and we'll be bailing out in the morning once I've had a chance to talk to Lace again."

"Toby is looking at the cameras on the highway," Gabe said. "But we don't know what we're looking for. If this person is on the road network, we're probably looking right at him. Unless you want us to run every plate…"

That would be time consuming and may not yield any results. They could run the plates of the assailant and unless it said on his record, "Manic with a penchant for artists," they could scan right past him.

"We're still investigating Graden," Will said. "And we're going to pull up what we can on his movements over the last few days. He knew the women were here and he would know how to get in and out of what could be a disorienting environment to someone who doesn't know it."

"We're lucky that we're ahead of the game on this one," Rocco said. "He was on the list after the gallery. We've already started gathering intel."

Ryder didn't like Graden. The guy pissed him off just by existing, but Ryder was aware his prejudice probably came from how close Elijah thought he was with Lacie.

"Keep looking into it," Ryder said. "But we can't get too fixated on that. Do the cops have anything?"

"Nothing in the system yet," Toby said from his place in the corner behind his computer screen. "No BOLO, no APB, no ATL, whichever frickin' code they use up here, and no arrest warrants either. I'm keeping one eye on their system though."

"Good," Ryder said. "We need to work out their point of entry because it wasn't the main road, we rigged it with the sensors. If we can do that, we might be able to narrow our search on the traffic cameras. We may even catch a vehicle coming out of the forest."

Unlikely because in this area there just weren't that many cameras because there was nothing to see. "Find out if there are any experiments or monitoring activities in the woods," Ryder said. "Fish and Wildlife might have something or the city college, they're more likely to have cameras or motion sensors planted around a forest than the state trooper."

"What would they be monitoring?" Will asked, but Gabe was already making his way to another of the computers.

"I don't know, migratory patterns or endangered species numbers. I don't give a fuck if they're monitoring mating habits, but who else is going to have monitoring equipment setup in the middle of nowhere?" Going over to a now nodding Will, Ryder planted a hand on his shoulder. "Meanwhile, I want you and Rocco going over all reported incidents for the last seventy-two hours, look for anything suspicious, traffic stops where maybe the guy had a syringe or a weapon or a kidnap kit…" Will was nodding, he passed his boss to pull up a chair beside Toby.

"This sonofabitch didn't roll into town ten minutes before he hit Lacie. He might have been sleeping in his car, but he might have had a hotel room, a meal in a restaurant, gone into a convenience store for a soda. I want eyeballs on every image we can pull up and cross-reference anything suspicious with license plates in those locations. If we can match that to vehicles who might have come in the same day as the primary, or just after, then we can find out if that car was on the road last night when Lacie was assaulted. We're going to find this asshole."

The room chorused a "Yes, sir" but no one looked up from their task.

Taking control and issuing orders gave him a distraction. This lunatic had drugged her once and loons tended to stick to the same MO. What he didn't understand was why the guy didn't take her, why he didn't assault her further. With the drugs he was using, he could have kidnapped Lacie and no one would have known about it until half a day later when Sorcha woke up to find Lacie gone.

This guy was playing a dangerous game and not being able to figure out the rules or the objective made Ryder very uneasy.

TWENTY-FIVE

Lacie

MORE THAN A week went by and Lacie tried her best to get back into a routine. She was unsettled and was getting only short bouts of sleep. But she was home now and safe. She had no intention of leaving this city, or going anywhere without security, until this was all over.

She hadn't seen Sorcha since they'd returned from Elijah's cabin. They had talked briefly on the phone, but when Sorcha had shown up on her doorstep that day, it was a surprise to Lacie. As distracted as Lacie was by her own troubles, she could see her friend fidgeting from the moment she'd walked in.

"What's wrong with you today?" Lacie asked her over the kitchen table after they'd been talking for around half an hour and Sorcha hadn't revealed the source of her agitation. "I thought I was jumpy, but you're... you can't sit still, you're looking all over the place and—"

"We got married."

Lacie's mouth was still open from her speech and she hung there mid-pout for a moment. "I'm sorry, what?"

"Bruce and me…" Sorcha said, shoving her coffee mug aside. "We just… I was crying and I don't know what happened, the next minute we were making love and then… I guess we just got swept into the romance of the night because the next day… we went to city hall and—"

"You got married?" Lacie said. Her need to stand made her push away from the table and stalk toward the window. "To Bruce? Bruce?"

Sorcha nodded. "Our parents made us get the license a few weeks ago. Bruce said he'd been fighting with his parents about him not working and they kicked him out… he was upset too. I think we needed each other."

Sorcha's desire for happiness and her tendency to be spontaneous had gotten her into bed with Shep, and with Bruce, in the first place. These snap decisions had consequences that Sorcha never took the time to think through. She did what made her feel good in the short term, but Lacie feared what this would mean for her friend, and her child, long term.

"What about Shep?" Lacie asked, trying to gauge her friend's reaction to the mention of the man.

"You were the one who said I had to make a decision," Sorcha said, displaying more impatience than longing. "What decision did you think I would make?"

"The right one," Lacie said, approaching the table. "You married a man you don't love because you were both having a shitty weekend and it made you feel better."

"It did," Sorcha said, rubbing a hand over her stomach. "He's stayed with us since then."

"And what happens when he makes up with his parents and moves back in there…"

"We'll deal with it," Sorcha said with a decisive nod. "We're having dinner with his parents tomorrow… I need to get something to wear, something… responsible."

"They're going to flip out when they hear you eloped."

"Probably not," Sorcha said, then brought her thumb nail up to her teeth. "Do you think so?" Lacie could only glare with disapproval and rest her hands on the back of the chair. "Will you come shopping with me?"

There was nothing else to do and with this revelation, Lacie knew she would have more questions, so work was out of the window. "Come on," she said, grabbing her purse from the table.

The pair got ready to go out and Sorcha was talking about the hotel she and Bruce had booked into for their wedding night when they got into the elevator. It stopped only a couple of floors down and Sorcha stopped talking to examine the illuminated numbers.

"What are we doing here?" Sorcha asked.

Lacie crossed the hallway, keyed in the code needed for access and pushed through the gray door. On this floor, there was a recreation room for the men to use when they had downtime. There, she found what she needed.

Hanging in the door, with one hand on the handle and the other on the door jamb, she looked past the half a dozen new S.I.S. men around the couches beside her. Rocco, Will, and Ty stood around the pool table on the far side of the room and it was them that she spoke to.

"Are you guys busy?" Lacie called to the men she knew.

All of the men in the room had noticed her entry, but Rocco and Ty were concentrating on the game at hand. "Not for you, Princess," Will said. With his arms folded, he was propped against the wall, watching his friends play. "What do you need?"

"Security," Lacie said. "Sorcha and I are going shopping. I don't really want to go out with—"

"Say no more," Rocco said, putting his cue on the table then all three came toward her.

Lacie hadn't realized that the three were paying so close attention until they jumped into action. "Whoa," she said, holding up her hands and using her hip to keep the door ajar. "I don't need the three of you."

The trio were already on her position. "There's two of you," Ty said, taking the door from her hip to open it further.

"Better more hands than less," Rocco said, grabbing a jacket from a hook beside the door and pulling it on before he took off another two to give to Will and Ty.

"We're not doing anything anyway," Will said, putting on his own jacket.

Ty got to the crux of the matter. "Plus, the boss would have our balls if something happened to you while one of us sat here on our asses."

Lacie nodded in concession and let herself be herded backward toward the elevator door where Sorcha was still poised. "You'll be bored out of your minds."

Sorcha had already called the elevator, so they all waited for it to arrive. "Let's hope so," Rocco said.

Lacie didn't like to be a bother, but she knew that they were right. Having three guards would make her feel safer and they would be able to keep an eye on Sorcha too. Ryder would appreciate his men being vigilant. Despite how self-conscious she felt, Lacie appreciated it as well.

TWENTY-SIX

Lacie

BY THE THIRD store, Sorcha was loaded down with bags and didn't have any inclination to slow down. Melting her credit card made her happy and Lacie would bet she was burning the one her parents paid off, hence why Sorcha didn't have to worry about the zeros on her receipts.

Seated on short leather benches perpendicular to each other, Lacie and Sorcha tried on the various pairs of shoes the attendant had brought them before Sorcha excused him.

"Bruce cooked dinner last night before staying the night," Sorcha said, sliding her feet into delicate gold heels then extending her legs to admire them from afar. Bruce had been the hot topic of conversation. It was amazing to see Sorcha glow again, but Lacie knew she was setting herself up for a crash. Hope as she might that Bruce was taking his role as husband and father seriously, Lacie knew he was a guy who took the easy way out when things got too hard.

"That's good," Lacie said, putting on a pair of shoes Sorcha had selected for her. Indifferent to them, Lacie bent to tidy away the various pairs Sorcha had tried into their boxes. "Did you have sex?"

"Yeah," Sorcha said, pointing her toes out and twisting her legs from side to side to check the shoes from every angle. "It's a bit weird. I was sort of getting used to Shep."

"Have you heard from him?" Lacie asked.

Glad that Sorcha had brought him up, she eased into the issue.

"He's called but I haven't answered the phone." Sorcha got up to walk in the shoes. Lacie slid the shoes she was wearing off her feet.

"You'll have to talk to him eventually," Lacie said, watching her friend walk back and forth in front of the low mirror.

Sorcha turned around and her smile lost some of its sparkle. "Get them," Sorcha said, watching Lacie return the shoes to their box.

"What do I need fancy shoes for?" Lacie asked, stacking the boxes. "Until my head is back to its old self, I am not tottering around in heels."

"Good point," Sorcha said. "Have you seen the doctor since you've been back?"

"I have an appointment tomorrow. I'm just so tired and distracted… I don't know if it's an after effect of the drugs, or maybe some sort of psychological aftereffect."

"You definitely need a pick-me-up," Sorcha said. Kicking off her shoes, Sorcha rushed over to grab Lacie's hands and pulled her onto her feet. "Next is the most important thing and there's no excuses for you getting out of that."

"What?" Lacie asked as Sorcha drew her toward a purple curtain in the corner.

Sorcha whipped it aside to show a store within the store. A vast but secret store. A very specific niche store. "Lingerie!" Sorcha declared and kept Lacie's hand to ease her inside.

This was more than lingerie. On the walls were mannequins wearing costumes and displays of sex toys, body paints, and how-to DVDs. But it wasn't sleazy. It seemed rather tasteful and catered to most tastes and requirements. Lacie didn't dare look over her shoulder at the three security men who would follow them in. Rocco, Ty, and Will had been respectful and gave the women distance to talk without fear of them eavesdropping. But they would not let her out of their sight, so they would have to enter this space.

"Shouldn't you have bought this stuff before the wedding night?" Lacie asked.

"There's always a reason to buy sexy underwear. We don't need an excuse," Sorcha said, picking up a leather paddle and running her hand over the flat surface. "Do you think we should get toys?"

"Ask Bruce," Lacie said, still absorbing the details surrounding them. "You know what he likes in bed."

Patting her hand with the paddle, Sorcha considered this before she responded. "We'll be married for a long time. It might be nice to experiment," Sorcha said, casting the paddle aside to rush toward what was probably considered the demurest corner, which was filled with babydoll nightwear and silky chemises.

Lacie followed on and caught up when Sorcha was searching a rack for her size.

"You have plenty of lingerie," Lacie said, letting her fingers run over the delicate fabric. "Will any of this fit over Bump?"

"A girl can never have enough lingerie, and I have to plan for after childbirth, not just before," Sorcha said, fingering the lace cup of a bra. Lacie was amazed to discover that her friend did forward plan—in the most frivolous area. "What are you going to get?"

Stumped, Lacie sealed her mouth and her thoughts because it hadn't occurred to her to make purchases of her own here. "Me?"

Sorcha was searching through another rail of lingerie and selected another piece. "We're here. Why not treat yourself and your boyfriend too?"

"I don't think so," Lacie said, shaking her head and taking her fingers away from the material she'd been fingering.

"Why not?"

Glad that Sorcha was preoccupied with her hunt, Lacie's brightening complexion went unnoticed... at least she hoped it did. Rocco, Ty and Will were somewhere on their periphery but Lacie didn't dare look up to seek them out for fear they'd be snickered about her reaction to Sorcha's suggestion.

"I don't... I've never... I don't even know if Ryder's into that," Lacie said. "He likes me naked. I think lingerie would just get in the way."

"Every man likes lingerie on his partner," Sorcha said, picking up a third swathe of fabric. "It builds the suspense, toys with them, teases them."

"More often than not I initiate sex," Lacie said, moving with her friend as she moved through the apparel. "It's hard to tease when you're the aggressor. And I've had sex with him a million times. I think it's a little late to be coy."

Sorcha stopped to frown at her friend before she dumped the things from her arms onto the rail beside her. "I've neglected you," she said. "With everything that's been going on I forgot that you're new to this sex thing."

"I think I'm doing okay," Lacie said, feeling two inches tall.

If it wasn't bad enough that her best friend had announced that she was terrible in bed, the three men protecting her could hear every word and everyone in their building would know it tomorrow. Lacie wasn't new to sex, she'd been with men before Ryder. But she was new to the kind of passion she experienced with Ryder. Before him, sex was something done for the pleasure of her partner and none of them had cared too much about how she might enjoy the experience.

Since her teenage years, orgasm was something she achieved on her own, with her hands or her toys. It was not something that she'd been capable of with her partners, probably because she was too tense and focused on not getting anything wrong since she got no encouragement from the men in her life back then.

"Men are far more likely to lose control of their hormones than women," Sorcha said, taking Lacie to a lush leather bench in the corner to seat them both. "Sex can be a lot of fun, I've always told you that, but you should always make sure that they work for it."

"Work for sex?"

"It's easy handing it out when you first get together but if you keep just handing it out, they get bored. Men like a challenge," Sorcha said, crossing her legs and leaning back to accommodate Bump. "It's like training a dog. There are treats and punishments. Their behavior dictates which they should get."

Lacie's nose crinkled. "Isn't that using sex as a weapon?"

"It's using it as a tool to make sure that you're looked after, to make sure you're treated well," Sorcha said, raising a hand as though she were delivering a college lecture rather than advising a friend.

"Ryder treats me well," Lacie said.

"Sure, now he does," Sorcha said. "You haven't been together for very long. You've been in intense situations, things are fraught. You have to get it right now or in the long term your relationship will never last. You have to learn when to give it out and how much. You can't be open for business twenty-four, seven."

"Why not?" Lacie asked, believing that fair was fair. "He is."

"He's a man," Sorcha said, returning to her educating tone. "We expect them to be horny dogs begging for table scraps. You have to claim power now or he'll be walking all over you for the rest of your time together."

"You think I'm being a slut?"

"I think you don't want him to think that. You have to let them know that you're in control, he'll only get it if you deem him worthy. There are a million men out there and you could choose any one of them, and if he gets too big for his boots you need to make him aware of that."

"You want me to withhold sex and flirt with other men to ensure I keep Ryder?"

"If that's what you want," Sorcha said and her serious expression gave way to a smile. "And every woman knows that any good sex war starts with the tease." Sorcha presented her hands to the store they were in. "And this is our armory."

Sorcha bounced up to go back to her shopping and Lacie glanced around to see what she might pick up. Playing games with Ryder was off the table for her and Sorcha didn't exactly lead by example when it came to how best to handle yourself in a relationship.

For now, Sorcha was happy, and Lacie would do all she could to maintain that delight in her friend. People went through such turmoil in relationships, she had too, before she met Ryder. He was a careful man, a responsible man, and she didn't need to toy with him. Still, it was nice to get a glimpse of the old Sorcha again.

TWENTY-SEVEN

Lacie

LACIE AND HER three security agents didn't get home until it was dark. Sorcha had gone on quite a spree then insisted on dinner. The five ate together at Lacie's insistence. They were all friends and she wouldn't have the men standing and starving in a place full of sustenance.

After they'd arrived at Sorcha's apartment, Ty helped Sorcha upstairs with her bags, and then the four of them traveled back to S.I.S. Lacie told them that they didn't have to follow her up to the residence, but they stuck with her, each wearing their own private smirk. They'd had quite a day and heard more than Lacie would ever have wanted to share with them.

As the elevator doors opened, Ty went out first though Lacie couldn't imagine what threat to her could exist here. Rocco draped his arm over her shoulders while Will stayed behind. No one was in the reception lounge, but when they got to the kitchen, voices warmed the air.

"What time do you call this?" Ryder asked, though he didn't sound upset or angry.

Ty moved aside and she saw Gabe, Sonny, and Toby at the table with Ryder who leaned back with his hands linked behind his head.

"Are you hungry?" Sonny asked. "We have lots of food."

"We ate out," Ty said, pulling out a chair for Lacie but she shook her head.

"I'm going to bed," she said.

"It's early," Toby said.

She just smiled and left the men to it. There was beer on the table, so the poker chips wouldn't be far behind.

"Lace."

The voice stopped her from entering the bedroom after opening the door. Glancing back, she turned when she noticed Rocco was traversing the hall to get to her. When he reached her, he gestured into the bedroom. Taking his prompt to go inside, he came with her and closed the door to give them privacy.

"Anything wrong?" she asked, folding her arms. There had been no incidents when they were out and if a threat had been identified while they were out, she would assume Ryder would be the one to give her the intel.

"Today was impromptu. You haven't had the standard client protocol discussion," he said. "There are a bunch of rules for us and we like to make clients aware of what to expect and how we deliver our service. I'm sure you'll be getting the briefing soon."

"Then I don't understand what—"

"We will never repeat what's said, what we see, what we hear, nothing," he said and although this serious side of Rocco was an anomaly, it wasn't unusual for him to be the one putting people at ease. Humor was his default way to do that, but when something else was required, he proved now that he was up to the task.

"Okay," she said with a nod.

"We wouldn't do it with any other client and you're no exception. We want to protect you. Our job is to protect you and that's exactly what we'll do, whatever it takes. I don't know how you'll want to configure your detail, which will be covered in your commencement briefing, and the fact that your boyfriend may take a turn on your rotation will be something you'll have to work out between yourselves. But as for the rest of us, we see nothing, hear nothing, and say nothing."

"While seeing and hearing everything," she said, her hands fell to her sides. "What you're saying is, I can have a torrid affair and you won't tattle-tale."

"Yeah, I guess that's it," he said, returning to a familiar smile.

"You've noticed my discomfort," she said, he nodded. "My concern isn't what you tell Ryder. You can give him a second-by-second account of my day; you have my permission."

"You squirmed all day," Rocco said. "You were obviously uncomfortable."

"About you and the other guys. Ryder knows everything about me, I'd tell him anything. But you and the others know me as Ryder's girlfriend. Now you get to see a different aspect of me. You'll all look at me differently, you'll know more about me than I do of you. My secrets will be out and that will change each of my relationships with you."

"You can follow the rest of us around if you want," Rocco smiled and his good humor made her release a short laugh.

"I suppose I still feel strange about this."

"You'll get used to it," Rocco said. "Soon you won't notice we're there."

Taking a long breath, she hoped that he was right. "Doubt that."

Lowering his smile, some of his solemnity returned. "Lace," he said, touching her shoulder. "We all love you. You're a member of the team and we look out for our own."

Teasing herself, she narrowed her eyes to peer closer. "Is this your way of telling me not to have a torrid affair?"

"This is my way of telling you that if you did, we'd kick Ryder out and keep you safe."

Lacie laughed, appreciating how he put her at ease and he had made her feel better. She gave him a hug which he returned until someone cleared their throat.

"Am I interrupting?" Ryder asked.

He stood in the doorway beside them wearing a smile. Lacie thought of Sorcha's claim she should make Ryder jealous. Yet there she was in the arms of another man, in a bedroom, and Ryder was completely unaffected. That fact only made Lacie love him more, though that it was one of his men probably made a difference to his reaction.

Rocco ruffled her hair then patted Ryder's shoulder as he negotiated his way out around Ryder who closed the bedroom door. Lacie kicked off her shoes and pushed the straps of her dress from her shoulders letting it pool at her feet. She stretched and flopped down on the bed.

"Oh it's been a day," she said.

"Heard you stopped for security before you left," he said. "Good girl."

"I thought you'd approve," she said, unhooking her bra and wriggling out of her thong.

"I do."

"I need to have a shower and wash the day off me," she mumbled closing her eyes as she buried her face in a pillow. "Sorcha's in her element. She and Bruce eloped; they're married."

"That's a surprise," Ryder muttered. "But as long as they're happy."

Lacie wasn't in the mood to get into the details of if Sorcha was happy, if she'd acted on impulse, or how long any of this would last. The bed shifted, indicating to her that Ryder had seated himself beside her. His fingertips touched the back of her knee and slid up the back of her thigh toward her butt.

Hiding her smile in the bed, she tried not to let it convey in her tone. "Uh-uh, I'm withholding sex."

"You're what?"

The grin in his voice widened her smile. From how he kneaded her glutes, he paid no heed to her words. "I need to train you," she said into the pillow. "So I'm withholding sex and I have to tell you that a really hot guy smiled at me today."

"Is that right," he murmured.

His hand left her but before she could mutter her disappointment, his lips touched the back of her knee and he crawled up her, kissing the path his hand had just trekked.

"That doesn't bother you?" she asked, turning her head out of the pillow to look over her shoulder as he kissed up her spine.

"Did he approach you?" he asked between kisses. "Or touch you?"

"No," she said.

"It doesn't surprise me that men show interest in you, you're beautiful. They can look all they want, but you're mine."

Knowing fine well that she had no intention of following through on her assertion, she kept teasing. "I'm withholding sex," she said, warmed by the possession in his feral tone.

"I heard you," he said, sweeping her hair aside to kiss her neck.

His weight pushed her down into the mattress. The rasp of his fully clothed body on her naked one made her wriggle and push her rear up into the buckle of his belt, seeking the solid want he impressed into her.

"Ryd," she exhaled.

"Mm, Dusty," he mumbled against her back. "Anything you want, anything at all."

"Your dick in me," she gasped, pushing her body upward to force him up so she could roll onto her back. He came in for a kiss, but she went straight for his belt buckle.

"I thought you were withholding," he laughed when she stuck her hand in his briefs to pull out his thick member.

"I did," she said. "That's over now. I'll withhold when you go back through to play poker with the guys."

"You want to have sex then kick me out of bed?"

"You talk too much," she said, pushing him to his back.

Climbing over to straddle him, she speared herself on the pleasure he offered to only her.

"I love you," he coughed out, curling into the delight her own engorged tissues gave his.

Driving herself up and down, she bowed her mouth to his but the kiss was short-lived. Taking control, Ryder flipped her onto her back and pinned her hips with his own, still deep inside her.

"What if I'm withholding?" he asked. "Did you ever think of that?"

Running her hands up his body, she got her hands into his hair and took it in her fists, forcing their mouths together again. "Stop talking and make love to me Ryder, now."

He was better at teasing than she was, but when their need was so urgent, it wasn't in either of them to deny the other.

TWENTY-EIGHT

Lacie

GETTING OUT OF her funk over the next week, Lacie resolved herself to move on from the second attack and to do that, she had to be able to go outside and conduct business without panicking. Taking Rocco's words to heart, she made plans to treat her security detail seriously. What this meant was she had to go through the same procedure their clients did.

After Ryder left their bed in the morning, Lacie slept in. Eventually she woke to get herself ready for the meeting that would help them all plan how best to keep her safe. Sliding her feet into her wide heeled court shoes that went with the gray cotton business dress she had only worn on a couple of occasions, she swept her hair into a tight French roll and smiled at her reflection in the mirror. She looked every inch the consummate professional, which was exactly what she wanted to be seen as. But the S.I.S. men would get a laugh at seeing her so buttoned up.

Getting herself down the stairs, she drew stares from the newest S.I.S. men in the reception and the blonde receptionist—who Lacie now knew as Chantelle—sat up straight.

"Miss Hart?" Chantelle asked.

"I have an appointment," Lacie said.

"Boardroom one," Chantelle stuttered.

Lacie nodded and made her way around the waterfall glass to the first door on her right. Knocking once, she went inside and paused to let the men look her up and down. They weren't used to seeing her like this with her neatly styled hair, discreet make-up, and the sophisticated business wear.

"Lacie Hart," she said while trying not to smile at the agog faces. "I have an appointment."

Ryder sat at the head of the table with Gabe and Rocco flanking him. Next down was Will and Toby, then Ty and Sonny. She had every member of the elite team.

"You are a sexy thing, Hart," Ty muttered.

"That's not very professional," Lacie said, allowing herself a smile. Coming inside, she closed the door, and moved past her amusement. "How does this work?"

Ty spoke again. "If you feel like taking your clothes off…"

Ignoring Ty, Gabe stood up. "We were just discussing your predicament," he said, moving down the table to pull out a chair for her to sit a few places down from Ty.

Rounding the table, she sat and Gabe pushed in her chair. Ty winked at her, if he was trying to make her laugh, he was on the road to succeeding. Lacie hoped this wasn't how he was with all the female clients, and somehow, she knew he wasn't. Ryder trusted men who were capable and professional, not those who were unable to stand up to the job. Ty just liked to tease her and rile Ryder in the process.

"Do you have a plan?" Lacie asked Gabe who appeared to be taking the lead. It was nice that Sonny was at the table, he was moving up in estimations and was no longer just their servant.

"This meeting will help us to determine a path that will be suitable for all of us. We work for you at the end of the day but we won't allow you to impede us in doing our job, that wouldn't suit either party."

"You all know why we're here," Lacie said. "We all understand what the threat is. I trust every one of you."

"Rocco's given you our position," Gabe said. "Our goal is to keep you safe, regardless of our own personal cost."

The implication of this statement made her frown. "I don't want any of you taking risks," she said flattening her hands on the table.

"Then you've come to the wrong place, Princess," Will said, clipping his words. "We do our job no matter the cost."

All of these men would give their life for hers; she'd heard it before. "Maybe this was a mistake," Lacie said, considering how she would feel if anything happened to any of them because of her troubles.

"A mistake?" Gabe asked.

"There are other security companies—"

"One of our competitors?" Sonny said, displaying the education he'd gotten from these men. Exhibiting the depth of his awareness earned him his seat at the table.

"I don't doubt your skills," Lacie said. "But if anything happened to any of you—"

"If we do our jobs properly no one will get hurt," Gabe said.

All too aware of how these intimidating men could railroad a person, she asserted her position.

"I'd rather not take that risk," Lacie said.

"Do you think we would trust anyone else with your safety?" Rocco asked.

"If you got hurt on someone else's watch, how do you think we would react?" Will asked.

As each man spoke, they got her attention. It didn't take her long to come up with an answer to Will's question. People would end up getting hurt in that scenario. If these men started a war with another security company, there was no guaranteeing anyone's safety.

She also knew that regardless of whether she authorized it, these men would investigate and would probably guard her as well, even if it was from a distance.

"We're considered the best for a reason," Toby said. He wasn't known for saying much but when he did speak, he made it count.

"Okay," she said, drumming her flat fingers on the table. Arguing was pointless, because even if she told them not to continue working the case, they would. "My boyfriend is picking up the tab so I suppose I can afford to waste your time and his money."

Her intention was to draw a reaction from said boyfriend at the head of the table who had been conspicuously silent, yet he remained so.

"When you're here in the complex," Gabe said. "We assume you'll be safe but will still post one agent on your detail."

"Even when I'm home upstairs?"

"Yes," Gabe said. "We can't be complacent. Only the truly arrogant would assume they were invincible."

His words were true but being constantly under scrutiny didn't complement her personality.

"I like to be alone," Lacie said. "Will someone watch me shower and dress too?"

"I volunteer for that detail," Ty said, raising a hand to the rest of the men who snickered at their flirtatious friend.

"We would offer wide perimeter at home," Gabe said. "Security is in the process of being stepped up in the building."

"What about out of the building?" Lacie asked.

"For external and high risk four agents. In familiar or scouted locations three agents."

The thought of being constantly surrounded was unsettling. Yet as foreign as it was to be watched, having these men around would increase her sense of safety, and Ryder's sense of it too. That would be worth the cost of her privacy for the duration of the investigation.

"Are there any provisos that I should be aware of?" she asked.

"Give us as much information as you can ahead of time," Gabe said. "We appreciate that there will be spontaneous events but if you know where you'll be or who with we'd appreciate the heads up."

Lacie nodded. "I can do that."

"Keep your panic button on you at all times," Gabe said. "We'll provide you with another for company purposes."

"Okay," Lacie said. "It all sounds straightforward."

"We'll start and end each day with a briefing," Gabe said. "We'll also intercept your mail and your email."

"What has my email got to do with it?" Lacie asked as she hadn't been expecting this.

It wasn't like her email was filled with secret messages to unknown lovers or anything. But email was her main form of communication with Monty, her aunt, and her family back home.

"Intercepting visitors is easy enough," Rocco said. "We're all here anyway. You don't have a private phone line so we don't have calls to intercept and you're terrible at remembering to carry your cellphone with you. Your mail comes here and we've been vetting that since this began."

"He's never contacted me by email," Lacie said.

"Is it a problem?" Will asked.

"Yes," she said and felt them all draw in closer around the table. "There's no intrigue here. If he gets in touch by email, I'll let you know."

"Guaranteed that the first thing I'll be doing when I get out of this room is getting Toby to hack her email," Ty said to the table.

"There's nothing exciting in there," Lacie said. "No naked pictures or secret affairs."

"So what's the problem?" Will asked in his signature confrontational way.

"If it's important—"

"We'll negotiate," Gabe said. "We have to request your instructions."

"My instructions?" she asked.

"You're the client," Rocco said. "Do you have rules for us?"

Everyone expected her to say something but her mind went blank. "You all show me respect and know to give me space if I'm working or... occupied with my better half. I don't think I have any rules, as long as you abide by your morals." Rocco smiled at her pointed look.

"Do you have plans today?" Gabe asked her.

"Yes," she said. "I have an appointment to keep then I'm having lunch with Elijah."

"Graden?"

"Yes," Lacie said, ignoring the wave of surprise that swept the room. "Ryder knows all about it before you all gasp in horror, and I'm more than happy for any of you to stay in earshot."

"You've got Will, Ty, Toby, and Sonny today," Gabe said. "The rest of us will be working out the details, working on identifying the threat."

"Sonny," Lacie said, smiling at the youngest team member. "You've graduated."

"I'll do my best for you," Sonny said still as sheepish as ever.

"I know you will," Lacie said.

"Dismissed."

The word came from the afore mentioned silent figure at the head of the table: Ryder.

All of the men followed the order and got up to go. Lacie stayed put. The door closed behind the men, leaving her and Ryder alone.

"You're a good girl," he said.

"Thank you," she said, stretching her arms across the table. "Letting Gabe take first chair?"

He didn't give much away in his expression or manner and she wondered at what was on his mind. "I'll take my turn on detail, but I want to investigate a few leads we've picked up."

"Promising?"

"Maybe."

"You were very quiet," she said, giving in to her need for his solidarity.

Revealing some of himself, he softened his expression. "I have to maintain a professional distance. There will be no more mistakes where you're concerned."

"A professional distance," she said, letting her eyes wander to the side while her smile grew. "Does that mean you'll be sleeping in the spare room?"

He almost laughed and she was encouraged by the way the corner of his mouth rose.

"Don't think so," he said. "I'm giving you space with Graden. It wouldn't be good for me to be on your detail when you're lunching with another guy."

Losing her will to tease, she felt it was her turn to reassure him. "He's a friend, nothing more."

"I know that," Ryder said. She believed his certainty. "If he won't accept that—"

"Why shouldn't he?" she asked. "I don't think he requested this lunch to make a move on me."

His perception of her naivety amused him. "That's exactly why he called this lunch, Dusty. If he pressures you—"

"I'll have my guards pin him to the ground while I run," she said without believing she would have the need.

"Good girl."

Lacie pushed away from the table and got to her feet, she faltered, then found herself smiling. "Can I kiss you goodbye?"

"Can I bend you over this table?" he asked with the same level of professionalism he'd maintained throughout the meeting.

Closing one eye, she mused on the point. "I don't think that's what my boyfriend is paying you for."

"Call it a freebie."

Lacie wandered the length of the table toward him as he rolled his chair back from the table. Upon reaching him, she sank onto his lap and linked her fingers around his neck.

"I wish I had time to let you," she said, pressing her lips to his. "I have to see a lawyer."

"That's your appointment?" Ryder asked, kissing her shoulder.

"Elijah was right that I need one."

"This is his lawyer?" Ryder frowned.

"Sorcha's," Lacie said, shaking her head.

"My lawyer comes here," Ryder said, resting his linked fingers on her hip. "If you don't like this guy, I can set it up."

"Thank you, baby," she said and this time she didn't relinquish his mouth.

Kissing Ryder brought her a sense of complete wellbeing. The jitters left her body in lieu of the heady union of his tongue with hers. His hands moved up her body to cup her breasts, then sliding his palms down her bare arms, he clasped her rear, crushing her hip into the solid want he reserved for her,

"Ryd," she whispered, grasping his hair when his lips moved down the column of her throat.

She was going to be late for this appointment if his hand found its way under her dress.

"Boss."

Lifting her head from his lips, the couple saw Ty hanging into the room with an emerging grin.

"What are you smirking at?" Ryder asked.

"Professional distance you said," Ty pointed out. "You're a legend."

"I should get going," Lacie said. Patting Ryder's shoulder, she kissed him goodbye. "Are you working tonight?"

"I'm on your detail," Ryder said, checking her out.

She straightened her dress and found herself smiling again. "This is going to be fun."

TWENTY-NINE

LACIE HADN'T LIKED the lawyer much. Whether it was his personality or profession that put her off, she didn't know. But her security team had remained alert, discreet, and had maintained distance. Having these men on her periphery gave her solace. She'd worried that the obvious protection would make her feel vulnerable and maybe it would have if she didn't know these men so well.

Lacie was comfortable with them, trusted them, respected and valued what they were doing for her. So while she sat at the restaurant table with Elijah sipping her water, she could have forgotten that they were there… if Elijah hadn't been so edgy about their presence.

Replacing her water glass on the table, she wiped the condensation from her hand onto the napkin on her lap. "If you ignore them, they'll ignore you," Lacie said to Elijah who was preoccupied with something behind her.

"They're not especially covert," Elijah said, glancing one way and then the other.

"I wouldn't want them to be," she said, forking up some of her salad. "I don't want to be attacked and their presence will ensure that."

"You have complete confidence in them?"

"Yes," she said. "What did you want to discuss?"

Elijah hadn't eaten much of his food, which put paid to her hope that this meal would be brief. "I had hoped we would be alone."

"We are alone," she said. "They're not here to report back."

"You're still with Stone?"

"Yes."

"I can't understand what you see in him."

At least Elijah's frustration was distracting him from her security detail. "No one's asking you to date him," Lacie said, stabbing more leaves onto her fork.

"Is that what it is? Casual dating?"

"We live together," she said. "There's nothing casual about it."

Elijah wasn't using his usually bold, confident demeanor. He leaned over the table and kept his hands on his lap. If he wanted to be discreet about disparaging her boyfriend then he wasn't succeeding. "Do you expect it to last? He's hardly your type."

"Of course it will last," she said. "Ryder wouldn't let us fail."

"He's controlling?"

Lacie smiled. "He's determined and I owe my happiness to him."

Just as Lacie began to think Ryder could have been right about Elijah's motivation for arranging this meal, she saw Will coming toward her. Worried that something had happened to Ryder, she put her fork on the plate and stood up without warning Elijah she was about to.

"What is it?" she asked Will before he'd got all the way to her.

"The hospital," he said and her heart sank into her guts, then he smiled. "Maternity."

"Sorcha?" she asked and he nodded and took her hand.

"It's too early," Lacie said, but dipped to pick up her purse.

Elijah was standing now too, trying to get the attention of a server, presumably to ask for the check. But she didn't wait.

"We have to get to the hospital," Will said and the rest of her security detail closed in around her.

If the baby came now, it would be early, but it should still be healthy, at least that was what Lacie hoped.

Without giving Elijah the chance to say anything, she went with the men charged with protecting her and trusted them to get her where she needed to go. It wasn't her intention to be rude or shut Elijah out, she was just in shock that this was it, this child who had already caused so many events in the world, was about to introduce him or herself.

THIRTY

Lacie

LACIE FOUND OUT having a security detail meant having transport too. They got her to the hospital in quick time. Sorcha was in labor; Bruce was on his way, but this kid was coming now. Lacie held Sorcha's hand as she breathed through the contractions. She kept Sorcha distracted during the epidural and spent what felt like hours comforting her best friend while she wept. When Bruce eventually did show up Sorcha screamed at him to get out again.

Lacie kept her moist palm pressed against Sorcha's and stroked her hair through every push, willing her friend on. After a seeming eternity there was a muffled croak then Sorcha's screaming ceased and a pair of tinier lungs took over the wailing. Sorcha blinked at Lacie as she was handed this little crinkle faced kid, who was very pink and smudged with blood. There the baby was, the new life that had been responsible for so much, including Lacie's own happiness, was here.

"Congratulations, you have a daughter," the midwife said.

"I… I…" Sorcha held the baby who still fussed but seemed to be sleeping at the same time.

"You did it, honey," Lacie said, swiping at Sorcha's tears. "You have a little girl."

"I…" Sorcha couldn't form words, Lacie had never seen her this speechless.

Lacie grinned. "Do you want me to get Bruce?"

Sorcha's saucer eyes never faltered but she nodded without focusing or speaking. Lacie kissed her temple, thanked the staff, and merged into the packed waiting space on the opposite side of the corridor from the labor suite.

The room was full of people. Bruce was there of course, as were Sorcha's parents, her sister, and a couple of friends. Elijah was there too with his own brother. But to her relief, her security was still here and with their cohorts including Ryder.

When she came in, everyone gathered close, fixated on her.

"It's a girl," Lacie said. "Six pounds two ounces, ten fingers, ten toes."

Everyone cheered and patted a suddenly ashen Bruce on the back.

"Can I…?" Bruce pointed behind Lacie.

She nodded. "Just you," Lacie said. "They're still cleaning Sorcha up."

Bruce disappeared out of the room to meet his daughter.

Lacie's own exhaustion left her rooted to the spot. Elijah was the first to come to her, though she was in too much of a daze to think about what he wanted to say.

"What a day," Elijah said, stopping in front of her.

Unable to react or play it civil, her own emotions began to well up and a lump formed in her throat.

"Ryder," she managed to squeak.

Elijah frowned, but she couldn't explain to him why she was suddenly so pale and shivery.

The jubilation in the room quieted. Lacie assumed everyone noted her odd behavior, but all she cared about was Ryder, who came to her at her request. Before he could get a word out, she fell against him and locked her arms around his body, clinging on for dear life as tears flooded her face. Sobbing, she hated making such a public spectacle, but the whole experience had been overwhelming.

"Is she okay?" came a wary male voice.

"She's fine," Ryder said, stroking her hair and keeping his mouth against the top of her head.

"Did you upset her?" Rocco said with an anger in his voice that was uncharacteristic.

She recognized Rocco's voice but saw nothing through her closed eyes. Ryder's embrace tightened. Lacie didn't want to fight it because her only chance of regaining her composure was to stay right here. Fumbling a hand in the direction of his voice, she sought out Rocco. Her hand landed on his abdomen and Rocco's own hand took hers to hold it against him.

The males must have shuffled off because Rocco melted away after a few seconds and Ryder walked them backward a few steps to give them some seclusion. Lacie tucked her hands into the back pockets of his jeans and tried to slow her breathing.

"Are you okay?" Ryder mumbled into the top of her head.

Grateful that he had been quick to reassure others that she was going to be fine, she also appreciated his condolence. Nodding, she rubbed her face up and down his torso in the process. With another couple of breaths she lifted her head so that only Ryder could see her expression.

"It was beautiful. It was terrifying… Promise me you won't leave me alone," she said as he smudged her tears from her cheeks. Barely aware of anything except the warmth and sanctuary he offered. She needed reassurance of a different kind. "When it's us, when I'm in there… don't leave me alone."

"I promise, baby," he said with an odd smile on his face.

Lacie wasn't in the mood to deconstruct his expression, so she nestled back into his embrace and let him hold her weight for a while longer.

THIRTY-ONE

Lacie

IT TURNED OUT to be more than a while. After Bruce emerged, everyone was told to wait until Sorcha was moved to a different room. They complied and were then allowed to visit with Sorcha and the nameless infant in small groups. Sorcha requested that Lacie should stay the night. She wasn't allowed in the room but Lacie agreed to sleep in the waiting room.

When Lacie told Ryder of Sorcha's request, he didn't fuss, though his men did. Elijah hung around longer than everyone else but was defeated when it became obvious that Ryder and his men weren't going to leave Lacie alone.

Elijah was putting his jacket on. Ryder was in the corner by the vending machine whispering with his posse. Lacie rested her head back against the wall and let her eyes close. Her solitude was short-lived. Someone sat at her side and she knew in the same second that it wasn't Ryder or any of his men.

On lifting her head, she saw Elijah sitting at her side. "You did well today, Lacie," he said and leaned in to kiss her cheek. What she might have thought was an act meant to provoke Ryder, became something else when she felt the corner of a piece of folded paper poking her hand.

Elijah leaned back and looked at her for a moment then got up and left, passing the growling S.I.S. crew.

"We'll take you downstairs for something to eat," Ryder said not as affected by Elijah's actions as the men he worked for were. "The canteen's still open." The door closed and the elite team relaxed. Ryder sauntered a few steps in her direction and held out his hand for hers. "Are you coming?"

Lacie was frozen and from the change in his expression, she'd say that Ryder noticed her discomfort.

"Did he say something to you?" Gabe asked, moving to Ryder's side with the rest of the gang at his back.

She shook her head and gripped the paper in her hand as though to prove to herself it was real. Elijah had something to say to her, in private it seemed, but the whole affair unsettled her somehow.

"Dusty," Ryder said, crouching in front of her. "What is it?"

Lifting her head from the wall, she opened her hand to show Ryder the folded paper in her palm. "He just gave me this."

"When? Just now?" Ryder asked and she nodded.

He took the folded paper from her and opened it. His men crowded in to read the message too. Lacie stayed put, unsure whether or not she wanted to know what it said.

Ryder read it then looked over the top of it at her. "I don't think I want to know," she murmured when she studied his features.

"In the museum, what did the threat say to you when he grabbed you, when he drugged you?"

"He said he knew what I was afraid of," she said. All the men focused on her. "What?"

Ryder turned the paper around and she read, "I know what you're afraid of. We have to talk alone, urgently." A phone number was scrawled on the bottom.

"What are you afraid of?" Ty asked and for once he wasn't teasing.

"I feel strange and unsettled," Lacie said, happy to edge her legs forward in the vee of Ryder's squatting legs.

Ryder handed the paper off to Gabe and came up to sit at her side. "I wasn't going to leave you alone here tonight, you know that. I'll have two of the guys stay too."

"It would be safer not to stay here at all," Gabe said.

Ryder had known better than to even ask. Lacie took Ryder's hand and rested her head on his chest when he curved an arm around her shoulders.

"Graden has had alibis," Gabe said. "That first night, he was at the exhibition in view of most of us. But he's involved, somehow, I don't doubt that now. Your instincts were right."

"I don't want to be alone with him," Lacie said, threading her fingers in and out of Ryder's. His fingers flexed, locking hers in place between his, as his strong arm tightened around her shoulders. "I don't want to talk to him. Do you think he was…?"

"What?" Ryder asked.

"Today he was very unhappy that I had security," Lacie said.

"She's right," Will said. "The guy was fidgeting, his eyes all over the place. He was acting guilty as hell."

"We thought he wanted to make a move on Lace," Ty said. "Just figured the guy was pissed our eyes were on them, screwing his chance to make a move on her."

"Maybe," Lacie sighed. "When Will came over to tell me about Sorcha, Elijah was trying to convince me that you and I were incompatible, that I would be happier without you. I told him straight that you were my happiness."

Ryder stroked her hair. "You guys really do tell each other everything, don't you?" Toby muttered.

Lifting her head from Ryder, she observed their friends. "I told you I didn't care if you gave Ryder a second-by-second account of my day. I meant it."

"Back to Graden," Gabe said. "He must have an accomplice."

"I don't know who was at the cabin," she said. "There might have been more than one, I don't know. I can't remember."

"You definitely didn't recognize the voice at the gallery?" Rocco asked.

"I wish I had," she said. "I wish I paid more attention to him. But… I… he was keeping his voice low, maybe he was trying to disguise it. Until he touched me, I wasn't sure what was going on and by then it was too late."

"Shh," Ryder said, bending his elbow at her back to rest a hand in her hair. "No one's expecting you to remember anything. We're still investigating and we're going to stop anyone from hurting you again."

"What do we do now?" Will asked.

"Now we get Lacie something to eat," Ryder said, standing up and taking her with him.

"If we talk to Graden now he'll know we've seen the note he passed her," Toby said.

Moving toward the door, Ryder didn't respond. "We're going to have dinner," Ryder said, trying to not-so-subtly tell his men to drop it.

They complied and switched their attention to the door. Lacie stayed put, which brought them all to a halt. "I don't hide things from Ryder," she said to the group. "And I don't hide that fact from anyone. Elijah might think that he can pass secret notes, but I'm not going to lie to him either. He should know that Ryder's seen the note."

"We might not want him to," Will said, coming back to address her outburst. "Keeping him out of the loop about what we know, might be our way to figure out how he's involved."

"I don't want any of you in danger or in any confrontation where someone could be hurt. But I don't lie to the man I love and I don't lie to anyone about that."

"You're about as straightforward as they come, Hart," Ty said.

They all smiled at her with a kind of pride that reminded her of their close ties.

"If you have to tell Graden that I handed the note over to Ryder, then do it," she said. "I'm not ashamed of our trust. But if you formulate a master plan, make sure you clue me in on it." Their esteem only grew and Gabe nodded in reassurance.

"When are you going to start squeezing out the sprogettes?" Will asked, they all appreciated the subject change and began to move out of the waiting room for the journey to the canteen.

"Are you kidding?" Rocco asked. "If the boss is this nuts about keeping his woman safe, how many men is he going to hire to protect their offspring?"

"Yeah," Ty said. "They'll have to name one after each of us so the boss has got his work cut out."

"You expect me to carry six children?" Lacie asked. That was enough of a shock to distract her from the possibility of one of her oldest friend's being her stalker.

"Probably more," Ty said, staying close. Having this group of men around her made her feel safe again and the needling helped to relax her. "You'll need six boys, there might be girls in between."

"I don't know," Rocco said, holding a door open. "Gabriella and Wilhelmina are girls names." He winked at Lacie who led them all in their laughter.

By the time her group had something to eat and she got back upstairs to Sorcha, Lacie was sure that she would be back in her normal spirits. Having a baby was such a happy blessing that Lacie didn't want any negativity visiting her best friend's bed, so for now, she wouldn't reveal what was going on with Elijah and his possible involvement.

THIRTY-TWO

Lacie

STAYING THE NIGHT in the hospital waiting room left them all stiff and cranky. After breakfast, Sorcha calmed a little and Bruce returned so Lacie was granted permission by Sorcha to go home.

She was thankful for the reprieve, not just for her own sake, but for security's sake too. Lacie hurried back to the waiting room and ordered everyone home to bed. The collective gasp of joy told her she'd been right about their wish to shower and sleep.

When they got back to base, Ryder joined her in her morning shower. He kissed and caressed her, working more than just the soap into a lather. Being so gentle made her ache with her want for him. But this wasn't him teasing. He drew comfort from appreciating her like this. Their intimacy was a demonstration of what they had and how much they wanted to hold onto it.

After the water was off, he carried her through to their bed and kissed every inch of her. Making tender love to her, he savored the chance they had to be together. If last night's development reminded them of anything it was to not take their proximity for granted. They'd been torn apart in the past and pure will couldn't stop it from happening again.

They hadn't spoken more about Elijah, about the note, or about what came next but as Lacie fell asleep in his solid embrace she told herself not to worry. There would be time to worry, and to plan, but Ryder would tell her when that time was.

For now they were together, safe at home. All threats remained outside this bed, this room, and this building. Nothing could touch them here. She'd told Elijah that this was her happiness. It was at times like this, in Ryder's arms with the pulse of his heart under her cheek that proved her conviction. This was her protection, her heart, her home.

THIRTY-THREE

Lacie

WHEN SHE STRETCHED herself out of bed, the balm of sunshine was satisfying, and with a yawn she wrapped the bed sheet around herself and padded out of the bedroom, finger-combing her hair. The kitchen drew her with the scent of coffee. When she entered, Lacie found Will at the table drinking from a steaming mug and reading the paper.

"What time is it?" she asked, holding the sheet in her fist above her breasts as she headed for the coffee pot.

"Fourteen twenty-one," Will said, leaning back in his seat.

"You drew the short straw?" Lacie asked, gulping from her newly filled mug.

"Actually this is the easy shift," Will said, taking his eyes back to his newspaper. "I sit around drinking coffee making sure you don't stub your toe."

Wrapping one hand around the mug, through the handle, she pressed it to the back of the hand that held her sheet. "I have to see Sorcha tonight."

"Are you working today?" Will asked.

"If I sit in my dome, will you come and watch me work?"

"If you want me to," Will said, still reading. "But the boss told us to leave you alone up there, he said even he doesn't watch you work."

"He doesn't, but it's not a request," she said. "When Ryder and I find ourselves alone, we… It doesn't take long for…"

Will held up a hand before she could finish. "We all know what happens when you two are alone… How are you feeling today about Graden and his note?"

"I don't know," Lacie said, letting her face sink toward the steam coming out of her mug. "I don't know what to think about any of it."

Will turned the page of his paper and then picked up his drink. "Don't worry about it. The boss will keep you right. He's not going to let you go easily."

Lacie took another mouthful of coffee then sighed. "I don't have to be at the hospital until seven. Do you want to watch movies with me in the den?"

Raising his eyes to hers, she shrugged and he closed his paper. "Oh well, I suppose if I have to," he said with mock irritation. "Just keep your hands to yourself."

Focusing on work was going to be impossible and she needed a day where she could just numb out. "You heat the popcorn and I'll get changed. I really need the distraction today, thanks Will.

With another slurp of coffee, she put her mug aside and went to get changed. She hadn't reacted well to having someone tailing her at home, but she hadn't seen the advantage. In need of company, she had a friend on hand to keep her mind off all her stresses.

THIRTY-FOUR

Lacie

SHE AND WILL had munched their way through several bowls of popcorn and watched several movies. Night had descended, cloaking them in a dark blanket. The present movie was almost over when a shard of light intruded from behind the couch, followed by the rumble of male voices.

"Working hard?" Rocco asked coming around the high back couch to seek them out.

Will sat in the back corner of the slouch couch with his elbows resting on his drawn-up knees. Lacie lay on her side across the width of the couch with her hand holding up her head. Their peace was further interrupted when Ty and Toby climbed over her to sit at the back with Will.

"Start it again," Ty said, clambering for the remote. Wearing Ryder's tee shirt and her hot pink boy shorts, she sat up to make way for the amplified audience.

"This doesn't look much like working," Gabe said to Will from his place standing at the side of the couch.

With his eyes trained to the screen, Will handed over the popcorn bowl to Ty. "She's alive, isn't she?"

Rocco sat at the front of the couch earning some groans from the back, so he slid down to sit on the floor. Gabe remained standing, and scanning those present, Lacie noticed two absent members.

"Where's—" The question didn't need to be finished because Ryder and Sonny entered.

"What are you all doing in here?" Ryder asked, looking from his men to the movie screen.

"The primary's in here," Ty said, gesturing toward her with a hand full of popcorn. "We're keeping her safe."

"She's alive at least," Ryder said. Sonny propped himself on the side of the couch to watch the film.

All of the men were transfixed by the movie, all except one of them. Letting her eyes slink upwards to fasten on the intensity of his, she smiled when she found his smoldering attention fixated on her. The corner of his mouth slid upward and she was naked in his mind's eye. The exposure of his violation made her tingle.

They might be in a room full of people, but they were the only two people in the world. His wide stance and his folded arms were professional, but his eyes were hot, heavy, and personal.

Requesting silent acquiescence, she kept a grip on the couch beneath her thighs and inched forward. With an almost imperceptible move on Ryder's part, Lacie got her agreement and sprang to her feet.

"I'm off-duty," Will said around the popcorn filling his mouth. "Ty, she's yours."

Lacie climbed over Rocco, keeping balance on his head, and all the men called out when she passed in front of the screen.

"Odds," Ty said to Toby holding out a fist.

"I've got her," Ryder said, hooking his arm around her neck.

"Bet you do, Boss," Ty said and they departed the den on the good-natured jeers of the colleagues.

THIRTY-FIVE

Lacie

A GOOD HOUR later, she was coiled in the sheets on their bed and reluctant to leave the arms of her lover. "I have to go to the hospital," Lacie said, kissing her way down Ryder's torso.

"You don't look sick to me," he said.

She kissed his groin and cupped her breasts around the steel length of him. Pushing them together, she squeezed him in her cleavage. He stroked her hair down to her shoulders as he sat up to take her into his arms and draw her up against his chest.

"What's wrong?" she asked. "Did I hurt you?"

"No, baby," he said, kissing her, then settling her in his arms.

"No more sex?" she asked.

While kissing her hair, Ryder's hands wandered over her bare skin. "I'd have sex with you constantly but you're going out and this problem isn't going away."

Sagging in defeat, their intimacy had to secede to reality. She stated what she believed he was thinking. "You want to talk about Elijah."

Still pressing gentle kisses to her, he nuzzled his mouth through her hair to her ear. "I don't want you to say his name in our bed."

"What is your plan?" Lacie asked. "I have to talk to him, don't I?"

"Does that sound like my policy? No," he said, grasping her derriere to haul her up to straddle his hips. He didn't let her sit up, he stole her in his arms and crushed her chest to his. Seeking her mouth, he sang her a sonnet with a sweep of his tongue and the gentle caress of his hands. The rasp of his chest hair on her taut nipples made her squirm closer. Getting the hard length of him between her folds, Lacie let him glide against her sizzling center and writhed against the heat of him.

"Easy," he murmured, stalling her hips from their motion.

"I thought we were finished talking."

"I'm going to sort this out for you, baby," he said. "You don't have to worry about it. And you stay far away from it. I'll take care of Graden."

Losing her desire in the face of what would happen if the two men came face to face. "You're going to talk to him," Lacie said, not thrilled at the notion. "What if he is involved? You could be hurt."

"I think I can take him."

"Don't be complacent," she said, pushing up a little to prop her elbows on his chest. "If someone puts a bullet—"

"I can handle myself. I have no concerns about that. Do you know if he has violence in his past?"

"He's been known to be adamant but I've never heard of him being violent. Why are you talking to me about this?"

"We've done a lot of digging; we've been tracking his movements. I'm talking to you about this because we're honest with each other. I don't want to bog you down with details but if you want me to give you every—"

"I trust you," she said without needing every piece of information.

They were in bed and this wasn't the place to talk about evidence and probabilities.

"I'm going to talk to him."

"Don't go alone," she said. "He'll want to talk about me, about us."

"My favorite topic," he said.

She didn't appreciate his glib attitude to what could be a fractious conversation. "I'm serious," she said. "He might want to rile you up or be disrespectful."

"I'll be cool," Ryder said, trying to kiss her again. "I've dealt with my share of lowlifes."

To ensure he remained rational, she played devil's advocate. "There's every chance he's innocent," Lacie said. "Don't go judging him based on your preconceptions. He could be a good guy, misguided, but not a dangerous man."

His stroking hands were distracting, but his attention betrayed how seriously he took this. "Do you believe that?"

"I don't know what to believe," Lacie said. "You're paid to be the brains in this operation. Just go easy on him… for me, you did get the girl after all."

His agreement came in a nod. "Don't kick a man when he's down."

"I'm not saying he's down…"

Taking her hair in his fists, he let them drag down and out, then repeated the move. "He's lovesick. I'd be down if I lost you too."

"He never had me," she said. "Plus, you're crazy in love with me and I still can't get the sex thing right."

That he recognized her coy tease for what it was made her desire him all the more. "You get it more than right and you know it. Stop fishing for compliments."

"I'm not fishing," she said and began to rock her hips. "Just hinting for the chance to keep practicing."

"You've got six kids to cook up," he grinned. "When do you want to get started on those?"

Talk of Elijah was over, but the concern for her safety would still be plaguing Ryder's mind. "Rocco had a point about protection."

As if he was confused, he leaned back a couple of inches. "To reproduce the protection has to go out the window. Do we have to have a talk about the birds and bees?"

Digging her elbows in, she slid them down to bring their bodies closer again. "That's not what I meant. We have to keep ourselves safe before we think about bringing more lives into the world who we'll be responsible for."

"I know," he said. His hands glided down her shoulders, her arms, then over her ass, up her hips and to her waist. "You're a tiny little thing."

"Uh, to you, because you're huge."

His brow slunk up in time with the corner of his mouth. "Thanks."

Digging her nails into his sides, she scowled at his swagger. "I don't know how I'll carry your babies. Your sons could be massive. I might break." After witnessing childbirth, Lacie wasn't sure she would be capable of the feat no matter what the size of the child.

His laugh rumbled through her like an electric blanket, warm and comfortable with a little buzz thrown in. "I'll look after you, Dusty, always will."

"Okay," she said, kissing his neck then his chest and then his mouth. She hummed at the delight. "Enough flirting, it's taken up our sex time. I have to get ready to see the baby."

She climbed off the bed and headed for the en-suite while he settled back down in the bed with his hands linked behind his head. "Does she have a name yet?" Ryder shouted to let his voice carry to her.

"Not that I know," Lacie called back. She turned on the shower. "She's so beautiful, so small and helpless, and to think of all the trouble she's caused already."

"I'm very thankful," Ryder said, keeping his voice raised.

Wiping the gathering fog from the mirror, Lacie stared at her reflection. "She brought us together," Lacie said. "I thought the same thing myself."

Ryder's voice sounded over the shower spray. "We should get her a gift."

With this being the only child in their lives, Lacie had a feeling this kid was going to be seriously spoiled by everyone. "I'll deal with that. Something tells me this little girl isn't going to be short of anything."

Ryder's reflection appeared in the mirror, making her turn to face him. "You're sure we don't have any sex time."

Laughing, she shook her head, and slid open the shower while extending her hand. "Yes. But you can soap my back."

"I'll take it," he said and came over to hold her hips and guide her under the spray.

THIRTY-SIX

Lacie

IN ALL THE TIME Lacie sat by her bed, Sorcha kept her eyes on the baby in the plastic hospital crib next to them.

Lacie might have expected Sorcha's terror, but the awesome wonder was a surprise. Most people must have a sense of incredulity that they had created a life. Sorcha experienced that and more, admitting that she had a fear of holding the baby because she didn't want to hurt her.

Lacie had hoped that Sorcha would embrace motherhood when it happened but she had worried that Sorcha might not take it seriously. Those worries proved to be unfounded because when a nurse had come in to take the babe back to the nursery, Sorcha had bombarded the staff member with questions. She'd gone to the length of retrieving a notebook to write down the nurse's answers so she wouldn't forget anything.

Conspicuously, Bruce was missing but Sorcha said nothing about it so Lacie didn't bring up the issue. Sorcha had enough on her plate at the moment.

Much as it was obvious that Sorcha wanted Lacie to remain, she couldn't stay all night. So after a drawn-out farewell, Lacie peeked at the baby once more then she and Rocco rode the elevator down to the main hospital entrance.

Walking outside Lacie thought of getting back to Ryder, to their home, to the cocoon of their safe nest.

"Hey, Hart!"

Lacie paused at the sound of the holler from behind her and spun around. There against the railing of the wheelchair ramp was Shep, lounging like he had all the time in the world. After a few seconds of nothing, Lacie nodded to Rocco to back off and he gave them space but didn't go far. Shep sloped away from his perch and crossed to her.

"What are you doing here?" she asked.

Looking the same as always, Shep wore a scowl and Lacie guessed it broke his heart to know that Sorcha was here in apparent bliss, while he had nothing. "We have to talk."

"About what?"

"The case," Shep said. "It's important. Meet me at my office?"

Glancing back at Rocco, Lacie waited for him to give the nod before she returned her focus to Shep. "We'll follow you."

Rocco was driving. They got back to the car and drove away from the hospital. Lacie used the time to bring Rocco up to speed on the sequence of events that had taken her to Shep again. While talking she realized she had no idea where Shep lived, because the only time she'd seen him on his own property was in his office.

Rocco parked and escorted her to the office. The door was open, so they went into the outer receptionist room where Rocco paused. "I'll wait out here," Rocco said to Lacie when Shep held the inner office door open. "No sneaking out the back this time."

"It's locked," Shep said. "I'll leave the door open."

Rocco sat in one of the plastic waiting room chairs and let Lacie and Shep recede into the office.

"What is it?" Lacie asked. "Either you found something definitive about his infidelity or…"

"You think I brought you here to hit on you?" Shep asked, taking his place behind the desk.

"Do you live here?"

"You interested in finding my bedroom? If you send Stone's lackey back to base then we can have all the fun you want."

She levelled her gaze on him. "You didn't bring me here for sex. You knew I would have at least one of Ryder's men with me, and you told me this was about the case."

Shep opened a desk drawer and retrieved a file. "He's cheating." Dropping the file in front of Lacie, he then sat back in his seat.

She didn't want to open the file. Shep had done the job that he'd been asked to do. He hadn't been happy at watching Booth when Sorcha was happy with him. Now Shep still didn't look happy, but the frustration was something different.

Knowing she'd have to face it eventually, even if only for Sorcha's benefit, Lacie opened the file. The first picture was of Bruce at a bar with a blonde. The next was with the same blonde at a restaurant, then at a second restaurant, different clothes, different day.

"Maybe she's a cousin, or—" Lacie flicked to the next picture to see Bruce and the blonde in a passionate clinch under a streetlight. The next picture was of them kissing in Bruce's car, the next was at a motel.

The pictures got worse but it was always the same woman. Though Lacie wasn't sure if that was better than indiscriminate cheating.

"Who is she?"

"Floozy from his father's staff."

"The household staff? Do his parents know?"

"I didn't interview them. Thought it might have given them a hint that Sorch didn't trust her fiancé."

"Fiancé," Lacie said, the pictures slipped from her hands back down into the file.

"Yeah."

"Seth…"

His brow furrowed. "I didn't know you knew my first name." That could be forgiven because Lacie wasn't sure she'd ever used it except when addressing Ryder in the early days.

"They're married." Lacie didn't think pussyfooting around it would help anyone but she witnessed the ice travel through his body.

"They're married?"

"They eloped. Bruce had an argument with his parents and…"

Shep moved up and away from the desk then took a long breath. Sorcha was impulsive, Lacie knew that. Shep knew it too but he could never have expected this and she wasn't surprised by his reaction.

"I figured she'd gone back to him when she dumped me again… I left it a couple of days, figuring she'd be back… she always comes back." He must have missed witnessing the wedding in those couple of days he'd left Sorcha alone. "When she didn't, that's when I found out about the blonde. He's been with her more in the last few days."

"Bruce was staying with Sorcha," Lacie said.

"Yeah, I saw that. The blonde lives at his parents' house. Both she and Bruce went back there last night separately after saying goodnight on the sidewalk outside… that's the picture under the light. I guess he was telling his parents about the kid… making up with them I guess."

After the argument with his parents, Bruce couldn't stay at his parents' house, so he had to be seeing the blonde on the side. Maybe he thought that relationship was over or it was a casual distraction while he was under his parents' roof. Either way, he'd stayed with Sorcha, and married her, not out of love, but because he had nowhere else to go.

It was no shock that Bruce had used Sorcha, and as much as Lacie wanted to believe that he cared for her best friend, how Bruce felt was nothing to how Shep felt, as was proven by how he clenched his jaw and glared into nothingness.

"You should've told her," Lacie said. Her spike of sympathy became a rush of anger. "You should've told her how you felt. If you'd—"

"You think I'd be faithful to her?"

His anger was hot too but ferocity like that confirmed what Lacie had known all along.

"Yes," Lacie answered. "You would be faithful. You got rid of Tiffany for Sorcha the last time."

Landing his anger on her, he snapped. "Who?"

"Your ex-assistant. You were screwing with her until Sorcha came back to you. When I was abducted, you were there for Sorcha, you were…"

His scowl was a mask that Lacie wished he would shed. "You don't know what you're talking about."

Thrusting onto her feet, she let out her frustration on the man who could have changed her best friend's life for the better. "You need to shape up. If you had shown Sorch that you were serious—"

"This is my fault?" he asked, pointing at himself. "Booth fucks around and I get the best friend giving me shit? You want to shout at—"

"It's not your fault. I'm pissed at you. I'm pissed at Sorcha. You've both messed up."

"And Booth hasn't?"

The truth only had power if people released it. Hiding behind fears led to unhappiness in their lives. "Ryder was right. We've known Booth was an idiot since the beginning, which is why I'm pissed. If you had stepped up, shown Sorcha that you could be a good guy…"

"Then what? We could've lived happily ever after? She's just squeezed out another guy's kid!"

That wasn't enough to assuage Lacie. To her that was no excuse at all. "You found out she was pregnant months ago. You were one of the first people to know! You knew it before her parents did," she said, dropping her hands onto the desk to press her weight closer. "If you had cared about Louise—"

"Who the fuck is Louise?" he said, screwing up his face as he leaned away.

"Sorcha's daughter," Lacie said. "They're calling her Louise… it's my middle name."

Shep's expression opened. "They're naming the kid after you?"

"Sorcha's calling her Lulu," Lacie said and her anger disappeared in light of the happy topic. "She's beautiful."

Shep's anger seemed to have diminished too, and he rubbed the back of his head with an open hand. "I'm happy for her." Dropping into his chair, he began to gather up the images that Lacie had just viewed.

Standing straight, she scrutinized his actions. "What are you doing?"

"She can't know now, can she?" he asked, stacking the sheets, and closing them in the file. "We'll just… we'll just pretend this never happened. That this meeting never took place." He took a few tries to get the folder back in his drawer. "It won't be tough for me, I probably won't… I probably won't see her again. She's married and… yeah…"

Sinking back into her seat, Lacie leaned over the desk to take his hand. Shep might be brash and vulgar, but his reaction to hearing this news of Sorcha was real. "It might not be too late," Lacie said. She could be speaking out of turn because Sorcha hadn't indicated that she would choose Shep over any other man. But Lacie didn't think her friend's feelings for Bruce ran as deep as her feelings for Shep and maybe all it would take was for someone to take the risk of putting themselves out there.

"She's married."

"He's cheating," Lacie said. She understood Sorcha's desire to do the right thing and marry the father of her child. But that meant nothing if the father was a dog who would only make Sorcha unhappy. "I want her to be happy and I'm not sure Bruce can do that for her."

"I'm not sure I can either," he admitted.

Someone who spent so much time making everyone believe they were lazy and good-for-nothing probably had insecurities about their own worth. Seeing Shep in front of her as he was now, dejected and heartbroken, she saw beyond some of that bravado.

She might have expected him to react with anger, to shout or even make insulting jokes. She hadn't expected to see him defeated. Dealing with her own demons was no excuse for abandoning a friend in his time of need. Despite his cranky nature, Shep was a friend. He'd been there for her in the past and had contributed to her release from Jamie Wallace's prison.

So after giving his hand a squeeze, she slapped a hand onto the desk.

"Have you had dinner? I know it's late, but I'm starved… Have you got your wallet?"

His slow smile knew that she was being kind because the truth of his hurt was written all over his face. But he got to his feet and took a jacket off the hat stand behind his desk.

"What are you going to do with the oaf?" Shep asked, referring to Rocco who was still seated in the outer office.

"He can watch us eat from the other side of the room," she said, linking her fingers with his when he came around the desk. "We'll eat too much dessert, drink a few cocktails and then when it's late and neither of us can stand up anymore, he'll drive us home… Having a bodyguard isn't all bad," Lacie said, hoping to prompt a laugh.

His smile broadened, but she didn't get the desired laugh. "Are we going to talk about Sorcha all night?"

"Do you want to talk about Sorcha all night?" she asked and he shook his head. "Then consider that the last mention of her name." Lacie would humor him because if she really did get him drunk then he'd probably start rambling either in love or anger about the woman who caused his current mood.

"If you get really drunk, will you show me your breasts?"

"If it will make you feel better, I might just do that," she said and finally got a laugh out of him.

"You know, you're all right, Little Lady," he said, tugging her toward the office door.

"I always knew you were a secret fan," Lacie said, following his lead. "You never showed up for my exhibition though. I think we'll find some time to talk about that tonight."

They went into the outer office and when she explained the plan to Rocco, he made no objections. He'd probably heard every word of their conversation as the office door was open. But as he'd previously promised her, he made no indication that he'd eavesdropped and was the consummate professional. So much so that he didn't even reference the placement of her hand, which was still in Shep's for comfort.

THIRTY-SEVEN

THEIR NIGHT ENDED up being much later than she'd thought. Shep had gotten drunk and got to the topic of Sorcha. He went through every emotion, as quickly as he hit one, he would swing in the other direction and find another. She and Rocco got him to bed and then Rocco drove her back to hers. She didn't pay much attention to the time other than to note it was after midnight before she fell into bed and found a deep slumber, one that had eluded her for days.

Waking up without Ryder wasn't uncommon for Lacie, but it did make her sigh every time. Having his form to curl into each morning was an indulgence she loved to lose herself in. She held out hope during her shower that he might surprise her, but he didn't.

Spending time drinking with Shep hadn't been in the schedule, but she felt good about taking the time to console him. Sorcha might be with a man who wasn't good for her, but she had a man and baby, Lulu, and a squad of family and friends to distract her now. Shep was alone and Lacie doubted Heather would be much of a remedy for what ailed the PI.

Getting dressed, she speculated on how Ryder's meeting with Elijah might have gone. But when she got to the kitchen, Ryder wasn't there. Gabe, Will, and Ty were there, but no Ryder.

"Good morning," she said, making a beeline for the coffee pot.

"Sorcha called from the hospital," Gabe said. "I told her you'd call her back, there's a chance she's getting out today."

"There are pancakes on the table too," Will said.

Slurping her coffee, she went to sit at the table and help herself to the pancakes which all the boys knew were her favorite.

Putting her mug aside, she put a pancake on a plate and dragged it to her. Pulling one foot up onto her seat, her arms came around her bent knee to tear a piece of pancake off to pop it into her mouth.

"Is Ryder downstairs?" she asked, raising her attention to the men who were frowning at each other.

"We thought he was in bed with you," Gabe said. "I haven't seen him this morning."

"I woke up alone," she said and the pancake in her mouth became and inconvenient lump that felt too big when she swallowed it down. "He said he was going to meet with Elijah, maybe they couldn't meet until first thing." If Ryder had work to do, he never woke her up, usually because she was restless at night. But with a few drinks in her last night, her sleep hadn't been nearly as fitful as normal.

"We'll track him down," Gabe said.

Dropping her pancake to the plate, she brushed the crumbs from her hands. "I'll call Sorcha and find out if she needs anything set up at her apartment before she brings Lulu home."

"Great name," Ty beamed. "You think she'll break hearts?"

"Under Sorcha's instruction?" Lacie asked, standing up and pushing her chair in under the table. "Little Lulu will have a lot of fun first."

The men appreciated her humor but Lacie made sure to straighten her face on her route to the bedroom because Sorcha wouldn't be in the mood for jokes. Once she'd settled into motherhood, she may be more relaxed and get back to her old self. The woman Lacie had seen at the hospital last night was tense and harried. As much as Lacie didn't like to see her friend in distress, it was nice to see Sorcha care about Lulu so much that the prospect of failing as a mother weighed on her as it should.

The conversation with Sorcha went on for about half an hour, but as soon as there was a cry in the background Sorcha cut herself off and ended the call.

She wasn't getting out until later in the day, which gave Lacie the time to make the arrangements Sorcha had asked her to. Tidying up in the bedroom, she collected her purse to head back in the direction of the kitchen to brief the guys on what her day would hold and to ask what their security plans would entail.

As soon as she walked into the kitchen, she could sense that something was wrong. Gabe wasn't here. Instead it was Will who came toward her while Ty skulked in the background with his head down. He only stole glances at her and seeing Ty so withdrawn chilled Lacie through to her bones.

Will tried to take her hand, but she dropped her purse and backed away until she came up against the kitchen wall. "What?" she asked, part of her wished she'd just stayed in the bedroom, because the look on Will's face was enough to distress her without whatever news he was about to deliver. "It's Ryder?"

"He's gone," Will said.

"Gone? What do you mean gone?"

"We can't find him," Will said. "None of us can get in touch with him and his security codes haven't been used in the building since yesterday."

That meant he hadn't come home last night. She'd been aware that he wasn't in her bed when she went to sleep, but it wasn't unusual for him to work late or workout at night, especially if she wasn't home yet. Ryder didn't like to go to sleep until he knew she was safe in her bed. Lacie had never considered that there might be a need for her to offer Ryder the same courtesy.

"Okay, but you're going to find him, right?" she asked. "You're going to… he can't have gone far…. This is Ryder—"exhaling a laugh, she swallowed, trying to quell the tingle in her sinuses—"he's… he's invincible." Except he wasn't and that was why Will's expression was so taut right now. Thinking that she wouldn't get what she wanted from him, she thrust an arm against Will to sweep him out of the way and began to move toward Ty, the flirt, he never took anything seriously. "Ty? You're going to find him… aren't you?"

"We'll do our very best for you, sweetheart," he said, but when he lifted his chin, he looked through her at Will and she didn't like the pinch in his eyes.

"Where's Gabe?" she asked. Determined to take a proactive role in tracking Ryder down, she set her mind on kicking his ass just as soon as they had him back safe.

"Downstairs," Will said and she whipped around. "He's setting up an incident room."

She didn't want this to be an incident, that sounded serious and serious could mean dangerous. Marching past Will, she didn't miss a step when she crouched to swipe her purse from the floor then set Gabe and his incident room in her sights.

THIRTY-EIGHT

Lacie

FOR WHAT FELT like an age, she had been placated while the men worked. The incident room had been set up in the same boardroom she'd had her client protocol meeting in and she was struck by how quickly the tables could turn. Paper piled up on the large table in the center of the room. Phones rang, keyboards clacked and still, no one had been able to pin Ryder down.

"Right, here's what we have," Gabe said loud enough to make everyone stop what they were doing to gather around the table. Everyone except Toby who just kept on battering his keyboard, which he glared at so intently she began to wonder if it had a brain-machine interface.

"We have the primary on camera leaving this building an hour after Lacie did," Gabe said, glancing at her.

"The primary," she said, wrinkling her nose. "That sounds so… detached."

"That's the point," Gabe said, maintaining his professionalism.

Except she didn't want them detached, she wanted these men to be as torn up inside as she was because that fire bred a sense of urgency that would make them work harder. Gabe kept on talking with that same impersonal demeanor and she had to trust that he knew what he was doing.

"He took his truck, which we traced through license plate recognition in the city and use of the CCTV cameras," he said, spreading out a series of images which showed Ryder getting out of his truck. "It's a block from the Graden Mining building about six miles from here."

"So he did see Elijah?" Lacie asked. A flutter of hope burst in her chest. "I can go over there, I'll find out what happened—" Will snagged her arm when she tried to turn away, glancing at that anchor point, she sought out the approval of the other men but was met with only frowns. "What?"

"You're still under our protection," Gabe said. "If you go out there then four of us have to go with you."

"You can't afford to relinquish that kind of manpower at the moment."

Gabe shook his head and Will let her go when she turned back to the group. "I could call him."

"This might be an appropriate moment to state the obvious," Gabe said to everyone, though Lacie was sure it was for her benefit. "You'll notice that the only men in this room are former employees of StoneWall. Our other contracts will be dealt with by the new men Mr. Stone hired. We don't plan to miss a step and as far as the outside world is concerned, it's business as usual around here."

"You don't trust them," Ty said.

"We don't know them well enough yet," Gabe said. "The men in this room are trusted. The information that's shared here is considered top secret until we know more."

For all the hours she had spent worrying about how Jamie Wallace's treachery had affected Ryder, it hadn't occurred to her to look further afield. Gabe, Rocco, Toby, Will, Ty, and Sonny all trusted Jamie and their other associate Eric who was involved with her kidnap. All of them had been bitten by betrayal and these weren't the type of men who would repeat a mistake.

"Is the truck still there?" Will asked, returning to the case.

"Yeah," Gabe said and the silence of these men intensified as their expressions became harder.

"What does that mean?" Lacie exhaled, desperately seeking someone to give her answers.

"It means he didn't get to where he was going," Will said.

"Or he did and he never left again," Rocco finished.

"There's no legitimate reason for that truck to be in the same place more than twelve hours after the fact," Ty said. "The only reason would be…"

"Bad," she said.

Now she understood, she wrapped her arms around herself and rolled her lips into her mouth. Letting her gaze fall to the pictures, she examined each still of the man she loved and considered unstoppable. They were right of course. Ryder wouldn't be spending the night anywhere by choice, there was no indication of him having an affair and even if he was the chances that his mistress would live so close to Elijah's building would be astronomical.

Clearing her throat, she didn't want to break down in front of this group of professionals. "Could it have broken down?" she asked. Ryder kept his vehicles in top shape because sometimes he and his men relied on them to get them out of dangerous situations fast. But considering all that had happened in their lives recently, it was possible he'd missed a service or something.

"Ty," Gabe said. "You get over there and bring it home if it moves… standard checks."

"Standard—"

"For tampering," Will said to her. "We have to check for devices before we attempt to move it."

She didn't like that idea. "Be careful," she said to Ty who winked at her.

"It's unlikely to be broken down or tampered with. We've watched footage through the night to see if the primary ever returns to it and he doesn't," Gabe said. "Still, she's right, be careful."

"I've got something," Toby said, still typing on his keyboard at a hundred miles an hour, he rose. His focus remained on the screen, but he lifted one hand to point toward the door. "Someone kill the lights."

Will left her side to go over and do that as the projector screen began to descend from the ceiling. When it was down and they were in darkness watching, Toby pressed a button on his keyboard and a video flashed onto the screen.

"This was minutes after he left the truck," Toby said, standing behind his desk, watching the same thing they were.

"What is—"

"That building on the left is Graden Mining," Toby said. "I took this from a security camera on the business entrance opposite, look at the top right corner."

A woman was walking down the street and Lacie saw nothing peculiar about that except she was heavily pregnant. From the shadow of an alleyway, a man ran out with a balaclava over his head. He grabbed the woman who tried to struggle and when he began to pull her backward into the alley, another man came into the shot and ran into the shadow of the alley as well.

"That was Ryder," Lacie breathed.

"Yeah," Toby said, pressing another button on the keyboard to rewind the footage. He paused it when the angle of the man who ran in was best and there was no mistaking his identity. "He doesn't come out again. None of them do."

The men considered this and Lacie tried to decipher what that would mean. If they didn't come out then they had to still be there. But the only reason they would be there all these hours later would be if…

"Is he dead?" Lacie asked and lost control of the tears she'd held in.

"Ty, take Will," Gabe said and the men headed toward the door.

"I want to come," Lacie said, but Will stopped her again and this time held her forearms to walk her back against the table.

"You're staying, princess."

"I can't just stay here and do nothing," she said.

"If there is anyone capable of surviving a lunatic on the street it's Ryder," Will said. "Just because they went in that way doesn't mean they left that way. The alley has to let out somewhere and even if it doesn't have an obvious exit point, there are buildings on either side. Ryder might have gone into one of those buildings and come out a different way, sometimes these buildings are interconnected. There's every chance he went up too, there could be a fire escape or a way onto the upper floors of each structure. Just because we don't see him walk out of there doesn't mean he didn't make it."

That did make her feel better, there was still hope, and she didn't want to witness what they might come across if there had been carnage. "Okay. But you be careful too."

"We will," Will said. "You have to stay here and keep the fire going under the asses of these guys."

He leaned in to kiss her forehead and she was amazed that the man who had always been an opponent to her presence was taking the time to console her. He and Ty went out and she went back to looking at the picture on the screen, which was still down.

"We have work to do," Gabe said and someone turned on the lights, which dimmed the image of Ryder on the screen, but didn't erase it.

It was just like him to see someone in trouble and run to their aid. But a woman, and a pregnant one at that, he wouldn't have walked away from her suffering. That he was such an honorable man was one of the things she loved about him, she just didn't want that honor to cost him his life.

When she had last been involved in an incident room such as this, Ryder had been in prison and they were working to get him out. At the time, Lacie thought it was one of the hardest things she'd had to endure, knowing her love was being imprisoned for something he didn't do. She had underestimated the power of knowing where he was though. This not knowing was worse, tenfold. Now she got a taste of what Ryder had experienced when she was taken from him.

Everyone went back to their bustling, then an intercom buzzed on the conferencing unit in the middle of the table. Gabe leaned over to press a button. "Chantelle?" Holding her breath, Lacie waited for news of Ryder.

"There's a man and woman here with a baby," Chantelle said with the snarl of disgust in her voice. "They say they are looking for Miss Hart."

It was nice to know that Lacie's first experience with Chantelle had taught the receptionist not to be so judgmental. That aside, Lacie glanced at a clock on the wall to see she'd missed Sorcha's release from the hospital.

"I'll take them upstairs," Lacie said to Gabe who nodded and went back to his work.

Lacie wanted to be helpful, but she didn't have the skills to find Ryder. Before she had been able to make calls in an attempt to gain information or pull strings. This time, there was no one to call, at least not yet.

So she went out to reception and Sorcha's snit vanished as soon as Lacie came into view. "What's wrong?" Sorcha asked, coming to her friend's side.

"Upstairs," Lacie said, with a sideways glance at Chantelle and Bruce. "We'll talk upstairs."

Lulu was in a stroller, so they pushed her into the elevator and went upstairs, using the new security code that had been updated this week. Bruce came with them and Lacie was uneasy. Shep had told her not to tell Sorcha about Bruce's infidelity. But Gabe had told them to keep the information top secret, so Lacie couldn't reveal all to Sorcha in front of Bruce.

But the man wasn't taking the hint. They got upstairs and Lacie took Sorcha into the kitchen on the hope of getting her alone, but it seemed that Bruce didn't want to be alone with his daughter because everywhere they went, Bruce followed on.

Lacie gave up trying to shirk him and settled them all in the living room that the elevator opened to, she didn't want to miss anyone coming in and she still held a hope that Ryder would come back and laugh at them all for making such a fuss.

"If you don't tell me what's wrong, I'm going to go crazy," Sorcha said, taking a seat beside Lacie and snatching both of her forearms. "What is it?"

"It's Ryder," Lacie said, glancing at Bruce who was standing in front of a tall window. "He didn't come home last night."

"He didn't…" Sorcha said and her shoulders fell. "Do you think something happened to him?"

"That's what we're trying to ascertain," Lacie said. "The guys are downstairs looking into the possibilities." Much as it pained her not to be doing anything to help locate Ryder, Lacie turned her attention onto Lulu. "How is she?"

"Loud and smelly," Sorcha said, unfastening the restraints from Lulu. Lacie smiled when she saw Sorcha smiling at the baby who was fast asleep. Sorcha might want the world to think that she was complaining, but this was a woman glowing.

"Can I hold her?"

"Sure," Sorcha said.

They talked about and to Lulu for the next hour and after her cuddle, Sorcha had one and Bruce refused so Lulu was put back into her stroller for a sleep. Sorcha did look tired, but really appeared to be taking to motherhood, which pleased Lacie because it was what she had hoped for.

When the elevator pinged, Lacie thrust up to her feet and all pleasantries were forgotten. It seemed to take an hour for the doors to open and she took an involuntary step toward them, praying for Ryder to walk through when they parted.

He didn't.

Gabe, Sonny, and Rocco were in the elevator. When they came in, she saw another man behind them. Shep. All thoughts of what drama could be caused departed her and she ran over to him.

Shep exhaled with a whoosh when she landed in his arms, but he held her all the same. "It's okay, Little Lady, we're going to find your fella."

Squeezing her eyes closed, a tear escaped each duct and she sniffed. Shep had helped Ryder to find her, maybe that was why she felt such an affinity for him now.

It could just be that they had bonded last night over ice cream and margaritas, and she needed some comfort now just like he had the previous night.

"What is he doing here?" Sorcha demanded.

"He's here to help and we need all of that we can get," Gabe said. Lacie noted an edge of aggression in his tone that made Lacie lift her head from Shep's chest to see the men were fixated on Bruce. "Mr. Booth, I think your business is concluded here, is it not?"

"You're kicking me out?" Bruce demanded and glanced to Sorcha. "Are you going to let them throw me out?"

Lacie turned around but stayed against Shep. "Thanks for your patience, Bruce," she said, pleased that she wasn't the only one creeped out by him. "But we really need family around us now."

"Family?" Bruce said, striding over the room with an outstretched finger in Sorcha's direction. "She's not blood. None of you are blood."

Lacie would cite Ryder's proclamation to her that she had blood in the game. Bruce could argue that he had spilled blood himself, but his trauma was born out of his own selfish greed. No one here had invited damnation the way that he had.

"You're also a criminal," Shep said.

"A criminal," Bruce said.

As long as he provided evidence in Wallace's trial, he wouldn't see the inside of a jail cell himself. Although law enforcement had an open investigation on him with regards to his embezzlement of money with his previous employer.

"Yeah," Shep said, moving her aside to approach Bruce. "And no one here trusts you. Not one person."

Bruce glanced back at Sorcha, as if he expected her to come to his defense. He was disappointed because she was wiping drool from Lulu's chin.

"Fuck all of you," Bruce said, and stomped his way to the elevator, which opened as soon as he pressed the call button.

When he was gone, Gabe bent to catch her hand and he led her into the kitchen to talk alone.

"What have you found out?" Lacie asked.

Gabe appeared serious, but didn't seem to be packing bad news, not if his unchanged expression was any barometer of his mood.

"We called Detective Deacon," Gabe said, Deacon was their cop contact. "We can't get anything more on our own. Toby is trying to find footage of how they exited the alley. Will and Ty are keeping their boots on the ground. They have surveyed the area and have found no evidence that any of the three marks are still in the alley. No bodies. No blood. No scuffle."

Hearing that Ryder wasn't dead was a relief. Until they could actually find him, her heart rate would remain erratic. "So you called the cops?"

"Getting his description out there is helpful and they have greater manpower than we do. Sometimes a random traffic stop is all that's needed. It would be foolish of us to assume that we were the only ones with the intelligence to crack this, not when our resources are limited."

"Okay. That makes sense," she said, she didn't care who found Ryder, as long as someone did. "Will he file a report?"

"Not at the moment," Gabe said. "If we don't have him back by the morning, you can go down and register him officially as a missing person."

"But?"

"He's a grown man and at liberty to go wherever the hell he wants," Gabe said. "I told Deacon about what we found so far. With the suspicion of foul play, we might get some airtime on the police radios but… they have other priorities."

Law enforcement went all out for missing kids or vulnerable adults. A man like Ryder who was capable and fit, it would be assumed that he could take care of himself, which was what everyone there had assumed too.

"We were all so busy looking at me," she muttered.

"What?" he asked.

"Could this be connected to what happened to me?" she asked.

"It could be and we've been working that angle," Gabe said. "But the setup doesn't seem right. Your pursuer didn't create a diversion. All evidence suggests that he was working alone. He couldn't have known that Ryder was going to meet with Graden or known that the woman was going to be walking along the street."

"You have suspected Elijah since the beginning, all of you have."

"Ty and Will are going to talk to him, try to get a measure of his honesty."

"He might not see them," she said. "He's a busy man and if he doesn't recognize—"

"Will and Ty can be persuasive when they want to be. Elijah's assistant is a petite redhead," Gabe said, resting a comforting hand on her shoulder. "Do you think there's a better man than Ty to charm a woman?"

"No," she said, embracing herself again while a smile found her face.

"We can't be sure of much at the moment," Gabe said. "But if this was just an assault gone wrong, Ryder would have come out or been left at the scene as would the woman. Something else is going on here, whether it's related to your crazy or not, we don't know and we're keeping our minds open."

"Two crazies at once seems unlikely," she said. Gabe's face remained static and she was impressed by his ability to conceal his emotions. "But you don't want me to blame myself, so you're trying to make me feel better." Groaning, her head fell back and she closed her eyes. "Ryder taught you all well. He's looking after me even when his own life could be in peril."

"I guess that's what love is," Gabe said. "Ryder told us that you were priority one and his orders remain current."

He'd said something similar to her, so all she could do was breathe through her frustration and be warmed that his love was still here even if he wasn't.

"I'm going to check on Sorcha," Lacie said and Gabe let her go.

Moving through the house, her brow came down when she heard Sorcha laugh. Creeping up to the entrance to the living room, she saw Sorcha and Shep kneeling on the floor together with Miss Lulu on a changing mat in front of them, diaper off and surrounded by every baby product that ever existed.

Sorcha laughed again and picked up a packet of wipes. "You have to be quick," Sorcha said, tugging out a few wipes and trying to hand them to Shep.

"I'm not doing it," he protested, but when Sorcha shook them closer, he grumbled and snatched them. "Well, hold her legs or something. Geez, kid."

Lacie couldn't see his expression, but he sounded sufficiently disgusted, though he still worked on cleaning Lulu up. "You're a natural," Sorcha laughed.

Tiptoeing backward, Lacie left the couple alone. Sorcha was reveling in motherhood and Shep seemed willing to embrace that. It was about time Sorcha had some security in her life. Lacie just hoped that Shep didn't fall as hard for Lulu as he did for Sorcha.

THIRTY-NINE

Lacie

TO GIVE THEM some space, Lacie had gone back to the incident room with the other men and been given the task of watching video footage of one of the alley's exits. Not all the exits were covered by cameras and those that were weren't always public cameras. Lacie thought it best not to question where Toby got this footage. She was set up in a corner and watched every second that was put in front of her, but she didn't see any of the three people who entered the alley together or any vehicles of note.

When she did see a vehicle, she noted the timestamp and what she could of make, model, and license plate then handed that information off to Toby for further investigation. No one had come back to her to say any of them were significant, so she assumed they were all dead ends.

No one ate dinner. No one even suggested food. Night drew in. Shep came in to work with them after he dropped off Sorcha, but when it got to midnight, he came over to her in the corner.

"Time for bed," Shep said to her and offered a hand.

Scanning the room, she didn't see anyone else showing signs of slowing down. "No. I have work to do."

"If Ryder comes back and sees you haggard, he'll tear us all a new one," Shep said. "You're only going upstairs. If anything breaks, we'll come and get you."

Gabe was in the far corner and he made eye contact with her and nodded. "I guess you guys have taken a vote."

"Yeah, and it was unanimous," Shep said, picking up her hand from the desk. "Come on. I'll tuck you in."

Rising, she followed in his wake. "You think if you hit on me that Ryder might materialize to kick your ass?" she asked, curious if that had been his reasoning and it didn't sound too far-fetched to her because Ryder didn't want any other man touching her.

"If you want to make out a bit or get naked, I'm your man," Shep said. He took her through the darkened S.I.S. floor, past Chantelle's abandoned desk, and into the elevator.

"I don't think you mean that," Lacie said as they traveled up. Shep was being polite in offering to violate her and she was surer than ever that he was in love with Sorcha. "What did you think of Lulu?"

"She's whiney and demanding," Shep muttered, lowering his gaze as if to hide his expression. A moment later, he inhaled and returned to his impatient self. "Just like her mother."

"No wonder you're in love with her then."

The elevator doors opened and Shep went out, so she followed. "You're looking out for Sorcha even when Ryder is God knows where."

"I'm looking out for you too," Lacie said, going into the bedroom with him. "You two need to have a conversation."

Shep closed the curtains and turned down the bed when she sat on the end and slipped off her shoes. He came to her and stroked her hair. "You're something special, Lace," he said. "We're going to find Ryder for you."

"I know," she said. "He wouldn't leave me. He promised he would never leave me."

"And we'll make sure he keeps that promise." Shep bowed and kissed the top of her head, then turned off the light as he left the room.

Lacie was tired, she had to concede that. Emotional fatigue became physical exhaustion and now that she had been given the excuse by Ryder's man, she knew it was pointless to object because they were right.

Going through her routine to prepare for bed, she told herself that Ryder was in bed waiting for her every time she was hit with a pang of sorrow.

The lights were already off. So when she was finished in the bathroom, she crawled into the bed with her eyes closed, still desperate to cling to her illusion of Ryder's presence.

Facing the truth that her illusion was in fact a delusion, she took a breath and told herself to keep hope alive. Just as she was about to open her mouth to talk to him through the darkness an intrusive ring pierced the silence.

Only one phone would ring that loud in this space—Ryder's private line. Just as in the old SW complex, Ryder had a private, direct line to the bedroom. Few people had the number, and Gabe was one of them. Throwing back the bed covers, she pounced out of the bed and ran to the handset, ripping it off the base, which was attached to the wall.

"Do you have him?" she asked, needing to hear Gabe say the words that they had located him and were on their way to pick him up. Desperation closed her throat. Ryder could have strolled in downstairs, he could be here in the building, and she needed confirmation of that because the alternative was unthinkable.

"Actually, yes." The male voice on the other end of the line was not Gabe's. Dread recognized that voice. Her pain identified each syllable and her devastation spotted his nuance. This was the man from the gallery. No doubt the same man who attacked her in the cabin.

Emptying her emotion, she whipped around, determined to act quickly. Seeking out her panic button, she didn't get two steps toward it when he spoke again.

"I wouldn't do anything rash, Miss Hart," the voice said. "I have your love and I have every intention of injuring him. But there is still a chance you could get him back in one piece. If you summon anyone else, alert anyone that we have had this conversation, I'll send him back, an inch of flesh at a time."

Clutching the phone with both hands, she kept focus on the panic button, which was on her bedside, but she didn't move any closer to it.

"What do you want?"

"He's alive," the voice said. "You don't sound very grateful. I didn't have to keep him alive."

"I'm grateful," she said, squeezing her eyes closed she tried to focus, tried to memorize details which might help them find out Ryder's location.

"Good," the voice drawled. Recognizing that the voice didn't sound entirely natural, she wondered if the man was using some sort of tech to distort it. "You and I are going to work together and you're going to keep our association a secret. If you tell a single person, I will know."

"How will you know?"

"To say I am watching you would be an understatement," he said. "You're not as safe in your ivory tower as you might believe. I would think that your encounter with Mr. Wallace would have educated you on the pitfalls of trust. Apparently, it didn't. I'm here to make sure you get that message now, loud and clear. If you think there's someone you can trust, I can tell you that you'd be mistaken. Someone you know, someone close to you, is close to me. I hear everything. I see everything. You and your life belong to me now, Miss Hart, and I took your boyfriend to ensure you didn't forget that."

"He's leverage? For what? What is it that you want me to do?"

"First I need your assurance that you will keep our relationship a secret."

A tickle in the back of her throat signaled her revulsion at the idea of having any kind of "relationship" with such a mad man. But this threat had Ryder and no matter what it took, no matter what this lunatic wanted her to do, she would do it, because she would do anything to keep Ryder safe. If their roles were reversed then Ryder would already have signaled his compliance.

"I'll keep it a secret. I won't tell a soul. Just please, give me Ryder back."

"You will get him back," the voice said with a curl of pleasure. "Provided you comply with my instructions."

"What do you want me to do?"

"The first task I have for you is simple and one you should've taken care of already yourself."

A few beats of silence increased her heart rate. If she lost this connection then she lost the only link she had to Ryder, the only chance she had of saving his life. "What is it?"

"Get yourself a good night's rest and then without provoking suspicion…"

"What?"

"Tell Sorcha about Booth's infidelity."

Lacie hadn't expected that. Her body prickled as her eyes gradually opened into the frown that adorned her face. "How do you know about that?" she whispered.

The callous laugh on the end of the line curled Lacie's lip with anger and disgust that this sicko could be getting pleasure out of the torment he visited on their lives. "I know everything about you and your life, Miss Hart—absolutely everything."

Again, the line went quiet and a clicking on the other end piqued her ears. But too soon the drone of the dial tone confirmed what she feared. He'd hung up.

FORTY

Lacie

A GOOD NIGHT'S rest was unlikely, but for his instruction not to provoke suspicion, Lacie had to give the impression that she had. The captor had given her no idea of how many commands he had or when he would be back in touch with her.

With hope that she would hear from him sooner if she got the first task done, she called Sorcha at seven a.m. As it was Sorcha had been up for most of the night with Lulu, so the early morning call didn't wake her.

"Can we have coffee?" Lacie asked.

"Oh, honey, I would, but it's just been crazy here. I'm not at all presentable."

"That's okay, it's only me," Lacie said, regretting every time she had begrudged Sorcha her girlie events. "I really need to see you."

"Is it Ryder? Did you hear something?"

To her credit, Sorcha did sound concerned and hopeful. Hearing her friend being so genuine fired a pang of guilt into Lacie for not being honest. She prided herself on privacy and loyalty and now that she was keeping secrets from her best friend. It felt so disloyal that her chest became tight.

"No. We haven't, but… I don't want to neglect you at this time. Gabe and the guys have got it under control. I really want to see you."

"You do?" Sorcha asked.

The silence that followed made Lacie slide from the corner of the bed she was perched on to sit on the floor. Drawing her knees up, she clamped a hand over her mouth to damn the gasp that threatened in time with the wobble of her lower lip. She couldn't tell if Sorcha was suspicious or touched. All Lacie could focus on was not revealing her deception. How people dealt with being duplicitous every day of their lives, Lacie didn't know. Her heart wouldn't be able to handle the stress of it.

"Maybe I could come over…"

"My apartment is a mess," Sorcha said.

Lacie didn't want to ask why Sorcha was hesitant. Either Bruce was standing over her or Sorcha didn't want to clean up. With a crying baby, she wouldn't have had the time to preen herself to her usual level of perfection. Sorcha prided herself on being stylish without a hair out of place. If Lulu was going to be demanding, Sorcha might have to get over that hang up.

"I don't mind mess," Lacie said, but she didn't want Bruce present when they had their conversation. Going out meant taking S.I.S. security away from their jobs.

She wasn't going to depress herself because she had the chance to save Ryder and falling apart would do him no good. "Can you come over here today?" Lacie asked. It was the only other choice.

"Lulu just went to sleep. I'm going to take a nap. How about I come over after?"

"Okay," Lacie said, through her fingers which curled over her mouth because she wanted to yell or object or question how long it would take Sorcha to get here. She should be considerate of her exhausted friend and how news of her husband's infidelity would affect her and her daughter's life.

Deciding to rip off the Band-Aid, Lacie decided that waiting wasn't an option. "It's just… Shep told me… he gave me news, about Bruce… I didn't know if I should tell you but…"

"We're always honest with each other," Sorcha said. "What did he tell you?"

The tinge of wariness in Sorcha's voice could be attributed to her nerves, but Lacie couldn't tell if Sorcha wanted the news or not. "You were right," Lacie said with no other option but to come out with it. "You were right about Bruce, right to send me to Shep." Sorcha didn't say anything. Lacie listened to the slight change in Sorcha's breathing and then she seemed to hold her breath for almost a minute before she swallowed. "Sorch?"

"It's fine," Sorcha said, sounding altogether too chirpy. "I mean we knew it, didn't we?"

"Yes," Lacie said. "That doesn't make it easier to hear… I wish I was there to give you a hug."

"I don't need a hug I… I'm going to take a nap."

"Sorch—"

"Thanks for telling me, Lacie. You're a real friend."

"Was it right to tell you?" Lacie asked, but she had no choice if she wanted to help Ryder.

"Yes. I wouldn't want to be that woman. You know, everybody whispering behind her back… Do you know who it is?"

"A blonde woman from the household staff," Lacie said.

Sorcha yelped and actually laughed. "How cliché! Wouldn't his father be proud? Bruce made up with them, he's been sleeping there since Lulu was born… or sleeping… somewhere else maybe."

Lacie didn't know Booth's parents. Sorcha had loved spending time with her mother-in-law, but it was possible that relationship was now doomed. "What are you going to do?" Lacie asked.

"Take a nap," Sorcha said, taking a deep cleansing breath. "Then I'm going to phone Shep and get all the details. Are there pictures?"

"At his office."

"Good. Bruce won't know what hit him," Sorcha said, regaining some of her confidence. "I'm glad I found this out now. Yes. This is all for the best."

"Do you want me to come over now?" Lacie asked.

"No. No. No. With everything that's going on with Ryder… you stay there. You're needed there. I'm a big girl. I can handle this myself."

Motherhood had done more to Sorcha than ruin her grooming routine. She was standing up and taking responsibility for a mess that she found herself in. Lacie couldn't be more surprised.

They rung off and Lacie stared at her phone for a while, long after her friend had hung up. Now that the first task was complete, she wanted the kidnapper to phone again and give her the next one. Racing through the gauntlet this maniac was laying down without flinching or retreating was the only way that she could deal with this. Getting Ryder back was all that she cared about.

FORTY-ONE

Sorcha

SORCHA PACED AROUND the perimeter of her living room, checking that nothing was out of place. Lulu was sleeping and instead of taking her nap earlier, Sorcha had done her chores. So it was all Shep's fault that she was exhausted. The doorbell rang, and she stormed out of the living room and down the hall ready to give her visitor hell.

"Do you know how rude you are?" she hissed, grabbing Shep's jacket to pull him inside.

"Rude?" he asked, producing a bottle of wine from behind his back. "I don't look rude from where I'm standing. I brought you a gift. You're the one bitching about—"

"I can't drink wine. I'm nursing." He hadn't been here for ten seconds and already she wanted to scream at him for being an idiot.

Using his sleeve as a leash, she dragged him down the hall and into the living room where she thrust him down onto the couch. "You don't ring a doorbell at ten p.m. when there's a new baby in the house," she whispered.

Having a baby around changed her way of thinking about everything. After the exhaustion of her day, she did not want Lulu to wake up because she wasn't sure that she had the energy to settle her daughter down in bed again.

"You could've left the door unlocked," he said, bending forward to put the wine on the floor, he traced his fingertips up the side of her calf as he sat back. "Like you used to."

Sorcha hadn't shaved her legs and going for a wax was out of the question with a baby in tow, so she shoved his shoulder to get his hands off her as soon as possible, in hope that he wouldn't notice her stubbly legs. "I'm married now."

"I heard," he said, lifting his eyes and his brows when he folded his arms.

"Is that why you didn't come over when I called this afternoon? You thought you weren't getting any, so what was the point of answering an ex-girlfriend's call?"

"I don't remember you being my girlfriend," he said, tilting his head and squinting. "And I did answer your call, sugar-hips, I just didn't jump at your command. I told you I'd come over later and here I am."

He opened his arms as if she should be grateful for his presence. Sorcha could only scowl because the truth was, she was pleased that he was here and she hated him for it. Spending another night alone might just bring her to tears. But she couldn't show weakness, not in front of Shep. She couldn't bear to have him laugh at her.

"I asked you to come over because I paid for a service, not because of the other thing."

"What other thing?" he asked. The curl of his lips betrayed that he knew exactly what she was talking about.

Squeezing her lips together, she silently fumed, and reminded herself not to raise her voice in deference to her sleeping child. "Lacie told me," she snapped while remaining hushed. "She told me Bruce was… that he was…"

"Screwing around on you," he said, resting his hands on the couch on either side of him.

Maybe she appreciated the superior position, or maybe she was just afraid of what might happen if she sat down, but Sorcha stayed on her feet in front of him, looking down her nose. "So show me," she demanded and held out a hand.

She expected a joke or a tease but received neither. Shep opened his jacket, reached into an inside pocket, and pulled out a stack of photographs that were folded once down the middle lengthways. Snatching the pictures from him, she was full of gusto and expressed that with the arch of a brow. Shep might have taken his sweet time about coming here, but he had come, and he'd done it because she'd ordered it.

The first picture didn't register, she flicked to the next and saw Bruce with a blonde, saw him kissing the blonde, and the truth of what she was looking at made her sink down into the seat beside him. She had known that her husband was cheating, at least she had suspected it. But part of her wanted to be wrong because all she wanted was the fairy tale. She wanted a man who would go to the ends of the earth for her and never look at another woman.

Her home life had never been secure. Her parents had busy lives and their own priorities, which didn't always include her or her sister. Sadie was flighty and popular. They had never been particularly close, choosing instead to compete with each other for the attention of their parents and then for friends and men as they grew up.

"He's an asshole," Shep said, curling a hand over her knee.

Sorcha had been staring at the pictures, though she didn't know for how long. When she looked up and met his eye, she realized he was there with her, sitting beside her at the front edge of the couch, knee to knee. One of his hands came up and cupped her face. He angled her head then leaned in to kiss her.

It felt good to be kissing him; it always felt good to kiss Shep. But when his tongue edged into her mouth and the weight of him grew more insistent, she had to part their mouths.

"Is that why you came here late?" she asked, throwing the pictures at him, and shooting to her feet. "You thought if you showed me this, I'd be vulnerable enough to let you into my bed? God, you're so predictable."

"I came here late because I was on a job today," he said, standing at her side and matching her fury. "I didn't want to come here at all. I told the Little Lady not to tell you about Booth's bullshit because I didn't want to see your heart get broken."

"You didn't care about my heart when we broke up!" she bit out.

Encroaching on her personal space, he threatened her resolve to dismiss him because he smelled so good… he always smelled good. "Every time we split it was you who did the heart-breaking, sugar-hips. Did I ever end it with you? Huh? No! I came running back like a dumb stupid pup because you cross those lush legs and lick those lips and I forget to notice that you're glaring down your little button nose at me."

"Uh, I have a baby! I have just been told my husband is a snake! Are you allowed to talk to clients this way?"

"Clients? You're not my damn client, Sorch."

"Then what the hell am I?" Her breath caught in her throat with a gasp when he grabbed her arm and hauled her against him.

"You're a superior, melodramatic bitch with a blind spot for good sense."

"It's a wonder you would come back to me at all then, isn't it?" she said, maintaining her patronizing tone, but deliberately licking her upper lip in a slow swipe meant to torment him and it worked, because his eyes dropped to her mouth.

"Little Lady is right," he murmured and swept his other arm around her to restrict her breathing with a tight embrace that brought her to the tips of her toes. "I come back because I love you, just like I have since the start."

She couldn't believe he meant it. If he did, it would change everything she'd ever believed about their relationship and the type of man he was. But if it was a ruse and she fell for it, Shep would use it against her in jest at least, and she just wasn't strong enough to face being betrayed by another man.

"You don't love me," Sorcha said and tried to use her bent arms on his chest to lever her freedom, but he hauled her back. "What we have is sex, hot, dirty, demeaning sex. We use each other because we tease each other… that's all it is."

"Is it? Then why do you keep coming back to me?"

"You're convenient."

"I'm anything but convenient," he said and tried to kiss her, but she leaned away and hit his chest.

"Get off me, you animal, I've just had a baby! I'm not having sex with you. I'm a mess."

"I don't want sex. I want to take you to bed and rub your back until you fall asleep—"

"Then you'll slip it in while I'm sleeping? That's rape, genius."

"You come back to me because you love me too," he said, rubbing his nose on hers though she tried to get away by wriggling in his arms.

"You're unreliable and lazy and—"

He let her go. She shook her arms then straightened her top, expressing her indignation with a tsk.

"Then why is it you come to me whenever something goes wrong in your life?" he asked.

"I don't."

He conceded a nod. "Okay, then why do you send Lacie to me every time something goes wrong? You want me to pick up the pieces, you want me to—"

"I didn't ask you to come to S.I.S. and bond with my baby, did I?"

"No," he admitted. "But Lacie needs us. Ryder needs us. They're the kind of righteous, altruistic people who would actually drop everything to help us if we needed it."

His face scrunched in a kind of disgust that made her smile. They weren't the kind of selfless people that Lacie and Ryder were, but some of that goodness appeared to have rubbed off on him, even if it did make him uncomfortable.

"I want to help too," she said, because she felt terrible for what was going on.

Ryder and Lacie were meant to be together, yet circumstances kept pulling them apart.

Stroking her arm, he moved closer. "You can come to S.I.S. with me tomorrow," he said. "After you dump your husband." Her head went back and she exhaled. "You have to talk to him, Sorch. You have to end it. Now that you know the truth—"

"Seth!" she said, holding up a hand. "I can't deal with this right now, please."

And she meant it. Lulu was keeping her awake at night. Bruce was going to ruin her reputation and wouldn't quietly agree to end their association because that would just be too easy. And Lulu… Sorcha wasn't prepared to be a parent let alone a single parent.

As if on cue, the lights on the baby monitor flared and she sagged before she actually heard Lulu cry. "Just leave the pictures and let yourself out," she said and turned to head for her daughter's bedroom. Except Shep snagged her wrist and pulled her back.

"Let me get her. I'm not walking away from you, Sorch. I don't care how long it takes for you to see it. You're not driving, I'm not going to limp away because you bench me. I'm sticking by your side until you can't deny it anymore."

He didn't give her a chance to answer, just took the liberty of going past her into the second hallway, presumably to get Lulu. She didn't know what made him an authority on babies, but she wasn't going to argue with the help, not tonight when she was exhausted.

Glancing down, she saw the pictures of Bruce scattered on the couch and floor, facing in various directions, some upside down and some obvious. Exhaling, she admitted to herself that she wasn't heartbroken. There had never been much love between them. The most overwhelming emotion in her was fear, as it had been from the start.

Except now that Lulu was here, she wasn't so scary. Being a parent was exhausting and it was constant, but when Sorcha heard Shep through the baby monitor talking to Lulu who quieted to gurgle, she smiled. Her daughter wasn't immune to the charms she had fallen for, but she couldn't take a chance on Shep as she had with Bruce. She would have to be sure she was making the right decision before she tethered herself to another man. Shep would have to prove himself.

FORTY-TWO

Lacie

NO MATTER HOW hard she willed it, the kidnapper didn't phone that day. It was heart breaking to see Gabe and the others working so tirelessly trying to find Ryder when all the time she was holding on to this tidbit of information.

Lacie did her duty and went downstairs to start looking through more footage for them in hopes that if she could find Ryder then she could put a stop to this crazy game. She underestimated how difficult it would be to be surrounded by people.

Most of the guys seemed to take her reticence as a reaction to what they were going through. But the truth was, she hated keeping secrets. In need of moral support, she considered calling Shep. Sorcha hadn't called back or come over and Shep had been absent too. Lacie didn't know if they were together, if Sorcha had gone to Sheppard Investigations to get answers or if her friend was curled in a ball crying her eyes out.

Calling Shep became such an attractive idea that she actually reached for the phone. Something stopped her though and it was that nagging doubt in her mind. The kidnapper had said he was watching. He also said he had someone on the inside, and that he would know if she revealed the truth to anyone. She and Shep had been the only two people who knew about Bruce's infidelity. That left no explanation on how the kidnapper knew.

Peering over her computer, she scanned the men working around her and got a glimmer of how Ryder must have felt when he began to suspect Jamie Wallace of betrayal. All the men there had been innocent of being in cahoots with Wallace and she had fought for them when Ryder doubted them. So how had the kidnapper known the truth of Bruce's infidelity? How did he get the number for Ryder's private line? How did he even know that there was one?

Ryder might have given out the number, but the kidnapper would have to ask for it first, and that would mean he was aware of its existence. The men in this room knew about the private line. So did Jamie Wallace and his accomplice Eric, but they were both out of the picture and had been for months. Sorcha and Shep had never been in Lacie's bedroom, but it was possible they knew about it.

That night she didn't need anyone to tell her to go to bed. She went upstairs, got ready for bed, and then lay in the dark waiting for the phone to ring, hoping that it would.

At exactly midnight, the phone began to ring and she dashed over to snatch it up.

"Very good," the voice on the other end said before Lacie had a chance to say a word.

"I did what you said," Lacie said. "Now you let Ryder go." She knew it was never going to be that easy, but she had to ask.

"That was your test, to see if you were going to comply, and you did."

"Why are you doing this?" Lacie asked, feeling the heat of anger replace her distress. "Why are you doing this to us?"

"I'm not doing anything to you," the voice snarled. "Not everything is about Lacie Hart."

"Why did you drug me at the cabin? Why did you show up at the gallery and drug me? Just to scare everyone?"

"That's exactly why," the voice said. "That was a good, old-fashioned case of misdirection. I didn't want anyone looking at Ryder. Your history gave me the perfect cover. I knew as soon as Ryder believed you were in danger, he would double his efforts to keep you safe. Security swarmed around you and you were cut off from the world. The focus was on you because everyone thought you were at risk."

"And while they were distracted, you went after Ryder," Lacie murmured and wandered to the bed to sink down. "But why?"

"Why is nothing to do with you," the voice said. "Why is for me and my prisoner to discuss. Your concern should be your next task."

"Which is?"

"In the morning you're going to pack your things. You're going to leave that building and move into the Grand Hotel."

"What? Why would I do that?" she asked. "The men here, they're working to… they'll think I don't care about finding Ryder."

"I know exactly what Ryder's men are doing. I have already told you that I am aware of all that is going on."

"I don't understand—"

"If you refuse, you give me my excuse to hurt this man you claim to love."

"I do love him," she said because there was no denying it. "I'm not refusing. I'll do it."

"You'll go alone," the voice said. "Leave without telling anyone. If you're discovered, you will refuse security or any kind of accompaniment."

"How do I know this isn't a trick meant to draw me out?"

"You don't. But as I've said, not everything is about Lacie Hart. If I wanted you, I would have taken you from the cabin instead of leaving you there, wouldn't I? I had you then and I could've kept you. Your precious Ryder would never have found you."

Lacie splayed a hand on Ryder's pillow, the connection with him was fading as his scent was, but she knew she had to hold on. "Why did you leave me?"

"Because if I didn't, Ryder would have had nothing to protect. They had to be looking at you and unconcerned about their own safety."

"They?"

"His men," the voice said. "What has come before is all a part of my plan and it worked. I have Ryder and now you are my puppet. You will do exactly what I tell you or Ryder will be hurt. Do you understand?"

"I understand."

"Good. You have your instructions. I expect them to be carried out."

FORTY-THREE

SHE DID EXACTLY as she was told. The next morning, she packed what she needed and left the rest of her possessions filled with hope that she would be back soon. Going out into the world alone might leave her exposed, but the kidnapper was right that he could have had his way with her before if he wanted to hurt her.

Pulling her bag off the bed, she worried her lip in her teeth as she descended in the elevator. If one of the guys found her now, they would be very confused and she didn't want to fight. Lacie wasn't used to keeping secrets, so she didn't know how good a poker face she had. Ryder's men were trained to sniff out a lie, which was part of the reason she'd tried her best to avoid them yesterday.

Checking into the hotel didn't take long. Once she was there, she had nothing but time to whittle away. It might take the guys a couple of hours or more to notice that she was gone because they trusted her, they assumed that she would stay in the safety of the building where they all were.

Just before lunchtime, there was a pounding on her bedroom door that told her she'd been found out. Flicking off the TV, which she'd put on to distract herself, although it didn't work. Lacie went to the door and checked through the peephole, something Ryder had trained her to do.

Gabe and Rocco were on the other side of the door and when her hand fell to the door handle, she closed her eyes and took a breath before she opened it.

"What the fuck do you think you're doing?" Gabe demanded, barreling in with Rocco before she had a chance to inhale. "Why did you sneak off and—"

"I didn't sneak off," Lacie said, closing the door. "You were busy."

The room she was in was a standard room and with these two bulky guys present, it began to look a lot smaller. Anyone else might be intimidated by their height and girth, but Lacie didn't fear these men, even in their current angry state. That anger came from a place of concern and it tore her up to know that she was betraying that and them in favor of pandering to a madman.

"Busy?" Rocco asked.

Rocco didn't get angry, Lacie didn't think she'd ever seen him wear a frown, but he was wearing one now. "I just needed to get away," Lacie said, running her hands through her hair, trying to indicate that she was harried. "Everything there, it's just… it's Ryder all the time, all over the place."

"If you were having a hard time, you should have told us," Gabe said. "You were not supposed to run away without security or—"

"I don't need security," she said, meeting his eye. "If this is anything to do with the same guy who took me then he'd proved he doesn't want me. He took Ryder and kept him. Me, he drugged at the cabin and left me there."

"And if it's not?" Rocco asked. "If we're dealing with two separate crazies?"

"It doesn't matter, if this is a second crazy then he doesn't want me, he hasn't touched me, has he? And if this all stems from that mugging gone wrong, or whatever it was…"

Now her eyes drifted downward.

Gabe wasn't having any of her detachment. He took one long stride and came up against her. "What?"

"Maybe the guy got rid of him."

Gabe shook his head and set his attention on her. Without blinking, and with deliberate words, he conveyed his determination. "We are not giving up. It's been a couple of days. We are going to keep working under the assumption that Ryder is alive. You cannot give up on him."

Gabe's anger was a great disguise, but even his stoic self couldn't hide his hurt at her actions. "How could you walk away from him? From Ryder? How could you give up this quickly?" Rocco asked. "We never leave a man behind. And it was you, before… it was you who held us together when Ryder was in jail. He wanted nothing to do with us and we were ready to disband. You came in and told us to get with it. You gave us the kick in the ass we needed to get working."

"You don't need that now, do you?" she said, skirting Gabe to head for Rocco because he was easier to look at right now. Gabe had a way of looking through her that made her feel like he knew every thought in her mind. "You are working hard, together, you're doing a great job."

"You're a part of the team," Rocco said. "If you don't want to watch the footage, we'll find you something else to do."

"No," Lacie said, shaking her head. "I just need to be by myself for a while. I need to… I need to think about things… to process this."

"What is there to process?" Gabe asked, causing her to about face. "Ryder is out there in trouble and he needs us… When you were out there, the guy barely slept or ate. He would never have considered abandoning you."

"I guess I'm not as strong as him," she said. Being gentle wasn't working. These men weren't going to slip out of her room and out of her life without a fight. "I need space, Gabe. Is that hard for you to understand? I want to be away from that building. Away from everything and everyone in it. I need to be away from you guys. Can I be any clearer?"

Gabe's eyes narrowed and she held her breath to remain as inscrutable as she could. "How are you going to face him when he gets back?" Gabe murmured.

"That's for me to worry about, isn't it?" she said and brought her hands to her hips. "Now if you'd excuse me…"

It wasn't like she actually had anything to do, but the longer they were there, the higher the chance she would be found out.

Gabe didn't make it any harder for her. He almost pushed her aside as he stormed toward the door. Rocco caught her arm to help her steady her, but he didn't say anything. He just looked at her like a hurt puppy then made for the door after his friend.

FORTY-FOUR

Lacie

PACING IN THE HOTEL room only got her worked up, so she tried going out for a long walk to exhaust herself, but still she didn't sleep. Without the private phone line, Lacie had no idea how the kidnapper was going to get in touch with her. But there had been a reservation under her name when she arrived at the hotel, which could only have been made by the kidnapper. That he had gone to that trouble, suggested he had a plan.

Dinnertime had come and gone. Lacie was whittling down the minutes until midnight. Still clothed, she flopped onto the bed on her back and began to count her breaths. A noise outside her bedroom door made her open an eye. Straining to hear if there was someone out in the corridor, she slid off the bed as quietly as she could. A proud knock made her leap to her feet and rush toward the door.

The kidnapper could be here to visit her in person. Or maybe he had decided to release Ryder right here on her doorstep. Checking the peephole, she was surprised to see Sorcha on the other side of her door.

Sliding off the chain, Lacie opened the door wide. Sorcha's chin was tipped down but her eyes were fixed on Lacie. It appeared she'd perfected the disapproving mother stare already.

"Hi," Lacie said when Sorcha didn't say anything.

"I'm waiting to hear your explanation."

"My explanation?" Lacie asked.

"I'm not fooled, Lace," Sorcha said, propping a hand on the doorframe to drum her manicured nails on it. "You didn't come here for space."

"Then why did I come here?" Lacie asked, fearful that she would reveal more of herself to her friend than was safe.

"I don't know," Sorcha said. "That's why I need an explanation."

Sorcha came into the room now and flicked on the light Lacie had neglected to turn on even as night drew closer. "Where's Lulu?"

"Downstairs, in the lobby," Sorcha said, going to sit in an armchair that stood in the corner.

Lacie's eyes slunk to the side. "In the bar with a martini, or…?"

"She's perfectly safe," Sorcha said. "Don't change the subject. Why are you here?"

"Why is it so hard for everyone to comprehend that I just need space?" Lacie asked, crossing to sit on the corner of the bed opposite Sorcha.

"I have a new baby," Sorcha said. "But I've been at S.I.S. all day, doing what I can to help. I'm pitching in."

That was a surprise that Lacie hadn't expected. "You are?"

"Yes."

"Why?" Lacie asked and her intrigue deepened the groove between her brows. "When I was kidnapped—"

"Ryder did everything humanly possible to find you," Sorcha said, leaning toward her to take her hand. "He went out of his mind doing what needed to be done. He doubted his own best friend for God's sake. He actually listened to and relied on Shep when the shit hit the fan. Saving you was worth forging an alliance with a man he'd always detested… Ryder's gone for a couple of days and you check out. It doesn't make sense."

"What happened with Bruce?" Lacie asked. She had neglected her friend duties. The kidnapper hadn't told her not to go out or follow up with Sorcha, so there was no reason not to have acted as she usually would with her friend. Except to do that, she'd have to have a conversation and that would mean lying.

"What happened with Bruce is irrelevant to this conversation," Sorcha said, loosening her hand from Lacie's and standing up. "There's something going on with you and—"

"I need some space!" Lacie said. Thrusting to her feet, she paced away from Sorcha. "My God, Sorch! Why can everyone else say they need a time out and people just accept it? But I say it and suddenly everyone wants to be a part of my business? Can't you see how much my life has changed? Last year we were just… we were free and single and none of this was a part of our lives. We didn't have men worries and kids and kidnappings to think about. It was just you and me living our lives and it worked!"

"Are you telling me that you're turning your back on Ryder? That you're walking away from your relationship with him? Dumping him when he could be out there getting tortured or something?"

Her chest sank when she exhaled a puff of breath. "No. I love Ryder. Everyone knows that I do… I just… I need you to trust me."

"Trust you?" Sorcha asked. "Trust you can have, but support? I don't accept this. I don't accept that you would flout your relationship with the man who has turned the world upside down to look for you… I can't support it."

Sorcha's morals were picking an odd time to assert themselves. But this wasn't about her being righteous, this was Sorcha's way of telling Lacie that she knew something was wrong and she was right. Lacie just couldn't tell her that.

"Thank you for coming," Lacie said. "I want to be alone for a while."

"You can be alone for as long as you like," Sorcha said, striding across the room with her nose in the air. "Just don't be surprised if trust isn't easy to earn back."

"Kiss Lulu for me," Lacie said, catching the door as Sorcha threw it open.

Sorcha hooked her purse higher on her arm. "When you get your head out your ass, you can kiss her yourself."

Judgment coming from Sorcha might seem rich, except Lacie couldn't blame her friend for her attitude. If Lacie could this easily turn her back on her lover then Sorcha had to be wondering if she would do the same if her best friend was in peril.

Lacie stepped into the corridor to watch Sorcha flounce to the elevator and disappear inside. No one else was around, so she went back into her room. As soon as the door closed, she turned off the light and slid down the door to hold her head in her hands.

Being separated from Ryder was hard enough, now the kidnapper had her isolating herself from her friends as well. This could be what the kidnapper wanted, to break her, and if it was, she started to believe that he might succeed.

A buzzing sound made her lift her head. It was coming from within the room and it grew in volume. Crawling toward the noise, she tried to figure its origin and found herself pressing her ear to one of the drawers beneath the TV. It was definitely coming from in there so she yanked it open and was dismayed to find a cellphone inside.

The number was unknown, but she picked it up knowing that it could only be one person.

"You are good at this, very obedient," the voice said.

"What is the point of this?" Lacie asked, collapsing back to sit on the floor with her spine flush on the bed. "Are you getting some sick kick out of alienating me from my friends?"

"Once again, I tell you, not everything is about Lacie Hart. I don't give a damn about you."

"Then why are you trying to hurt me?"

"I would think it was obvious that the person we're trying to hurt here is your lover not your heart."

Then they were getting two for the price of one because hurting her lover meant hurting her heart. "You know what? You can go to hell," Lacie snapped. "I have spent all day fretting and arguing with the people I care about most. My friends think I've gone off my rocker and they're not far from right."

"Cursing at the person who has your prize, do you think that's wise?"

"You tell me that you have him, why should I believe you?" she asked. "How do I know he's still alive? Maybe this is just some sick game."

"Killing Ryder would relieve me of my leverage. No, keeping him alive is your goal and to do it, you have to do exactly what I say."

"No," Lacie said, tipping up her chin in unison with her rising determination. "I won't do another thing, not one thing, not until you let me talk to him."

"Talk to him? Why would I do that?"

"Because if you don't, I'll assume that he's dead. I'll go to the police and I'll tell them everything I know."

"That would result in his death."

"He might already be dead," Lacie said, grabbing the entertainment unit to haul herself onto her feet. "I want to talk to him, now. If he's alive, I don't see why that would be a problem… unless you don't have him at all."

"We have him!"

Pushing the patience of this tormentor had paid off already. "We" suggested that there was more than one person involved, that or the kidnapper had a split personality.

"Then let me talk to him," Lacie said.

The line went dead. Lacie took the phone from her ear to look at it in case they'd lost signal. They hadn't. Fixating on the reflection of herself in the wall-mounted mirror through the shadows of night she'd let encroach on her room, the deafening silence was punctuated by her short, sharp pants. Had she made a mistake? Had the kidnapper understood his misstep? Now that she'd annoyed him, he could be taking out that annoyance on Ryder.

Clutching the phone to her chest, she prayed that Ryder was safe, and prayed that the kidnapper would call back. Seconds, which felt like hours, passed and her breathing got faster. Though she'd been begging for it, she was startled when the handset burst into life and began to ring again.

Answering the call, her hand shook as she brought it up to her ear. "Hello?" she asked.

"Dusty?"

"Ah," she croaked and collapsed onto the floor again. "Baby, oh my God, Ryder. Are you okay? I love you."

"I love you too and I'm fine," he said, speaking as if there was some urgency at his end. "Listen to me, you go to Gabe, okay? You go to him and you tell him to forget it. Tell him I'm gone. Tell him I'm dead."

"Why would I—"

"Just do it, baby," he said. "I love you. I'll always love you."

"Why are you—"

"Don't do another thing that he tells you to, okay? He's going to kill me anyway, you have to know that."

"No," she said. "No, I'm not going to let that happen. We're going to get through this. I need you to fight. Believe in me like I believed in you. I knew you would figure Wallace out and I'm going to figure this out for you."

"No, Lacie's it's—"

"Time's up," the kidnapper's voice came onto the line and Lacie heard a scuffle in the background.

There was some swearing, but Ryder's voice was quickly muffled and then there was nothing but the usual silence behind the voice that tormented her.

"If you hurt him—"

"What?" the kidnapper sneered. "You're not capable of hurting me. You don't even know who I am. Don't know where Ryder is, what's motivating me, or who I have on the inside listening to every word you say."

Her attention drifted up and she began to glance around the room. If he had been in there to plant the phone, it was possible he'd planted cameras or listening equipment too. Lacie wished she could speak to Toby. He would be able to tell her how to seek out bugs. He'd be able to tap into the hotel security system and check cameras that could reveal the kidnapper's identity.

Discovering her own conniving streak, she began to think of how she could get Toby to do what she needed him too without betraying her motivation for being here.

"What's your next instruction?" Lacie asked.

"Plan to ignore your love's suggestion to return to your former residence?"

"I plan to do whatever is necessary to protect Ryder."

"Good," the kidnapper said and the thread of pleasure in his tone made her scowl.

"Your hotel stay was temporary. A stepping stone to take us to the next stage."

"Which is what?" she asked, sitting on the bed.

"A good friend of yours is out of town at the moment. He'll be back tomorrow around lunchtime. I want you to call him and invite him to dinner tomorrow night."

"Dinner?" Lacie asked, trying to fathom where this was leading.

"Yes, dinner," the kidnapper said.

"Who?" she asked. Lacie didn't know which one of her friends was in town or out. She hadn't been paying attention to much since the kidnapping event, which she knew now was exactly what this guy had wanted.

"Mr. Elijah Graden of course," the kidnapper drawled with a heightened enjoyment in his voice.

"What has Elijah got to do with this?" she asked. As far as she knew, Elijah didn't know that any of this was going on. Unless he was related and somehow was using this situation to his advantage. "Is he a part of your scheme?"

"No, Elijah has been out of town for the last couple of days. I'm sure he'll be very surprised to receive your call. But he'll be even more surprised about your request."

"What request?"

"In this time of need, I wouldn't want you to think that it was my goal to isolate you," he said, but the kindness was contrived and he made no secret of that. "You're going to ask if you can stay with him."

"What? Because you think that me being there will upset Ryder? Ryder knows that I would never—"

"Never what?" he snapped. "You will do what you are told and you'll have no say in that."

Could this person be considering using their current positions to coerce her into Elijah's heart, into his bed? That was something she could never imagine. She couldn't imagine any man except Ryder touching her. But she wouldn't protest, wouldn't put the idea in this man's head. All she could do was hope it wouldn't come to that.

FORTY-FIVE

Lacie

"I WAS VERY SURPRISED to receive your call," Elijah said over dinner the following night.

Lacie had asked him to meet her at the hotel because it was the least amount of effort and she didn't want there to be any confusion that this was a fancy date or anything of that sort. They had gotten through the awkward first drink and the starter. The entrée in front of her didn't appear to be appetizing, but food had lost its taste the minute she heard Ryder was AWOL.

"I just needed a friend," she said, using the kidnapper's line because she was too tired to come up with her own. "I've been… struggling for a few days."

She had told Elijah about Ryder's disappearance already. Though as she said the words, she felt like he already knew. That made her suspicious about his involvement. But this kidnapper wanted to play with her mind. This could all be a con. A ruse cooked up to make her crazy with paranoia. Even if Elijah did know about Ryder, it was likely he'd been told by a colleague or friend who may have used Ryder's services in the past. That he was missing was no longer a secret. Even the police were investigating and she knew that because Deacon called her only to be surprised to hear that Lacie wasn't a part of the S.I.S. investigation.

"I was having my own men investigate your assault," Elijah said. "I had no idea that Ryder was at risk."

"None of us did," Lacie said, fumbling with her napkin in her lap.

"I don't see security here for you."

When they'd gone to lunch together on Lulu's birthday, her security was visible. Today, she was alone. "They have to focus their efforts on finding Ryder."

"And you are not taking part in those investigations?"

"I needed to get away, get some space, you know? I had to get out of that house but was just filled with Ryder."

"Yes, of course," he said. "Given your own history, this abduction must be bringing back painful memories."

"Yes," she said.

The experience wasn't bringing back memories of her abduction as it was bringing back memories of betrayal. When she discovered that Ryder's best friend, Jamie, was behind her abduction, her heart had broken for her love. Every time Jamie came to talk to her, she wanted to spit at the man who would spit on her love.

Lacie was betraying those around her because this lunatic wanted her to. Lying to her friends was difficult. But it was harder to look at the faces of the men and women you had trusted with your life and not know which of them were in league with the person causing this torture.

They kept eating. Lacie was psyching herself up. This particular task was distasteful, she didn't want to use Elijah. If he was not involved then leading him on could hurt him. She also dreaded the idea that the next task could lead on from moving in with Elijah and she couldn't see any avenue other than an intimate one that they could take.

Elijah sipped his wine. "This is a very nice hotel."

"It is," she said. "But…" She didn't want to ask, didn't want to be social with a man who could be overbearing, not when her heart and body still belonged to Ryder. "I wanted to ask if I could stay with you." The sentence came out in one long rush of breath and she forced herself to make eye contact as she said it.

Elijah lowered his glass to the table then reached over to take her hand. "Of course you can, Lacie. I'm so pleased that you would ask. That you would choose to come to me for help. That's all I've ever wanted, Lacie. I want to help you."

His smile wasn't pitying, but it wasn't really genuine either. Lacie was asking a favor of someone who was likely to read too much into what was going on. The kidnapper would call her again tonight and she would demand more answers because as far as she could see, this sequence of events had no purpose other than to humiliate and damage her and Ryder.

FORTY-SIX

EXCEPT THE KIDNAPPER didn't call. Lacie went home with Elijah, who settled her into a guest bedroom. All night, she lay on her side staring at the cellphone she had brought from the hotel and it didn't ring once. At some point, she drifted off to sleep and she was awoken by staff bringing her breakfast in bed.

Elijah was at the office. But his staff had been briefed to provide her with every luxury possible. In his vast mansion, he had the facilities to entertain and pamper her. Lacie tried to keep up the façade of gratitude, but she really just wanted to scream at these people to leave her alone so that she could brood and worry in peace.

A second day passed with no contact and a third. Elijah treated her to lavish dinners and took her out to the opera. None of it meant anything to her, yet he was trying so hard to win her favor. If he saw this as an opportunity to steal her heart from Ryder then he was going to be disappointed. She wanted to believe that he couldn't be that cold-hearted and callous, but he had tried to tempt her away from Ryder on the day Lulu was born, so it was no secret that he believed himself more worthy of her.

Her nerves were fraying with every second of radio silence, she kept the cellphone on her person at all times now, never sure when it could ring. She believed that it may never ring again. Maybe this was what the kidnapper wanted, to set her up here until she gave into Elijah's charms. Maybe something had happened with Ryder, if there had been a fight maybe someone was hurt or worse.

If the kidnapper had no leverage left, he could have tucked tail and run. In which case, Lacie didn't need to be here anymore. Except how could she know? How long should she give it before she gave up hope of hearing this phone ring?

In the bedroom, she sat on the bed to pull on her pantyhose, then she slipped into the dress Elijah had bought her for dinner that night. She still hadn't been back to S.I.S. for the rest of her things. The men there hadn't kicked her out, but they hadn't sought her out either.

Before she could put on her shoes, the bedroom door burst open and she leaped to her feet, believing Elijah was the only one as bold as to storm in. Except it was Sorcha who threw the door shut behind her with such a bang that it made Lacie jump.

"Elijah Graden?" Sorcha said, thrusting her hands to her hips. "You're living with Elijah Graden?"

"I'm surprised it took this long for you to find out. I've been here for three days."

"I heard about it on day one, but I assumed you would come to your senses. I made excuses for you with Gabe. I told him that you would have a reason. Three days later, you're still here… do you want to tell me your reason?"

"What are you doing with Gabe?" Lacie asked, taking a step in Sorcha's direction.

"What am I doing there? The question is, what are you doing not there? I can't believe you, Lacie. I really can't figure you out. I am supposed to be the flake. I am supposed to be the one who needs to have a man in her life in order to receive validation… Are you sleeping with him?"

"No!" Lacie exclaimed. "Of course not! This is a guest room. I have my own private bedroom… Do the guys think I'm sleeping with him?"

"Probably," Sorcha said. "They don't say it in front of me, they don't want to upset me when I'm still hormonal."

"Where is Lulu?" she asked, looking around as though the baby would magically appear.

"She's in the car. We're not staying," Sorcha said. "Some of us have work to do."

"You can't leave a baby alone in a car," Lacie said, hurrying toward the door.

"It's a private driveway and it's night outside," Sorcha said, which made Lacie stop. "Besides, I didn't say she was alone."

"You're still with Bruce?" Lacie asked, peering at her friend. "How can you—"

"How can you? Do you not love Ryder anymore? Do you know something about this that the rest of us don't? I just can't figure out why you would run away like this. Ryder needs you."

"I know," Lacie said, clamping her back teeth together. "I know he needs me."

"So what are you doing here? Lounging around in some pretty boy's mansion being waited on by the staff. This isn't you. This has never been you! You used to argue when we were at my parents' house that you had to help in the kitchen even though we had a four person dedicated staff. I never knew why you felt the need, but you would still go in and peel or stir, do whatever the chef told you."

"I know."

"Then what the hell are you doing here?" Sorcha asked, throwing up her hands then grabbing Lacie to shake her. "Enough, Lacie, you can't run from this anymore. We need you. Ryder needs you. Why are you trying so hard to make us believe that you don't care?"

"I do care," Lacie insisted, but the tears were already blurring her vision. "I do care. I care more than you know. More than any of you realize."

"Can you blame us? We're busting our asses to do whatever is needed to get Ryder home safe and you're swanning around in hotels and going to the opera. It's like you couldn't care less. He could be dead out there!"

"He's not dead," Lacie said, shaking her head so fast that she shook her tears loose. "He's not dead."

"It seems like you wouldn't care either way."

"I do! I do care! Keeping him alive is all that matters to me!"

"You have to face it, Lacie. Face the truth that he could be dead. I need you to face it."

"He's not," Lacie shouted, wrenching her arms away from Sorcha. "He is not dead!"

"You can't possibly know that, none of us can."

"I can!" The quiver in her voice came before her desperate gasp. "I do know! He's not dead! He's not!"

"How can you—"

"Because I spoke to him," Lacie said and immediately drew her lips into her mouth. Her face was numb, her tears skidded in haphazard waterfalls down each of her cheeks and dripped onto her dress. But with wide eyes she fixated on Sorcha. When she couldn't take it anymore and had to breathe, she gasped in oxygen and let her knees release her weight and crumpled onto the floor.

Her sobbing brought Sorcha down with her. Lacie was gathered up against her friend who let her cry without any questions for a couple of minutes. Sorcha stroked a hand down her hair and then eased her back.

"When did you speak to him?" Sorcha asked.

Sorcha was so calm and Lacie was grateful of that strength now. It was possible that Sorcha believed her insane or that she had dreamed a conversation. Now that she'd said the words though, Lacie couldn't take them back. Trusting Sorcha was easy. With a new baby and a love triangle to deal with, Sorcha probably had little time left to be duplicitous.

"Five days ago," Lacie said, having felt every minute of their separation since then. "It was five days ago. I had dinner with Elijah the following night and I've been here ever since."

"You mean you spoke to him after he disappeared," Sorcha asked, now registering the weight of what they were dealing with. Lacie nodded and wiped her tears with her hands. "Why didn't you—"

"He told me not to. He swore me to secrecy."

"Ryder swore you to—"

"Not him," Lacie said. Revealing the truth was the only way to get Sorcha to keep quiet. Having a cohort may ease her burden, but Lacie was lumping a burden onto Sorcha by asking her to perpetuate the secret. "The kidnapper."

"Oh my God," Sorcha said, falling off her perch on her own heels to bump down onto the carpet. "You've spoken to the…?"

"Yes," Lacie said with a nod. "He called me the first night after Shep took me to my room and told me to get some sleep."

"Why didn't you tell anyone?"

"I couldn't," Lacie said, hoping her friend could understand her dilemma. "He told me not to. He swore me to secrecy. He said that he was watching and listening. He told me that he had a mole and that I couldn't trust anyone."

"But you're telling me now," Sorcha said, Lacie hadn't noticed her blink, Sorcha's eyes seemed to be getting wider and wider.

"I haven't heard from him in the three days I've been here. The last time he called me was the day I spoke to Ryder. After he took the phone from Ryder, he told me to call Elijah, to have dinner with him and ask him for a place to stay."

"So you did?" Lacie nodded and swiped away her new tears. "God, this must have been hell for you."

Sorcha crawled over to hug her again. Having someone to lean on who didn't judge her almost made her cry tears for a different reason.

"I'm sorry I didn't… I didn't know what to do and when he told me not to trust anyone…"

"It's okay," Sorcha said, taking her hands when she sat back. "We just have to figure out what to do now."

"You can't tell anyone," Lacie said, clutching at her friend. "Please, Sorch, I don't know who to trust."

"You can trust me."

"I know that," Lacie said, pursing a smile. "I just didn't want to burden you with this when you have Lulu and Bruce—"

"I kicked Bruce out," Sorcha said. "I saw Shep after I spoke to you and he showed me everything, then he came with me to confront Bruce."

"He came with you?"

Sorcha shrugged. "I think he wanted to look after me," she snorted. "Like I need looking after."

Before Lulu, Lacie would have laughed at that assertion because it sounded ludicrous. After Lulu, Lacie actually believed that Sorcha was capable of anything and was beginning to see that herself.

"So who has Lulu in the car? Elijah would—"

"Shep," Sorcha said and when she turned her smile to the carpet Lacie's jaw loosened. Sorch was blushing like she was actually playing coy. "He's been… helping out."

"Has he?" Lacie asked. Sorch deserved happiness and Lulu deserved a stable male figure in her life and that man was never going to be Bruce. Sure, he might have visitation, he was Lulu's father. But Shep had done a lot of growing up since Lacie had met him and she wondered how he'd take to the role of father.

"Lulu and Shep are fine," Sorcha said. "We have to focus on how to help Ryder."

"No one can know that I told you, Sorch. I mean it, no one." Sorcha wasn't known for her ability to keep a secret.

Her friend was nonplussed by the constant reminder for the need of secrecy. "Who do you think is behind this?" Sorcha asked, folding her knees to one side.

"If I knew that then I would call the police… or Gabe."

"You miss him, don't you?" Sorcha leaned over to curl her fingers around Lacie's.

"I miss them all," Lacie said, regretting that she ever complained about Ryder being vigilant when it came to security. "I miss being in Ryder's bed and having them all there to look out for me … I promise that once we get Ryder back, I will never complain about another of his rules. But I'm going to make him follow them too. From now on I'll expend as much energy keeping him safe as he does on me."

Sorcha smiled, then the moment was over and she became more serious. "So what's your plan?"

"My plan was to do as I was told and to get Ryder back," Lacie said, pushing up off the floor to stride to the bed. It wasn't much, but she had to feel like she was doing something. "Now that he's stopped issuing instructions"—she whirled around and sagged to display her exhaustion—"I have no plan."

"We'll come up with one together," Sorcha said. "We always work well as a team."

In the past, Lacie had been the one cleaning up Sorcha's messes and now it appeared that Sorcha was ready to pay her back for every one of those times with her allegiance now.

"I have to go to dinner with Elijah," Lacie said, picking up the edge of her dress. "He keeps asking me to go places and I don't feel right saying no. How can I beg a place to stay one day and then shun him the next? That's how I ended up going to the opera with him. I think that he thinks…"

"He finally has you," Sorcha said. If there was one thing Sorcha knew, it was men. "We'll just have to remedy that. Shep is outside with Lulu, why don't we join you for dinner tonight?"

That suggestion perked Lacie up, eating in a group would lessen her need to follow along with conversation. With her thoughts constantly sliding back to Ryder, sometimes it was difficult to keep track of what Elijah was talking about.

"Would you?" Lacie said, so grateful that she actually lunged at Sorcha to pull her into a hug. "I would appreciate that. I would… just to have others there…"

"Shep was supposed to be going over to S.I.S., but I figure we can make excuses."

"The guys might be suspicious if he doesn't turn up when he's supposed to. Especially if they hear that he was with me. I don't want them to think I'm poisoning their effort to find Ryder."

"All this guy told you was that you shouldn't tell anyone, right?" Sorcha asked. "So if they find out on their own then that's not your fault, is it?"

"Sorcha," Lacie said, meeting her eye. "You cannot tell them."

"I won't! I promise. Anyway, it's Shep, how reliable is he?"

Sorcha made a valid point. People expected Shep to be lazy and fickle, so skipping out on work to have dinner with three females was completely his style. "What if Elijah says no?"

"Pah," Sorcha said, waving a hand to dismiss Lacie's concern. "Men don't say no to me… You stay in here and keep getting ready." Lacie was ready, but Sorcha was giving her cover to avoid the conversation with Elijah. "I'll tell Elijah there's been a change of plans and then tell Shep. We will all fit in one car, so we can travel together."

"I can handle that," Lacie said. "Sorch, I'm so happy that you know."

"You should've come to me right away," Sorcha said. "We deal with everything together, highs and lows, we're a team."

Hugging Sorcha gave Lacie the first comfort she'd experienced in days. The kidnapper still hadn't been in touch and she was no closer to an answer as to why. But now that she had Sorcha on her side, Lacie felt like she was a step closer to victory.

FORTY-SEVEN

Ryder

RYDER HAD BEEN stuck in this room for days. The chains on his arms didn't give him much freedom. Not that it mattered because there wasn't a window in the place and the door looked to be steel reinforced. It didn't help that they'd kept him drugged for most of his time here. He hadn't gotten a good look at his captors either. The only one to come inside was male, but the lights were kept off so that Ryder couldn't look at him and they didn't talk to him either.

He knew that there was more than one person involved because he'd heard muffled conversation from the other side of the door. At first, he'd tried to call out, but no one had come and he had given up within a couple of days. His wrists were already raw from his struggle against his restraints and he began to worry about infection and how it would weaken him if he was here for a considerable amount of time.

Noise from beyond the room made him stand up, he had the ability to do that at least. But no matter how hard he craned his neck, trying to listen closer, he heard nothing specific. The last thing he'd heard clearly was her voice. Lacie. The male captor had come in and demanded that he speak to Lacie once he dialed the phone, but he was not to give her any indication of where he was or the conditions. That was fine by him.

Ryder didn't want Lacie coming anywhere near this place, not that he knew the location. And the conditions he existed in were irrelevant in the face of her suffering. He would not pity himself or have her feel sorry for him. These people would let him know eventually what they wanted and if that cost was his life, well, rather his than Lacie's was his thinking. He didn't want his girl or his men walking into anything that might be a trap.

The noise outside was closer now and it was split into two separate voices. One was deep, and the other was higher pitched, so he would suspect they were a male and a female, and they were right outside the door. From the hurried intonation and the way the voices overlapped, he assumed they were arguing. Conflict was good for him. He tucked that piece of information away because it could save his life. This couple was at odds about something. Whether they were family or romantically involved, it didn't matter.

The conflict was a crack in unity and that was one of the first things he told his men never to reveal in front of enemies. If an enemy got the chance to turn them against each other he would take it and that was what Ryder would do at his first chance. Getting a wedge in between this pair and prying it as far open as possible might be his ticket out. Invariably, there was one person with more invested in a kidnap job like this and if Ryder could befriend the other one it might get him out.

From everything Lacie had told him about her time in captivity, Jamie Wallace had been the only one to come near her or talk to her. Ryder had trained Jamie, so it didn't surprise him to hear that. Jamie probably had a lot of strain in his lower ranks. That and most of the guys were idiots. If Ryder was only dealing with two people, his odds of getting out of here relied solely on him getting out of these chains. Once he was out, he could take out both of them.

The overhead light flashed on and Ryder blinked his eyes trying to adjust them to the illumination as quickly as he could. Any chance he got to get loose and get back to his girl, he would take it. No one had come in and there were no switches on the walls, so the light had to be controlled from outside, which meant it could have been turned on by accident.

The concrete walls and floor were bare and gray, perfect for keeping a person in lock-up, and there wasn't a stick of furniture in sight, so he had nothing to use as a weapon if things got physical. Focused on the door, he willed it to open, and sure enough after another few tense seconds, he heard the click of a lock. Although the door was sturdy, the lock didn't sound it, if he could get out of these chains and strike when no one was around, he might just make it out of here under his own steam.

The door began to open and he braced to see who was responsible for keeping him here. But when his captor came around the door from the blackened hallway, Ryder was surprised. He'd expected a big guy, built with muscle and with a mean look on his face. This man had too fine a bone structure to be considered mean, but from the scowl on his face Ryder believed he thought himself dangerous. There wasn't a scar on his face, not a sign of having ever been in a fight and as soon as he put a finger on the guy's identity, he understood the slacks and opened cuffed shirt.

"You're Elijah Graden's younger brother," Ryder said. His linked hands came up to his forehead as his head went back and he laughed. Any fear he'd had dissipated. This guy had to be a flunky. In Ryder's time investigating the elder Graden brother, the younger one, Evan, came across as plain. So plain in fact, it would be an insult to call him vanilla. "This is about getting Lacie into bed."

"My God," Evan Graden said, coming in and pulling the door over at his back. "Do I have to say it to you as well? Not everything is about Lacie Hart."

"If you're not working with your brother then who are you working with?" Ryder asked, lowering his hands, and taking the time to listen to his captor hoping to discover clues of how to ingratiate himself. He kept one eye on the still open door too. The door was only open a couple of inches, but if he could get the chains off, that would be all he needed.

"What makes you think I'm working with anyone?" Evan asked. He was tall, about Ryder's height, but Ryder would be surprised if he could press fifty pounds.

"Okay then, Mastermind," Ryder said, leaning on the wall and picking up a boot to prop it on the wall too. "What can I do for you, huh? You've had me in here about a week. Isn't it time for the big reveal or was your entrance supposed to make me quiver in my boots?"

Evan said nothing for a few seconds and then his face contorted into the oddest smile that was pleased and smug, yet it didn't reach vicious. "Do you think much about Lacie?"

"Is that what you want to talk about? My girl. You could've just called me on the phone. I would've told you to go to hell then and there without you having to go to this trouble. Was it you who drugged her in the gallery? You who attacked her in your brother's cabin? What am I thinking? He's working with you, right?"

"Elijah is far too busy to deal with you," Evan said. "He's at dinner with Lacie and Sorcha and baby Lulu. They make quite the picture… She's living with him now, you know."

Grinding his teeth, Ryder tried not to give Evan the satisfaction of riling him. "She's a beautiful woman. Sorcha too," Ryder said.

"You never did get along with Sorcha, did you? You just pushed and pushed. It's nice to see Lacie's best friend get along so well with the new man in her life."

"Try as hard as you like to convince me that Lacie's being unfaithful… it's not going to make a difference to me."

"You're not as invincible as you believe yourself to be," Evan said. "I would think that this experience would prove that. You're not as smart as you think. Lacie's kidnapping, that incident at the gallery, it was all theater. Sleight of hand if you will. I wanted you to look at the left hand so that the right hand could take the prize from under your noses."

"And I was the prize," Ryder said, losing eye contact and tilting his head to convey he was unthreatened. "Well done. Touché. Is that it? Was that the whole point? Because we both know you don't have it in you to hurt anyone."

"Don't be too sure about that," Evan said. "Maybe I don't have your strength and if we were to go man-to-man, maybe you could take me out."

"Maybe?" Ryder asked, letting his own amused smile grow. "Why don't you undo the chains and we'll see? I'll let you throw the first punch… hell, I'll give you the first two. That's sporting, right?"

"Who needs sport?" Reaching behind himself, Evan pulled something from a rear pocket and he held it up to show Ryder what it was, a capped syringe filled with a clear liquid. "Drugs are cheap and they come in all sizes and flavors. I'll bet a man like you knows a thing or two about pain… all it takes is the right cocktail."

As far as Ryder was concerned, sticking a guy with a needle then running away was the epitome of cowardice. If someone was going to go to the effort to kidnap a person, they should at least have the balls to see the experience through to the end.

"I can use this to control you," Evan said. "It's what you were stuck with in the alley and you were down in a second. And I can use you to control Lacie… You see"—he began to saunter closer—"she is my puppet. She is dancing to my tune. All I have to do is issue a command and she complies, which is why I know that when I tell her to visit my brother in his bed, she will do exactly that. As long as we have you, she will do whatever she's told."

Ryder pushed away from the wall to get in Evan's face, but the bastard was still just out of reach. "Leave her out of this."

"You were right in one respect, Mr. Stone. I'm not working alone. And I know Lacie will get everything she deserves, just as you will. I knew she was afraid of it happening again. Of experiencing another trauma caused by the betrayal of someone close to her… or to you. That's Lacie's greatest fear. She's so paranoid right now that she trusts no one, not your men, or her own best friend. Lacie is mine, no one else's."

"If you want her so bad, why are you sending her to your brother?"

"I don't want her," he said, spitting out the words. "I don't want any of those stuck-up bitches. All of them believe they're better, believe they deserve the world and I'm tired of it."

"Ah," Ryder said. Opening his mouth to draw in a breath. He bobbed his head in understanding. "Trouble in the sack, is it? Never happened to me, not with my girl, but… there are medications and shit… or is it getting one as far as the bed that's the problem? I bet they take one look at you and one look at your brother and know they'd rather have the original model. No woman wants a guy who'll never be any better than second chair."

"You are just as bad," he sneered. "What gives you this arrogance?"

"If you lay one finger on Lacie, or force her to go anywhere near your brother, I'll rip every limb from your body," Ryder said, slowly. "Do what the fuck you want to me. But after your brother is convicted of rape and he's rotting in that shit-stew of a maximum-security prison, I'll get to you and when I do, I'll teach you something about pain."

"You'll keep," Evan said and smiled again though the polished exterior was slipping, his chin had lost some of its starch. "I have a phone call to make… would you like me to pass on a message to your former girlfriend?"

"Yeah," Ryder said, seeing an inch of opportunity to help Lacie even when he couldn't help himself. "You can tell my Little Lady that she's safe and that all orders remain current."

"And you think I have trouble charming women," he mocked then left the room. The door closed, the lock snicked, and the lights went back out. He couldn't be sure. But if Evan delivered that message verbatim then maybe Lacie could gain herself an ally.

FORTY-EIGHT

Lacie

SHE HAD FEARED this was coming. Since the madman started giving her instructions, she had feared him telling her to betray Ryder. As if it wasn't bad enough that she had already turned her back on Ryder's men and the quest to find her love, now she would have to do that which could not be undone.

Dinner the previous night with Sorcha and Shep had been the most relaxed she'd been since this began. Her worry for Ryder remained as intense, but she had an ally in Sorcha now. Once she and Elijah had gotten back to his home, Lacie had made her excuses and gone straight to bed. Not that she slept. As she had done for days, she lay staring at the cellphone, begging it to ring. When it actually did begin to flash, she sat up and froze for a second believing that she may have drifted off to sleep and imagined the whole thing.

When she hung up the phone, she felt no more reassured, in fact she felt sick down in the pit of her stomach. She'd sworn to do whatever it took to keep

Ryder safe, to get him back alive, and now she had to make the ultimate sacrifice. To save his life, she had to be unfaithful.

Elijah had called her from work to make dinner plans and she had dressed herself up as she always did. Descending the stairs to meet him the foyer, she took one look at him and knew she had to bite the bullet, to do it now, or she would lose her nerve.

"You look sensational, as always," he said, coming to the bottom of the stairs to meet her.

"Thank you," Lacie said. "Can we sit down for a minute?"

"Of course we can," he said, guiding her from the bottom stairs around to the chaise lounge that sat beside the staircase. "Is something wrong?"

"No," she said, trying her best to smile, but the nausea in her stomach grew and she had to grit her teeth and clear her throat to prevent the acid in her guts from making an appearance.

With shaking fingers, she took his hand and moved it onto her lap. Her digits were icy cold and he must have felt this because he used his other hand to rub some heat into her, but it didn't work. The frost that had overcome her was not because of the temperature in the room. It came from the realization that when she did this, when she followed through, she would never be able to take the act back and that she herself would be delivering that fatal blow to Ryder's soul when he heard of what she'd done. She wouldn't be able to deny it.

Privacy and loyalty were the words that kept circulating in her brain. But when she lifted her chin to look Elijah in the eye, his concern made tears blur her eyes. Elijah wasn't a bad man, not as far as she knew, and he would be heartbroken to discover he'd been used. One way or another this situation was going to end and when the kidnapper relinquished his grip on her, she would have to tell Elijah the truth too.

"What's the matter, Lacie?" he asked and kept rubbing her hand.

Bringing her other fingers up to his face, she tried to imagine Ryder, tried to imagine that he was the one here with her and that he was going to make everything okay. But Elijah's skin wasn't like Ryder's, their gaze was different, everything about them was different. More than that, Lacie knew that Ryder didn't like Elijah, that he'd been suspicious of his feelings for her since he learned of their association.

"I have to do something," she said, parting her lips just enough to say the words.

Straightening her spine, her height grew enough to bring her lips near to Elijah's. Squeezing her eyes closed, tears skittered down her cheeks, but she kept on going.

"Lacie, what is the matter?" Elijah asked, moving away from her advance.

Sagging back, her face fell into her hands and she admitted defeat. "I can't do it."

"Can't do what?" Elijah asked. "You're acting very strange. I know that things have been difficult for you recently. But this isn't you…"

Her tears were in free-fall now and she curled as low as she could. By refusing this instruction, she may have just signed Ryder's death warrant and all because she couldn't bring herself to be intimate with the man who was so gracious in his kindness toward her.

The front door opened, but Lacie didn't care about who was coming in or what else was going on around her. Elijah rubbed her back as she cried, but he didn't question her. Then she heard Sorcha's voice.

"What's going on?" Sorcha asked. "What did you do to her?"

"Nothing," Elijah protested. "She asked to sit down and then… I don't know. She's acting very strange."

"Lacie?" Sorcha soft voice descended on her. When Lacie let her hands part from her face, she saw her friend crouched in front of her. In the background, Lulu fussed, but the stroller wasn't in her eye line. "Honey, what's wrong? Did you get news?"

Lacie stared into Sorcha's face and the numbness grew until she glanced at another person behind Sorcha. Lifting her attention, she noticed Shep standing a few feet away wearing an expression of concern and suddenly she understood.

Thrusting to her feet, she strode past Sorcha to Shep. "You," she whispered.

"What about me, Little Lady?" Shep asked.

"You… I can trust you."

"Why would you—"

"He called last night and he gave me a message from Ryder. In that message Ryder called me Little Lady. Ryder never calls me Little Lady."

"Ryder?" Shep asked at the same time Elijah did, giving her the effect in stereo.

In her distress, she had forgotten that Elijah was there. When she spun around, he was on his feet and coming toward her. "How could you receive a message from Ryder?" Elijah asked.

Looking beyond him to Sorcha, Lacie hoped that her friend could offer some way to salvage this situation, but Sorcha just shrugged. "Tell him."

"Are you in on it?" Lacie asked, searching Elijah's expression for proof that he knew or didn't know about Ryder's predicament.

"In on what?" Elijah asked, glancing to every face in the space. "What is going on?"

"Your note in the hospital," Lacie asked. "What did that mean?"

"I…" His face brightened and he glanced at the others. "Your fear… that you would be hurt by another of Stone's men. I knew you had to be afraid of that and I wanted to offer you protection from them."

"From them?" Lacie exhaled. "So you're not involved?"

Elijah's patience vanished. "Would someone tell me what is going on?"

"Lacie has been called by the kidnapper," Sorcha said to him.

"What?" Shep snapped. "When the hell did—"

"She told me yesterday," Sorcha said. "Maybe we should all sit down and talk about this."

"Sorcha, I…" Lacie was still hesitant to reveal all when she'd been told so explicitly not to. But the genie was already out of the bottle. Ryder's message told her that she could trust Shep. By breaking down in front of Elijah and failing to follow through on the order she'd been given, if Elijah was in on the scheme, she had already given him all he needed to blow apart the whole affair.

FORTY-NINE

Lacie

"HE WAS TELLING me to go home," Lacie said into the glass of wine that Sorcha had poured for her.

Seated in Elijah's private dining room, she and Sorcha relayed the facts to Shep and Elijah and braced for their responses. Lulu was in her seat at the head of the table sleeping soundly and Lacie envied the baby her peace.

"What, honey?" Sorcha asked.

"The second part of Ryder's message was that all orders remain current. He once told me that I belonged at home, with him, and that was an order."

"Either that or he was saying you belong with him," Shep said from his place in front of the window. "Meaning you shouldn't screw around on him with rich bastards like Graden here."

"Now see here," Graden said, leaving his position near the fireplace to point at Shep. "I knew nothing about this, nothing at all."

"So you say," Shep said. He didn't shrink in light of Elijah's anger. He put his own glass of liquor aside to march over and meet Elijah. The men were both mad and stood close enough to each other that she recognized men on the brink of getting physical.

"Please don't fight," Lacie said, rushing over to them. "Please. I know that… emotions are running high and…"

"Shep!" Sorcha declared. "Don't you dare start a fight with Lulu in the room! What would she think if she saw you fighting?"

All of them glanced up at the baby who was still sleeping. Lacie didn't think that Lulu would know any different if the men were fighting because she was still so young. But Sorcha's warning got through to Shep who left Elijah and went up to tuck Lulu's blanket around her.

"I care more about this little girl than you do," Shep said, smoothing a hand over the blanket then standing in front of her as though to shield her from Sorcha. "You wanted to leave her with that lunatic Booth tonight."

"He is her father," Sorcha said, storming up the table. "We can't stop him from having contact with her forever."

"Maybe not, but we should at least try until after the courts have decided what to do with him."

"How come you think you know so much?" Sorcha argued, slamming her hands onto her hips. "You went into a mood when I suggested a sitter too."

Shep's finger came up but his expression became more open. "A babysitter is no substitute for a parent. Especially when she has one like your crazy ex."

He turned to run a hand over Lulu's blanket again.

"Stop pawing at her. You'll wake her up," Sorcha said, elbowing him aside to raise the hood over Lulu's seat.

Watching them argue like a married couple was endearing. They had both fussed over Lulu last night at dinner as well. From what Lacie could tell Shep had moved into Sorcha's place and was taking full-time responsibility for Lulu, sharing parenting with Sorcha. Maybe Lacie wouldn't have pegged him as the parental type. But he would do anything to please Sorcha and maybe along the way of doing that he'd fallen in love with Lulu too.

"Lacie," Elijah said, drawing her attention around. "I really wish you had told me about this."

"I was told not to tell anyone," Lacie said, accepting his hand stroking her arm. He was being supportive, but he had to be embarrassed or angry that what he'd thought was a relationship between them turned out to be a con.

"The pressure of it is just too much," Sorcha said, grabbing Shep to drag him away from Lulu. "Lacie should never have had to deal with this alone. Whoever this man is, he's a crazy person. We can't argue about what's happened already. We have to figure out a plan on how to deal with it now."

"While trying to get Ryder out," Shep said. "We can't leave him there to rot."

"Agreed," Sorcha said.

This couple argued about everything every chance they got. To see them agreeing was a definite indication that their relationship had moved onto something deeper. Lacie wanted that depth to last and now that Lulu had brought them together, they had the best chance they'd ever had of making a relationship with each other work.

"How do you want to deal with it?" Elijah asked. "How should we proceed?"

"You want to help?" Lacie asked having half expected to be thrown out after he discovered the truth.

"I am your friend," Elijah said, resting a hand on her shoulder. "I can't deny that I'm disappointed in your choice of partner. But you've made it clear that Ryder is the man you want to be with. I'll just have to find it in myself to accept that. I do hope that this situation will not affect our friendship."

Lacie imagined that this situation would affect many aspects of her life and her friendships with everyone had been tested. But she didn't have the time to deconstruct that now.

"Of course not," she said and turned to bring Sorcha and Shep into their circle. "Now we have to decide what to do next?"

"The first thing you have to do is make sure the kidnapper believes he's still got the power," Shep said. "Much as I hate saying it… you two have to fake it if you find yourselves in public."

Lacie glanced at Elijah because she wasn't sure how he would react to such a thing. "Of course," Elijah said. "But we must bring this to a head as quickly as possible."

"I'm sure there's no one who thinks that more than Lacie," Shep said, seizing her shoulder to pull her over between him and Sorcha.

It was odd because Ryder and Shep had always butted heads, yet here Shep was being territorial of her too. Was it because he was trying to get into Sorcha's good graces or did he feel felt obliged since Ryder singled him out as trustworthy in his secret message to her?

"What about Gabe?" Sorcha asked. "Can we trust him and the guys?"

"I would suppose that Lacie refrained from telling us about this until now because the person responsible has warned of repercussions for Ryder."

"That's right," Lacie said. "He told me that I couldn't trust anyone. He said he had ears everywhere."

"I would suggest that we use my team to investigate," Elijah said and held up his hands to silence Shep's protests before he could make them. "I will not give them any specifics. I can simply ask them to dig up what they can, given the emotional state of my new girlfriend."

Raising his brows he looked at Lacie for agreement with his plan.

When she noticed this and glanced at the other two, she saw that they were all staring at her. "Okay," she said.

The pressure was supposed to lessen now that she had allies, but she could see that they were all still expecting her to make the decisions. Lacie had missed Ryder since she left him to go to the hospital. But she hadn't grasped just how much she had grown to rely on him. If he was here, he would be the one taking over and making the decisions.

Lacie didn't mind being decisive. What she fretted was what would happen to Ryder if she made the wrong choice. He was relying on her now. She couldn't screw this up because if she did, she would never have the chance to apologize for her mistakes.

FIFTY

Ryder

RYDER HADN'T SEEN his captor again since he'd left with the message Ryder gave him for Lacie. Thinking about his girl was what kept him trying to manipulate the chains on his wrists. He had to tell himself he was doing something, even if that something wasn't showing any progress.

The clang of the lock was his first clue that anyone was coming back to him. The light came on just a split second before the door opened. As he was blinking into the brightness that made his eyes sting, his captor came over with a paper cup filled with water. He put it on the floor and backed away.

"You're going to meet her."

"Who?" Ryder asked, crouching to pick up the water. He could spit it back in the guy's face, but he needed to keep his wits about him and if he was dehydrated then his wits would be the first thing to go. His captor didn't say anything, he just backed away to lean on the wall opposite Ryder's. "What's your name? I forget."

Ryder remembered his name. Getting into this guy's head, making him feel insignificant under his queen, would expand that wedge he wanted to pry between them.

"Evan," he spat.

"Evan, that's right," Ryder said, finishing the water and balling up the cup. "How did you get involved with this?" He didn't respond, so Ryder began to speculate. "I'm going to bet it started with sex, right? That's how most women get us to do stuff. Especially things we don't want to do… Either she gave you sex and you thought there was more to it so you started thinking you owed her. Or she has promised you sex but hasn't delivered yet." From the way Evan's jaw worked, Ryder thought the second was on the money. "She probably never will. Trust me. If a woman doesn't put out in the first few weeks of a deal, she has no intentions of ever doing it… doing you… But we talked about you having problems the last time you were here… Is that what happened?"

"I don't have any problems," Evan snapped, shoving himself away from the wall. "And you are way off base. You couldn't be more wrong."

This guy was the emotional sort and getting a reaction from him was almost too easy. That would mean he was easy to manipulate too, naïve maybe, and definitely not street smart. "Then enlighten me," Ryder said. "Tell me where I'm wrong? There are only two motivators for women, sex or money. Men, we'll go to war over just about anything, pride, territory, on a bet, on a dare… but I guess that falls into the pride category."

"What's your point?" Evan asked with a snarl in his voice and a curl in his lip. Ryder was riling him, he was too easy, and that was just perfect for Ryder.

"My point is that your mistress is only doing this for one of those two reasons. Now I doubt she wants to sleep with me, since, you know, I'm down here locked up and unless there was some super-potent Viagra in that water you just gave me, I'm not getting it up for anyone but my lady."

"How do you know she isn't the one who orchestrated this? Maybe she and I are playing you," Evan said, elevating his chin and letting triumph contort his smile.

Ryder pushed his bottom lip out and shook his head. "Nah, this isn't Lacie's style. Besides, she wouldn't have to do something like this to me."

"What does that mean?" Evan asked, deflated, though he tried not to display it.

"Because whatever Lacie wants from me, she gets. If this was about money, all she would have to do is ask for it. There's no need for her to get revenge, unless she's been secretly blaming me for what Jamie did to her all this time. If that was the case, all she would have to do was tell me to cut myself open and bleed for her and I'd do it."

"You're pathetic," Evan said, disgust returned to his demeanor.

"I'm in love," Ryder said without attempting to hide his smile. "Love, man, it's freeing. I have a singular focus now. A partner in life. A companion. When you have love like Lace and I do… you never have to be afraid."

"Oh, she's afraid, all right," Evan said, returning to his smugness. "You should have heard her scream when I spoke to her last night and gave her the instruction to share herself with Elijah."

Clenching his jaw, Ryder tried not to react. He tried not to let Evan get him riled when it was supposed to be Ryder's job. But he could imagine how Lacie would have reacted to that command, much as he would react if a similar one was given to him.

"Me and my lady don't need money, you see," Evan said, moving toward Ryder. "Between us, our families have enough money to buy a dozen islands."

"So it's sex," Ryder said, though his own confidence was waning. Lacie needed him now. She needed him to save her from the thing she didn't want to do. While he was stuck down here, he was powerless to save her from the fate she dreaded.

Evan opened his mouth with an inhale, but a voice from the corridor spoke before he could. "Didn't I tell you not to engage with him?" the female voice was cool as it echoed down the corridor. Ryder recognized the tone but couldn't quite put his finger on who the voice belonged to until she sashayed into the doorway and paused before letting herself smile.

"Hello, Ryder."

"Sadie," he said, almost unable to believe that Sorcha's sister could be responsible for this kind of a scheme.

"How are you?" she asked, sauntering into the room. "I suppose that's a ridiculous question given the circumstances."

"Why would you do this?" he asked more interested in her motivation than his own liberation at this point.

"Why?" she asked and glanced around at Evan before she spun on him. "Because of you, my sister, and her prissy little friend! Because you ruined my life and stole the only good thing I had!"

"I don't—"

"I tried to get your attention, but you never saw me," she said. "You were all business, just like Elijah. You come over and you talk to my father like he's so important, but me? You all… you just ignored me! Well you can't ignore me anymore, can you?"

"You tried to get my attention?" he asked.

When he'd worked security for the Reynolds, he was aware of the women of the family, but he would never have abused Lawrence Reynolds' trust by taking advantage of them. Plus, Sorcha and Sadie were trust fund heiresses who would have more money than God when their father and mother passed. When a woman had that much money, she had a lot of choices, and a working grunt like him made pennies in comparison to their bank balances.

Sorcha had taken a while to recognize him after he got together with Lacie. She eventually did after she learned his last name and company name. With Sorcha paying him such little attention he'd have assumed Sadie would have as well.

"Yes! First it was Elijah, I loved Elijah," she said in a dreamy way that made her pause and stare off into the distance for a second. Behind her Evan's mouth pinched into a tight circle. He was a lesser specimen than his more charming brother. It had to hurt that even after doing all this for her, Sadie still preferred his older brother. "But that bitch of yours was all he could see."

"My bitch?" he asked, knowing that she meant Lacie. Sorcha, Elijah, Lacie and Sadie had known each other for years, probably since Lacie met Sorcha at college. Graden's crush on her must have started early.

"He always wanted Lacie and Sorcha always told him to stay away from her."

"Why?"

Sadie's eyes scrunched like she couldn't care less why. "I don't know. My bitch of a sister has always cared more about her precious Lacie than about me."

"So while Sorcha was telling Elijah to stay away from Lacie, you were trying to get his attention?" Ryder asked.

"Not that it mattered, he was as blind as you."

"And this is supposed to teach us all a lesson?" he asked, looking from his chains to her and Evan.

"No, I'm over that, I don't give a damn about any of you anymore," she said, turning her nose up for good measure.

"You've got a really good way of showing it, honey."

"Don't honey me," she snapped. "I am not your honey."

"Sadie, sweetheart, you're not—"

"You took him from me!"

Ryder tried to get some sort of translation from Evan, but he was too busy examining his shoes to be of any use. "I took—"

"Jamie!" she exclaimed. "He noticed me. He didn't ignore me like the rest of you did! He cared!"

"You were screwing Jamie," he muttered and brought his balled hands up to his forehead.

"Not screwing him, we were in love! We were going to be together and then you and that bitch of a girlfriend screwed everything up for us!"

"How many times have you seen Jamie since he's been inside?" Ryder asked, exhaling as he brought his hands down and his face up. "None."

"You don't know that!"

"I do." Ryder nodded. "I've been getting copies of his visitor logs, his phone records, I know what he has for his breakfast. Do you think I would take my eyes off him for a split second when he could be a danger to Lacie? The woman that I love? Jamie doesn't care about you. He didn't care about anyone except Jamie."

"No!" she protested and inched nearer. "No, I'm going to save him and then we're going to be together."

"You're going to save him?" Ryder asked, tipping his chin down to try concealing the smile that wanted to meet his lips. "From a maximum-security prison? How are you going to do that? With your Prada clutch or—"

"Don't belittle me," she sneered and scrunched her face again as she looked him up and down. "Look at where you are because of me."

"Well done," Ryder said. "The pair of you pulled off a convincing enough mugging to get me into an alleyway where you drugged me to drag me down here. Then what? What are you going to do with me now? Messing with mine and Lacie's relationship—"

"You don't have a relationship now," Sadie said. "She does what I tell her to. She wrecked my sister's marriage, turned her back on all of your friends so she's no longer under their protection. She lost their respect. Now she's screwing his big brother. She's having sex with him, Ryder." Her mocking tone was meant to upset him and he hated that it was working. "All night long in his bed, sweaty bodies, creaking springs the lot. He's a billionaire, Ryder. You can't beat that! You won't beat that."

"Why would—"

"Because wrecking her life, having her sleep around and act erratically... she'll have no credibility, maybe we'll get her to dabble in some drugs or have more casual sex... Hell, maybe we'll just have her top herself and be done with it."

"If she's screwing Elijah then I don't give a fuck what you do to her," Ryder said, exuding nonchalance and propping his boot up on the wall again.

"What?" Sadie asked and her triumphant smile disappeared to flicker back then vanish again. "What are you—"

"Why would I want to be with a slut who's going to mess around on me? If you're right, if they've really had sex then fuck her."

"Really?" Sadie asked, glancing over her shoulder at Evan who had perked up again. "You really don't care?"

"You think I like what happened to Jamie? Yeah, sure, I'm pissed about what he did to Lacie, she was my girl and we were supposed to be best friends… But the rest of the stuff? I wouldn't have cared about him embezzling or selling drugs. I know that sometimes a man needs to do the unthinkable to get by."

"You really wouldn't have cared about that?" Sadie asked, taking another step in his direction.

"I guess you want to discredit Lacie on the stand," Ryder said. "Is that how you're planning on springing Jamie?"

"Well, I…"

"Eric will be a problem," Ryder said. "He's in protective custody, but if you bribe the right guy then getting his address won't be difficult."

"Elijah has friends at the State Department," Sadie said. "Evan can't get him to spill, but I figure his precious Lacie will have better luck and now that they're sleeping together and she's doing our bidding… Lacie will find out Eric's whereabouts for us."

Widening his smile, Ryder made eye contact and nodded in admiration. "Very good, very good. I'm impressed, honey. Booth, now he's the one who kept the paper trail and that could hang Jamie bad… Taking him out, well…"

Sadie's gumption increased; his ego stroking had bolstered her. "Lacie just told Sorcha about his cheating. I mean it was so obvious. I slept with Bruce like two weeks after he and Sorcha met. Sorcha kicked him out. So now that he's just lost his wife and Lulu, his baby daughter… His parents were already mad at him for the embarrassment he brought on their family and he can't even find a job… his family will be mortified. Suicide's not outside the realm of possibility."

Still smiling, he drew her in. "How do you plan to do it?" Giving them both a pointed look, he made it clear he expected to hear their plan. "Come on, you had to have spoken about it."

"Getting you all paranoid about Lacie and getting you here to manipulate her, those were the main things we focused on," Sadie said. "After Lacie gives us Eric's location… Well, taking Eric and Bruce out was supposed to be his responsibility."

Sadie backed away to bring Evan into the fold. He was intent on her but from the lack of color on his face, he hadn't gotten to the planning stage yet. Seeing his chance, Ryder laughed, startling both of them.

"Him?" Ryder said, no longer hiding his amusement. "Man, baby, you picked the wrong partner. How many men have you killed, Graden?"

"Uh…"

"How many have you killed?" Sadie asked actually defending her colleague, which would be admirable if he wasn't intent on punishing them both.

Drawing his features together, Ryder stopped laughing to portray offense. "You don't do what I do and not learn how to take a fucker down."

"Great," she said, letting her arms fall to her sides. "Then all we have to do is bring them here and you'll do the dirty work."

"Why would I do that?" Ryder asked. "You've got balls, honey, I'll admit that. But I have no reason to help you."

"How about if you don't, we'll get your lady to screw every one of your men."

"Do it," he shrugged. "Getting her together with Elijah was a dumb move. If she's fucking him, she's not my responsibility anymore, is she? Truth is, if it wasn't for her, I'd probably be doing exactly what you are and trying to get my best friend out of jail."

"You don't care what we do to Lacie?" Evan asked.

Shaking his head slowly, Ryder scratched his chin with his bound hands. "Why should I? I won't go near some slut looking for an excuse to bang another guy. I could see it the first time I saw them together. I knew he wanted her and she led him on, didn't she? I'll bet she wanted to do this all along."

"Why should we trust you?" Sadie asked, peering closer. "How do we know you're telling the truth?"

"I don't give a damn what you think," he said, rattling his chains. "You've got me chained up here like an animal. You better be worried about when I get free of here because there's nothing stopping me ripping you both apart. Jamie is your only chance of survival."

"Jamie?"

"Sure, he's my best friend, isn't he? If you get him out, you better hope he tells me to leave you alone."

"You would do that?" Sadie asked, glancing between him and Evan like she wasn't sure what to think and he couldn't blame her.

Here was her captive telling her that her plan was falling apart and there was no one to save it.

"He's my best friend and I just found out that I turned my back on him for a woman who's a fucking whore." Rattling his chains again, Ryder grit his teeth and called out his frustration. "Let me out of here!"

"No!" Sadie said, retreating a few steps. Her nervousness was understandable because he kept pulling and shaking at the chains letting his anger build.

"You let me out of here and I'll do it for you. I'll take Eric out, that bastard was supposed to be my man too and he fucked me over. He fucked Jamie over! You never turn on a friend. Your men are your family and keeping their secrets is sacred. Now look at him, the prick is cowering in some secret location hanging out with cops! That bastard has it coming! I can do it for you… you don't need that bastard!" Nodding at Evan, he curled his lip in disgust. "He's a prissy little bastard who's more likely to cry for his momma than pull the trigger. I know what needs to be done. I've seen combat. I can take care of you."

"Of me?" Sadie asked.

The glitter in her eye was intrigue and playing the beast apparently did it for her because she was looking at him with female interest. "Sure, you're my friend's girl, aren't you? Looking after you is my job. We can work together. We'll get Eric, we'll get Booth, we can probably make both of them look like suicide and then no one will be looking for us, will they? Why would they? Everyone thinks that I'm with Lacie and you've been real smart about playing down your connection to Jamie."

"I only did that because I knew I could be of more use to him if people weren't asking questions."

"I understand that, sweetheart," he said.

She might believe that, but the truth was, she was never going to stand up in front of her family and admit to being with a guy like Jamie, not when said guy was locked up behind bars and unable to take care of her, which was probably exactly why she hadn't told anyone about their relationship.

Jamie always did like his women classy. Sure, most of them were down and outs, but he was old-fashioned about women, believed they should be taken care of and shouldn't swear etc. Ryder was old-fashioned about taking care of his woman too and he couldn't do that here.

Convincing Sadie to let him out was a long shot, but the woman obviously wasn't in her right mind. Teaming up with a wet blanket like Evan and believing that they could pull off this kind of op by themselves was a long shot too.

Women like Sadie were spoiled and didn't have street smarts, one only had to look at Sorcha to realize that. They did what they wanted because they believed that they were entitled and their wants could change on a dime. Sorcha portrayed this too, the way she flipped from one guy to the other depending on her mood and what the man was providing for her.

"Come on, Sadie, honey, you know that I can be of more use to you than this guy," Ryder said, softening his expression, he raised his chains toward her.

"Don't do it," Evan said. "He's playing you!"

"He has a point," Sadie said, turning her back on Ryder. "You're not going to kill anyone, are you? If you were going to then you would've done it already. Every time we talk about it, you get this wimpy look on your face. I need a real man to help me."

"Let's approach one of his men then, there must be someone else who can help us," Evan said.

"He's not even denying it," Ryder said. "See, honey, he's not going to be strong for you. You need someone who can take care of business and protect you. I have as much invested in this as you. We can get Jamie out… I need to see him. I have to apologize; we have a friendship to fix. We'll do this, get Jamie out and then the three of us can blow out of the state. I have plenty of money to see us right for a long time."

Tapping a finger on her lower lip, she turned to look him in the eye. "All three of us?"

"You'll have me and Jamie, we'll look after you. You know that we'd never let anyone harm you. We can do this, Sadie, you and me together… let's go get Jamie."

She was tempted and it was that temptation he played on. "How do I know this isn't just some ruse?"

"What have you got to lose?" he asked. "You've still got those drugs, right? If you think I'm fucking you around or I don't do the job then you can shoot me full of that shit and bring me back here. You've done it once, right? Why not do it again if you need to? But you won't need to, honey, come on."

Moving forward, he got as close to her as he could and raised his chains with the lock facing up. "What about Lacie?"

"Lacie, who?" he asked and smiled into her eyes, trying his best to appear unthreatening and maybe just a little impressed that she'd done this. "You've come so far on your own, I know this was your plan, not his. You're so smart, and I never gave you credit for just how intriguing you are. I love a woman who can take care of herself. A woman who sees what she wants and goes to get it. You don't let anything hold you back. You're a wonder, Sadie, you really are."

"Will you kill her?" Sadie murmured, arching her back and creeping toward him. "Will you take out your precious Lacie? She's a threat to Jamie too. Her testimony will be the most damning… Maybe if you promise to take her out… If you do her first then I'll know… I'll know that you're being honest. We have Lacie under our control. We can tell her to meet us somewhere and then… that's when you'll do it."

"See," Ryder said, widening his smile. "You're so fucking smart… Let's take the cheating bitch out together, sweetheart. You and me."

FIFTY-ONE

Lacie

"I DON'T LIKE THIS," Lacie muttered to herself. Not that she had believed this would be a pleasant experience. There were very few reasons why one would be called to a dark alleyway in the middle of the night. This alley was all the more sinister because it was in an industrial area that was abandoned at this time of the night.

Whatever was going to happen, it was overdue. Lacie had been here for twenty minutes. Either something had gone wrong, the event was late, or this was the whole plan. Maybe they wanted to humiliate her by leaving her here all night. It was cold enough that maybe she was supposed to die of exposure.

Having cohorts gave her some sense of security, although she was putting a huge amount of faith in them because she hadn't traveled here with them. She just had to assume they were out there protecting her whilst protecting themselves at the same time.

The call she'd received last night told her to use her connection with Elijah to get the address of where

Eric, Jamie Wallace's number two, was being protected by the cops. She was told to bring that information to this meeting point tonight and with a piece of paper in her pocket bearing the information, she began to second-guess what was going on.

Whoever was doing this to her was somehow connected to Jamie Wallace and that made the danger involved ratchet up. Coming here had seemed like the right thing to do. Compliance was more important now that she'd broken the rule of secrecy and failed to follow through in sleeping with Elijah. This situation was precarious and if Ryder's captors found out about her deception, they'd kill her love for sure.

Regret began to seep in and she wondered if she'd set herself up. Maybe the kidnapper was watching her every move. Maybe one of the people she'd confided in was really in league with the kidnapper and she was about to get her just desserts.

The scuff of a boot on asphalt made her spin around and although there wasn't much light, she was sure there was a figure in the shadows at the end of the alley.

"Hello?" she asked. Holding her breath as the shadow moved forward, she let out a yelp when she recognized Ryder's features. "Ryder!" Her impulse to go to him was interrupted when he held up a hand toward her.

"I gave you everything," he said, pausing in his own journey. "I… you were everything to me."

"What's going on?" she asked, not reassured by his tone. "Baby?"

"Is that what you call him?" Ryder asked and began to move toward her again. "Is it?"

"Who? I… you… they told you about Elijah."

"Yeah," he said, gritting his teeth. "About you and Elijah… I knew you two were hot for each other, but you told me I was paranoid, said there was nothing to it."

His hand moved and she glanced down to see the line of a gun barrel pointed at the concrete. "You're not going to hurt me, Ryder," she said, backing away. "You can't… you don't have it in you. I don't know what they told you or… this isn't you. Listen to me, baby—"

"I'm not listening to you," he said with a disgust in his expression that broke her heart. "You're poison… just like she told me. She was right… to think that I… I turned my back on my best friend…"

"Wallace." The shock of his reference to Jamie made her stop and her panic vanish. She couldn't think of any reason that Ryder would miraculously forgive or sympathize with Jamie Wallace. "No. You would never—"

"Don't talk! I've heard enough… She was right. She was right about you."

Raising the gun, he kept on coming until she had nowhere to run and her back was pressed into the wall. When he was in reaching distance, he grabbed her arm and hauled her forward. Forcing his mouth over hers, she opened to accept his kiss, hopeful that the reminder of their connection would quell any jealousy he might be feeling.

But she couldn't correct him, not when his captors could be anywhere around listening to everything. So taking hold of his shoulder, she pulled herself nearer and smiled when his mouth slid across her cheek to her jaw. She thought he was going to kiss her neck, instead he took his lips to her ear for the briefest of seconds.

"Play dead when I shoot," he murmured and then half a beat later the gun went off and the brickwork behind her exploded.

He backed off and she did as he'd said and fell to the ground. Trust was all she had right now, because falling onto the damp concrete face first, she closed her eyes and waited for what would happen next.

The gun had been between them, but he had to have shot under her arm because nowhere on her body hurt. Either that, or she was numb because of the shot. But this was Ryder and he would never hurt her, not if he was in control of his faculties and if he wasn't then he would never have warned her to go down after the gunshot.

"Oh my God, you did it!"

Lacie didn't need to have her eyes open to recognize that voice and she was pleased that Sorcha wasn't here to witness what had to be the shock of the century. Her best friend's sister was involved in this. Sadie was no criminal mastermind. She hadn't bothered with college because she believed herself too pretty to need it and she hadn't been wrong.

Sadie was satisfied in the world of the mani-pedi, having affairs with her tennis coaches and any other male who happened to cross her path.

"I told you I would, didn't I?" Ryder said.

The tinge of familiarity in his tone made Lacie want to open her eyes because if she wasn't mistaken, her boyfriend was flirting or maybe even intimate with the woman who had somehow condoned this.

"Is she really dead?"

A foot nudged her hip and Lacie saw her chance. Pulling her arm back she stabbed forward with the tranq dart and got Sadie in the ankle.

"Oh my God!" Sadie said, kicking her leg out in front of her, trying to get the dart out. But it was too late, the sedative was strong and this was the same kind of dart that had taken Jamie Wallace down. Taking Sadie down was child's play.

When the woman was on her back, slumbering under the effects of the drug, Lacie pounced up to her feet.

"Ryder?" she asked, but he was crouched next to Sadie, turning her onto her back to search her coat pockets. "What are you doing?"

"This," he said and stole something from Sadie's pocket.

At that moment, another figure came out of the shadows to hurry toward them. "What happened?"

Lacie stumbled back to the wall when she saw Elijah's younger brother, Evan, hurrying over.

"Nothing to worry about," Ryder said and lunged at Evan, stabbing something into his neck.

Lacie shrieked, but Ryder caught Evan and eased him onto the ground beside Sadie.

"Piece of cake," Ryder said, recapping the needle Lacie hadn't seen him use. "Baby, are you—"

"Are we safe?" she asked, looking around for any further parties who may sneak up on them.

"We're safe," he said, coming over to gather her up. "Are you safe? Are you hurt? I'm sorry I—"

"No," she said, clasping his face. "No, baby, I'm sorry—"

"I understand that they told you to—"

"I didn't... I couldn't... I... I was terrified they would punish you if they found out."

"You mean you and Graden didn't...?"

"No," she said, smiling when she saw the breadth of his.

"Thank fuck for that," he said, stealing her mouth in a kiss that made her toes tingle.

"Lovely reunion, but what the fuck is this?"

Ryder relinquished their kiss, but Lacie grabbed hold of him to prevent him from attacking Shep who had been hiding on the periphery throughout.

"You got my message?" Ryder asked her and she nodded. "Good girl." He kissed her head. "We have to call the guys and—"

"I already pressed the panic button," Lacie said. "Gabe has been working with the cops on your disappearance."

Ryder nodded and stroked her hair. "We should call the cops too."

"I already called them. What the hell is this?" Shep asked, examining Evan and Sadie.

"She seduced him into doing her dirty work," Ryder said. "Except he was lacking the killer instinct"— Ryder gazed down at her—"something I told them I could follow through on. It was the only way to get out of there and—"

"I understand," she said, caressing the stubble on his jaw. "You did the right thing."

"Thanks for playing along."

"This is lovely, but… Sorcha will be livid," Shep said.

"No doubt," Ryder said. "Especially when she finds out Sadie was having an affair with Jamie… she wanted to bust him out. Taking out you and Eric and Booth, that was her grand plan. If there was no one to testify then she believed he'd go free."

"And be with her," Lacie said and felt a pang of sympathy for Sadie. "That's sort of sad."

"Not sad enough to keep me from you," Ryder said. "You really didn't—"

"Would you stop?" Lacie asked but couldn't stop smiling. "I haven't been with anyone except you. Yes, I've been staying with Elijah, in a guest room. He knows about this and Sorcha does too."

"You were lucky," Ryder said. "I think that's how they were getting their information, their siblings, it's probably why they wanted you living with Elijah because either Sadie or Evan could question him about you and pretend to be a concerned friend."

"Or Evan wanted to see his brother used and abandoned," Shep said. "Sorcha says the guy is a bit of a loser and not the brightest crayon in the box."

"That's an understatement," Ryder said. He held her so close that her ribs ached, but it was the most wonderful pain she had ever been in.

Sirens faded in from the distance and she knew that the S.I.S. men wouldn't be too far behind. "I'm going to have a lot of explaining to do," she muttered.

"You saved my life. Playing along, or letting them think that you were playing along, gave me time to convince them of my usefulness."

"I hope the guys see it that way."

"They will," he said, kissing her head again. "Believe me."

EPILOGUE

"I DON'T CARE," Sorcha said over her shoulder to her fiancé who was bouncing Lulu on his knee.

"Yeah, right, but—"

"Shep," Sorcha said, spinning around to glare at him. "I said I don't care. Your opinion means nothing to me."

"It's probably best to leave them to it," Ryder said from his place opposite Shep.

Lacie tried not to laugh at Shep's eye roll because she had to show her solidarity with her fellow bride-to-be. They were in their coffeehouse having a girlie lunch. But their men were at the table just behind theirs because Lacie wanted approval from Ryder before making final decisions and Sorcha didn't want to be far from Lulu.

After Sadie and Evan were arrested, the trial of the century began because both families had enough money to fight the case all the way. Evan ended up giving evidence against Sadie to save his own neck and the Reynolds had Sadie evaluated and she tried an insanity plea. She was given a suspended sentence and the Reynolds were watching her like a hawk.

Needless to say, Ryder stopped working for them and Lacie stopped visiting. Sorcha was rarely near her family home anymore and after she and Booth got their quickie divorce, he moved back to his parents' home and Shep moved into Sorcha's place with her and Lulu.

"We're going to be beautiful brides," Sorcha said to Lacie and smoothed out the magazine they were sharing. Sorcha had a tote bag full of them. Lunch could go on for some time.

"Yes, we are," Lacie said and glanced past her to Ryder who hadn't taken his eyes off her all day.

It seemed to make sense that they would have a double wedding because Lacie had accepted the huge diamond from Ryder and had struggled to make plans on her own. Sorcha and Shep had been living in each other's pockets and Sorcha had actually taken to helping Shep out at the office, though he was working in collaboration with S.I.S. a lot more. Of course, Heather had been shown the door not too long after Sorcha was ready to admit that she and Shep were actually together.

And Lulu, she adored Shep and he was excellent with her. He didn't shy away from any role and was very protective of her, sometimes even from her own mother.

Wallace had been sentenced to thirty years after evidence of conspiracy to commit multiple homicides was corroborated by Eric and by Booth. Lacie had given her evidence but hadn't been there at the sentencing with Ryder and the other S.I.S. men. She had worked with a therapist and had processed what had happened to her and learned how to channel that torment into her work.

She loved the privacy and security she got at Ryder's place in her dome and couldn't imagine working anywhere else.

"Are you listening?" Sorcha asked her. "We have to coordinate."

"We will," Lacie said, still fixated on Ryder. "All that matters is that we're joined with the men we love at the end of the day, right?"

Sorcha reached over the table to pat her hand. "You have a lot to learn about wedding planning. Thank goodness you have me."

"Thank goodness," Lacie said, but her thoughts were on Ryder.

She was thankful that she had him and that no matter what came at them, they survived it. The positive thing they could take from all the trauma was that every time adversity came for them, they grew stronger. Their lives were one, entwined as one, and she wouldn't have it any other way.

~~~~~~

Ryder Stone also features in the Roxiverse series
~~~~~~

Thank you for reading this tale!
If you can, please take the time to review.

~

Ask your local library for more Scarlett Finn
novels!

~

For all things Scarlett Finn
check out:

www.scarlettfinn.com

Try out the Roxiverse:

www.ingramcontent.com/pod-product-compliance
Lightning Source LLC
Chambersburg PA
CBHW060735190726
48285CB00001B/218